DARK CONSORT

DARK CONSORT

Dark Dreamer

Book Two

Amber R. Duell

For Ryan

No matter how much darkness the world throws at you, I hope
you always stay as kind as you are now.

Chapter One

The Sandman

Somewhere, a Dreamer screamed.

It was the type of scream that quickened the blood and curdled the stomach. I'd heard the same cry over and over from different mouths since I'd reopened the barrier keeping Dreamers from the Nightmare Realm. Baku was right to scoff at my plan to keep it intact until Nora returned to claim her title as Lady of Nightmares. Five months of pent-up energy had the nightmares tearing themselves apart; if I hadn't let Dreamers trickle back in to appease the ravenous creatures, there might be nothing left to claim.

Not that I would mind a major culling of nightmares, but Nora needed them. Rowan was gathering nightmares to her side from the safety of the Keep in a bid to become the next Weaver.

To do that, she would have to kill Nora. Ideally, Rowan would first have to go through thousands of nightmares pledging loyalty to Nora. Unfortunately, this wasn't a battle I could win on Nora's behalf—not if she wanted to earn the respect of her subjects. So there I was: constantly chasing down Dreamers in the Nightmare Realm before they died both here and in the Day World.

Shame tightened my chest as the scream cut through the air again. Baku and I froze and listened. This landscape was particularly fearsome, composed of roughly fifty acres of steep, sudden valleys and hills, as if an enormous creature had dragged its claws repeatedly across the ground. It threw sound in whatever direction it felt like. The scream came again from just below our current position only to bounce somewhere to the north. *Finally.* The source was close enough to catch the cry before it was carried away.

I threw my hood up, feeling the hum of my sand at my hip. "Ready?"

Baku flicked his elephant ears once in response.

White sound waves spiraled silently up the grassy hill toward us, the rings widening the closer they got. I pulled sand from my satchel to form a barrier against the unseen nightmare's attack, but before I could give it shape, the force of a coil whipped it from my palm. *Not good.* Without sand, there was little I could do to defend myself, let alone the Dreamer. The closest known shelter was nearly four hundred yards away, but we'd never make it to the small, rundown shack in time.

I dug my boots into the dirt and looked straight into the tunnel of sound waves. "This is going to hurt," I said through clenched teeth.

Baku widened his stance, the black and yellow brindle fur on the back of his neck rising in anticipation.

The waves slammed into us, and a high-pitched whine pierced my eardrums. My bones rattled. Baku lowered his head and pressed forward. His ears laid flat against the side of his head, and his tiger paws clawed up patches of grass with each step. The hunger I was so accustomed to seeing in his eyes had faded and was replaced with anger. At me. At the nightmares. He didn't speak, so I had no true way of knowing without reading his dreams, but he was a loyal friend, even after everything. Of course, I often left a trail of dead nightmares in my wake. Hunting them down was a thrill for Baku, but having his meals handed to him didn't hurt either.

The Dreamer bellowed again, his low tones a clear contrast to the nightmare's, and I shuddered. Movement caught my eye ahead. A young man in a white t-shirt and plaid boxers climbed from one of the deep gouges and scrambled toward the shack at the edge of the forest.

"No!" I shouted, but the landscape carried my voice off. We had to get to that shelter before the Dreamer did. There was no telling what sort of nightmare waited inside, but there was undoubtedly *something* there. There always was. I veered toward the man, but moving sideways through the rings was harder than heading straight toward them, and I slipped in my rush. My ribs banged into a rock jutting from the ground. Baku lunged after me, struggling not to be swept away himself.

A puff of black fur, no larger than a hedgehog, rolled up the hill. The nightmare had no visible legs, no eyes or mouth, but the sound waves twisting off its back moved to follow the Dreamer. I braced myself against the shifting noise as it proceeded with clear purpose.

The moment the waves released us, I was on my feet, gripping a handful of sand. I barreled forward while forming the sand into two ski poles. There was only one path that would let me reach the Dreamer in time. Without thinking, I took a deep breath and leapt back into the waves. My eyes instantly watered as the noise filled my head, but I pressed on, the dirt giving way beneath the pointed poles.

The puff of fur froze, and the sound waves slowed. I knew in that moment that it could see, with or without eyes. I felt its invisible gaze pierce me as hard as the rings beat my eardrums, but I kept moving. There was no other choice.

Then the sound cut off.

I blinked, too stunned to take another step, but Baku wasted no time sprinting toward the small creature. Saliva dripped from the base of his tusks. The puff let out a single small chirp, and the ground rumbled. I wasn't about to stay to find out why. I hurried after the Dreamer, catching up to him just before he reached the shelter. "Wake up," I snapped, ripping him back by the neck of his shirt. "You're having a nightmare. Wake up."

My hood had fallen back, and the man met my eyes for the briefest of moments. He relaxed for half a second, and I thought he would take my advice. Instead, he shoved me away with a punch to my chest. "Stay back," he demanded.

I raised my hands between us and tilted my head sideways to check on Baku. He was nearly at the puff now, but the ground trembled so hard the rickety shack behind the Dreamer swayed in time with the earth's movements. "Listen to me," I said slowly. "This isn't real."

He bent and snagged a fist-sized rock from the ground. "*Stay back."*

I blew out a breath. Whose idea was it to let the Dreamers back in again? *Right.* I scowled. *Mine.* And now I had the privilege of traipsing all over the Nightmare Realm saving them when I should've been training Nora to do it herself—as useless as that had proven so far.

"Just wake up," I grumbled as I tossed a pinch of sand in his face.

The man swung out with the rock, nearly colliding with the side of my head before he vanished. The rock crashed to the ground, then bounced back up as a chorus of chirps raked the air. I winced, knowing without looking that there would be more screeching puffs behind me, and sprinted to Baku's side.

Nothing could've prepared me for what the nightmares were doing. Thousands of them scurried up to the first nightmare, creating a sea of black. Then, one-by-one, their fur fused together. They formed paws as big as Baku, legs wider than I was tall. Their creation grew quickly—too quickly. More puffs raced up the legs to form an elongated body, and my stomach dropped.

"We should go," I suggested.

Baku pranced closer to me but continued to eye the growing nightmare with a predatory gaze.

The body rounded, a tail stretching out behind it, and its head morphed with three rows of pointed teeth. A massive fisher cat stared down at us as the last few puffs rolled into place.

"Now." I stepped back. "We should go *now.*"

Baku shook his head.

There was little I wanted less than to fight this thing. It was mindless, driven by instinct, and would align itself with whomever exerted dominance. It was no threat to Nora if she didn't allow it to be one, and I hated to kill a potential ally. She would need everyone she could get when the time came.

"Baku, we can't—"

He charged the nightmare, mouth curled in a wicked smile.

I hesitated. Maybe the nightmare would run when we proved we weren't an easy target, or maybe Baku would give up when he realized I wasn't helping. Or not. Because Baku could handle himself. I groaned and reluctantly followed him.

When the nightmare saw Baku coming, it lunged toward him. I moved swiftly, throwing sand-made blades through the air. They glinted, their path true, and a single puff of fur fell with each slash. My jaw tightened. *Seriously, Baku…* I didn't have enough sand to take each one out individually.

The nightmare lifted a massive paw, and Baku slid beneath it on his side. Once under the beast, he climbed its hind leg as easily as a cat climbed a tree. His sharp claws shredded through the puffs, and they fell one after another. The fisher cat rose onto its back legs and threw itself over. My breath stuck in my throat. I rushed forward, sand at the ready. The fallen puffs popped like balloons beneath my boots. "Baku!"

The fisher cat lifted itself back onto all fours and swung its head in my direction. A collective hush from the puffs chilled my body. Then each one bellowed, sending countless sound waves in every direction. They knocked me flat on my back, and I struggled to breathe. My sand would only be swept away again if I tried to use it. Where had I put those ski poles?

An orange and black blur shot across the nightmare's snout and dove between its teeth. "Baku, you idiot," I hissed. I was nearly back on my feet when the sound came to a sudden stop. The smaller balls tumbled down on each other in one giant mound with Baku sitting at the top, shoveling them into his mouth with his trunk. The chorus of chirps sounded across the landscape, both far and near, as they began to reform. I took a heaping mound of sand from my satchel and flung it at the base of the pile. Baku leapt out of the way and circled to my side. The fisher cat was forming yet again when I called on the sand's magic to mimic the puffs' own cry. I compressed the sound into one wave that blasted through the entire mass.

Black fur wove gently back and forth in the air around us and settled in the creases of my clothing, my hair, my bag. My head rang. I rubbed the soft spot in front of my raw ears and my fingertips came away sticky with blood. "That was unnecessary." I could barely hear my own voice. My shoulders hunched, and I squeezed my eyes shut for a moment. "They could've proved useful to Nora."

Baku lifted a flattened puff with his trunk and stuck it slowly, defiantly, into his mouth.

"Fine," I said with a sigh. "I'm going home. Are you coming with me?"

He scooped up another trunk-full of dead puffs, slid them into my open satchel, and nodded with an amused glint in his eyes.

"Baku!" I stared at the half-deflated nightmares, my mouth open. "You're finishing these before we get back to the beach."

His only answer was a swish of his cow tail as he walked away.

I chuckled and followed him, ignoring the heat leeching through my satchel. Baku reached in and grabbed one after another as we made our way through the Nightmare Realm, and I tried not to shudder.

The only cries we heard on the way back to the Dream Realm were inhuman. At one point, something resembling a giant cabbage bounced past us, followed by what looked like a radioactive rabbit, but neither entity spared us a glance. Baku watched them, popping another puff as if it was popcorn.

"Please tell me they're almost gone." I peeked inside my bag to find it empty. *Thank the stars.* Baku's ears perked up and the fur rose on the back of his neck. "Relax. I'm sure you'll find something else to—"

My magic snapped against my chest like a rubber band, reaching out for sand I didn't have. Something was wrong. Very wrong. I raced to the barrier of the Dream Realm with Baku at my side. Barbed grass bit at my boots and pants, but Baku didn't seem to notice it beneath his tiger paws. What I saw waiting for me turned me to ice.

A half-emaciated giant stood at the edge of the Dream Realm wearing nothing but black pants with thick chains wrapped around his torso. Pieces of orange flesh had rotted away, leaving putrid wounds and exposed bones. He hoisted a five-foot sledgehammer, nearly half his size, over his bald head and swung.

"No!" I screamed as it sailed toward the barrier.

How did he know it was there? Intelligent nightmares had ways of tracking the Dream Realm even though it reflected the surrounding nightmare landscape, and sure, some of the others stumbled upon it occasionally, but giants were far from smart.

The hammer smashed into the barrier. Blue light burst at the impact and webbed over the dome.

"You will pay," came a tiny voice. Then another and another. Hundreds of them, saying the same thing, their voices overlapping until I could barely make out individual words.

"Leave us be."

Then I saw them. Hundreds of spotted red mushrooms with knobby arms and legs scurried through the tall grass at my feet. The grass parted for them, keeping its razor-sharp barbs from impaling the small nightmares. Beyond them, the giant lifted his hammer again.

Absolutely not.

I would not allow these creatures to destroy my realm. My *home.* What I was doing wasn't an act of war—it was an act of preservation for everyone involved. They needed the Dreamers' fear, but I needed the Dreamers to stay alive. And Nora needed a realm that wasn't imploding. There would be no fight between her nightmares and myself.

But that was the problem—they weren't Nora's yet. Right now, they were Rowan's. And Rowan… She *did* mean war, though this was the first time she took an offensive position against me.

I called on the sand within the barrier. It burst from within, using the place weakened by the giant's attack, and formed a spear the second it was clear. The tip pierced the giant between the eyes, and he fell backward, landing with a resounding boom.

The mushrooms fell silent at the sight of their dead comrade, and I flicked a look at Baku to see if he wanted the kill, but his intense gaze was fixed on the giant. So I let the sand rain down. Tiny squeals mixed with the clink of metallic barbs as the grass sought to protect itself from the acidic raindrops. The attack didn't stop until every blade of grass before me fizzled away.

I walked further down to where the grass was still alive, happy to leave the steaming pile of liquefied nightmares behind. Baku trotted over to the giant's corpse like it was a Thanksgiving feast. I shook my head and crossed back into the Dream Realm. With a flick of my hand, I sent sand in every direction to make sure nothing got inside, then set to work repairing the gaping hole in the ceiling.

The longer I wove my magic, the more my hands shook. It wasn't exhaustion—I had more than enough power now—but fury. And fear. What would Nora be walking into in three weeks? How many more attacks would Rowan send to my doorstep before then? Rowan had used Nora to kill the Weaver; now all she had to do was use her growing number of followers to bring Nora to her doorstep, and the realm would be hers. Rowan had to know the time for Nora's return was close. Things were only going to get worse from here, but I had no idea how to tell Nora that.

Baku waltzed through the barrier with a piece of the giant dangling from his mouth. As he chewed, he dipped his trunk down and wrote in the sand. When he was finished, he shoved a glob of muscle between his lips and sauntered away.

Six.

The word stared up at me. *Six.* The number of months I promised before Nora returned from the Day World, and time was nearly up. I ran the toe of my boot through Baku's note. I didn't need the reminder. Every time I saw Nora with her golden eyes and stained hands, it was glaringly obvious I was on the cusp of losing her.

Chapter Two

Nora

Once a week I was trapped in a light blue room, suffocating from the scent of eucalyptus-mint. The candle in my therapist's office was supposed to relieve stress, as was the rest of the décor: a brown, buttery leather sofa, ceiling-high windows that let in just the right amount of sunlight, and a barely audible soundtrack of crashing waves to top it all off. None of it negated the fact that I couldn't leave until the minute hand hit twelve.

That was my life now. *Waiting.* Waiting and suffering. I had to run mental rings around everyone in my life, and my body was absolutely finished with the Day World. But just like I was stuck in therapy for an hour, I was stuck in this world for another three weeks.

I glanced at my watch, the silver band stark against the black stain of the Weaver's magic on my skin. *My* magic. Of course, the therapist couldn't see the glove-like markings creeping toward my elbows, the golden veins throbbing beneath, or the gold that swallowed the green in my irises. Not that she would know what to make of it if she could.

Colleen sat in a matching chair, quietly tapping her pen against her knee. "Nora," she said gently. Always gently. Always kind. "You've been coming to see me for a little over five months now, and you've barely said two words."

I slid my sunglasses up my nose, the smallest bit of light too much for my new eyes to handle, and crossed my arms. It wasn't that I didn't want to talk about what happened, but how could I? *Well, you see, Colleen, the Nightmare Lord killed my friends because the Sandman stashed a secret in my dreams. Then I killed him, which means I get to spend the rest of eternity weaving horrible new creatures into existence in his place. Really, it's all Rowan's fault though. She's a nightmare with branch-like wings and a crown of raven beaks that can zap you into oblivion with a single touch. Or, as I like to think of her, she's a double-crossing demon with an army of moaning heathens and an angry, pointy-beaked sidekick, Kail. Anyway, they set me up with this magical knife…* Ugh. It sounded crazy even to me.

So, though I had a lot to say, sweet Colleen with her perfectly curled grey hair and grandma sweaters wouldn't get a single secret from me. This, the coming here, it was for my mother. Because no matter how strained our relationship became, the least I could do was try until the day I returned to the Nightmare Realm.

"This won't work if you aren't willing to talk to me," Colleen said.

I shrugged one shoulder and glanced at my watch again. Five

more minutes.

She sighed and shut her notebook. "Will you at least remove the sunglasses?"

"Why?" I asked, my voice dripping with suspicion. Wearing the glasses got me a few too many strange looks, so I tried not to wear them, but some days I couldn't help it. It just so happened that driving twenty minutes to the therapist's office in the middle of the afternoon exceeded my limits, especially with the pain getting worse each day.

"You've worn them for our last three meetings, and I want to make sure you're all right."

All right. When was the last time I had been all right? Before the Weaver went on a crazed killing spree? Before I met the Sandman? Did a time even exist before him? It felt like another lifetime, like I was another person. I shifted uncomfortably on the couch. I *was* a different person.

"I'm not hiding black eyes or anything, if that's what you're worried about." It certainly felt like I took a couple punches straight to the orbital area though. Actually, that would have been preferable, since that pain would only be temporary.

"I didn't mean to imply that you were." Colleen scooted forward in her chair and leaned toward me, smelling of peppermint. "Have you been crying?"

I laughed, the sound hollow and bitter. I hadn't cried since that day in the hospital.

"Did you fight with your boyfriend?" she further pried.

I took a deep breath and sat up straighter, removing the dark glasses. The sunlight immediately dried my eyes and each blink felt like sandpaper, but I refused to let myself shrink away from the growing discomfort of the Day World. Even the air hurt. It felt too dense against my skin and the universe itself seemed to shove and tug simultaneously in an attempt to be rid of me. My body had grown accustomed to the sharp pain of it all, leaving me with a constant dull ache.

"Ben and I are fine," I assured her.

She set her fingertips on my kneecap, and I fought the urge to slap them away. The pressure felt as if it would crush my leg, though I knew she was barely making contact. "Nora, a lot happened this summer."

"I'm aware." I scratched at the back of my hand, but of course the black stain didn't budge. "I was there."

"I want to help you," she said, almost pleading.

A soft click sounded from the timer on her desk. I forced a smile and settled the glasses back on my face. "Time's up, Colleen. Maybe next week."

"Actually, Nora, I think this will be our last session."

"What?" I froze, halfway off the sofa. "But I—"

"You don't want to be here." She stood and adjusted her cardigan. "I can give your hour to someone who does."

"My mother—"

She raised her hands in surrender. "If you need me to tell her, I will. She can call me tomorrow."

"No, no. Listen, just give me two more appointments, okay? That's it." I held two fingers up. "Two tiny little hours."

"Why two?" she asked with a hint of curiosity.

Because after that I'll be gone. "Let me get through Thanksgiving without letting her down. You can ruin Christmas instead."

"Not coming to therapy isn't going to ruin anything, Nora." Her expression softened. "It's not for everyone, and that's perfectly okay."

Yes, it was okay, but the problem wasn't that therapy wasn't for me. Someone like Colleen would've been a great help if my problem five years ago had truly been my parents' divorce. I stood and slung my bag over my shoulder. "If I promise to talk next Friday, will you let me come back?"

Colleen studied me for a moment, and just when I expected her to say no, she nodded. I let out a breath and grabbed a peppermint candy from the bowl on her desk. Anything to temporarily mask the permanent taste of sulfur that now lived in the back of my throat.

"Thanks. See you then," I called and bolted for the exit.

Outside, the sun was warm, the air cool, and I shivered against the extra jolt of pain the small breeze inflicted. I gave the street a quick visual sweep to ease my paranoia. All day, it felt like someone was watching me, but I was ninety percent convinced the feeling was only caused by my ever-growing magic. Either way, the quiet, residential street seemed safe enough. Nothing rustled in the neighbors' hedges or peeked up from cement storm drains.

Not that I needed to worry when the Dream Lord had my back.

The Sandman leaned against the carved stone railing outside Colleen's home office. My heart attempted to spring from my chest as it did every week, every day, every minute that I saw him. His dark t-shirt pulled against his lean muscles, and the midnight blue and silver flecks tattooed on his arms shone weakly in the sunlight. He turned at the sound of the shutting door, and a smile lit his entire face. My pain faded away, all the tension pouring from my limbs. I took the steps two at a time and flung my arms around his neck. He felt warm and sure against me. The scent of lilacs and something distinctly *him* was intoxicating. I closed my eyes and leaned into his embrace.

"Hi," he said. His breath was warm on my ear.

I smiled into the crook of his neck. "Hi."

"Ready to go?"

"More than ready." I tugged him toward my car, parked on the side of the road, but he didn't budge. "Aren't you coming?"

His violet eyes roamed my face as if he were seeing me for the first time. Or the last. It shook me to the core right there on the sidewalk. A couple walking their dog skirted around us, the woman accidentally nudging me with her shoulder, but I stood firm. I'd learned his expressions quickly over the last few months, but this one was the worst because I still wasn't sure what it meant.

"What's wrong?" I asked in a hoarse whisper. My mind raced over all the problems in the Nightmare Realm he'd brought up recently. We'd agreed on solutions. Did they not work? Was it something new? Something big? It had to be big—the look he gave me almost guaranteed it.

The Sandman's hand came up to cup my face, his thumb skimming my bottom lip. "Maybe we should take the day off from training and do something together."

"Skip training?" I jerked my head back. Sometimes I wondered who pushed harder for training, me or him. He knew the true situation in the Nightmare Realm. Not only *knew*. He saw it while I'd only heard second-hand. New ruler or not, the nightmares would eat me alive over there. Probably literally. "I don't understand," I continued. "Did something happen?"

His eyes flickered with concern, and he pulled me closer, leaning down. Our lips met. The kiss was soft, though anything but careful. It was a kiss of reverence and passion. Sweet. Desperate. I lost myself in the taste of him for the briefest of moments. In the feel of him, of being far away from all life's problems. Right then, it was just me and the Sandman. Like it used to be. But it was a lie—things would never again be like before.

I sighed, easing away so our lips were an inch apart, and tugged at one of his soft brown curls. "You're not telling me something."

"I'm just glad to see you." He nudged my nose with his. "And we've been working so hard."

"Mhm." I didn't believe that for a minute. Our training had turned into make-out sessions more than once, but we'd never skipped one in favor of the other. I really wanted to take him up on it, but time was short, and I wasn't where I needed to be as a fighter yet. "I have to be home for dinner, so we should probably get going."

He winced, and I instantly wished I'd agreed instead. Maybe he really did want to spend time together without all… *this*. I glanced at the black staining my arms, the gold veins throbbing beneath the skin, and heat crept over my face. Deep down, I wanted a day of normalcy too.

But before I could say so, the Sandman walked around my car and opened the door for me.

***

The hour-long drive out of downtown Cedarbrook was a silent one. The Sandman chewed the inside of his cheek instead of briefing me on the Nightmare Realm, which only made me more

17

curious. I knew whatever was on his mind would come out when he was ready, but that didn't make the wait any easier. Especially when I had a sinking feeling it involved nightmares.

We'd already agreed to let the Dreamers back in despite the risks of me not being there to keep the peace. If it wasn't enough, what else could we do, short of my going back early? Not that three weeks was going to do much good. I scowled out the windshield and cranked the radio to fill the booming silence as we followed the now-familiar roads far away from my mother's network of spies.

Nora skipped therapy today.

Nora jaywalked.

Nora did this. Nora did that.

I tightened my grip on the steering wheel. Leaving my family on a good note was easier said than done, but spending time with the Sandman helped. Going on a *date* with *Ben* gave my mother the impression I was trying to move forward, which cut her constant complaints about not having my GED in half. Sure, I promised I would get it, but only to earn her forgiveness for dropping out of high school. That and the therapy. I had read through a study guide, which apparently didn't count, but I doubted nightmares cared about their Lady's formal education. All they cared about was fear. Theirs. Mine. Dreamers'. Who had the most and who had the least.

I eased the car into the small dirt parking lot near a walking trail and cut the engine. The Sandman stared, unseeing, out the window.

"We can go back," I offered. "Maybe see a movie?"

He pressed his eyes shut and shook his head. "No. You were right. We only have a few more weeks."

"Let's make a deal." I grinned. "If I knock you off your feet first, we leave and do something fun."

Amusement glimmered in his starlit eyes, though not quite as brightly as I'd hoped. "And if I knock you down first?"

I leaned across the car to whisper in his ear. "Winner's choice."

I stole a quick peck on his mouth and darted from the car. The swell of his laughter brushed through my mind but quickly disappeared. Still, that his emotional control slipped even for a second widened my smile. I raced up the trail, jumping over branches, stones, and mud. I didn't have to look to know he was behind me. That's where he stayed until we reached our usual training spot.

At least one good thing came from our training: I could now run and run without getting breathless. I was fast too. Everything else on the other hand… I slowed to a stop in the middle of our clearing. Thick pines circled the oblong patch of overgrown grass, shielding us from the eyes of anyone hiking nearby. Our own little oasis, where I got my butt kicked over and over and over. The Sandman might've taught me how to throw a knife and dodge a punch, but I would never be good enough to beat nightmares like Rowan and Kail if I didn't learn how to use the magic foisted onto me. Magic the Sandman admittedly had no idea how to harness.

"Do you want to warm up first?" the Sandman asked.

It was doubtful any nightmare would give me the chance to stretch, so instead of answering, I bent and swung my leg out to knock the backs of his knees. Despite the lack of warning, he was ready for me and jumped aside. I leapt toward him. He swung out. The moves felt mechanical, rehearsed. Because they were. The same drill on repeat for five months, and I still couldn't figure out how to change it. To be better. To spot an opening and know how to take it in the blink of an eye.

I ducked beneath the Sandman's arm, pivoted, and shoved my palms against his chest. He flew to the ground, his head smacking against the dirt. I blinked down at him in shock. When I suggested knocking him down first, I hadn't believed I would win. I never won. It was an unspoken rule that he never went easy on me, no matter how much it hurt—the nightmares certainly wouldn't. And that was most definitely not him *letting* me get one over on him.

"What's going on with you?" I asked.

He sat up and rubbed the back of his head. "I suppose I'm feeling a little guilty today."

Uh-oh. "Guilty about what?"

The Sandman leaned forward and rested his elbows on his knees. "Baku and I destroyed a nightmare that could've been useful to you."

"So?" *This again?* I wiped the sweat from my forehead. "They aren't exactly in short supply, and I'm sure you had a good reason. I can make more in a few weeks anyway."

"I think—" He winced.

I tensed at the realization of where this was all headed. "If you're going to say a few weeks isn't long enough, the answer is no. We aren't delaying anything."

"It's chaos there, Nora. Anarchy. And Rowan—"

"I don't care," I shouted, then reigned my anger in. "The *only* thing keeping me together right now is that this is almost over. The physical pain, dealing with my family, all of it. I'm tired of standing at the edge of goodbye. The bandage needs to be ripped off so I can learn to be whatever it is I need to be."

He raked a hand through his hair, and a spark of dread flickered inside me. *His* dread. I hated him for it. For letting me know exactly how afraid he was when I was already terrified enough. And I hated that I couldn't hide my feelings. No matter how much I practiced, it was never enough to keep him from knowing everything through our emotional connection as Night World rulers.

"I know," he said quietly. "Don't be angry. I'm just worried about you."

"Then get up and fight me," I growled. Before he had the chance, pain flared in my back, and I let out a soft cry. It felt as if two daggers scraped against my spine. Hateful eyes, hungry and dangerous, tore into me like I was nothing more than fog.

"What is it?" The Sandman was on his feet, his hands on my arms. I couldn't answer. "Nora? What happened?"

"You don't feel it?" I asked, the words barely a breath.

His brow furrowed. "I feel *you.*"

"I think someone's watching us."

He removed the pouch of sand from beneath his shirt and turned it upside down while his eyes narrowed, glancing at the edges of the clearing. The sand spread all around us and shot straight out at the trees. A moment later, he let out a breath. "There's nothing here that shouldn't be."

I rolled my shoulders, and the pain lessened. "The stress must be getting to me," I lied. I felt it. Something was out there.

"Hang on a little longer, okay?" He kissed my forehead. "Come on. Let's get out of here."

"But—"

"You won," he said with an encouraging smile.

My phone rang, and I jumped straight into the air. "Sorry. One second." I skipped to my bag, hanging from a low branch, and dug the cell out with shaking hands. *Mom.* My nose wrinkled in disgust. What did she want?

"Hello?" I answered.

"Nora, where are you?" Someone laughed in the background. "Are you on your way home?"

"Not yet." I put my free hand on my hip and stretched my side.

"Well, you need to be."

"Why?"

"I expect you back in half an hour," she said and hung up before I could argue.

I squeezed the phone hard to keep myself from chucking it into the woods. *A half hour.* It was impossible. Now I would have to hear about being late all night. The sinister grin lurking inside me surfaced, a darkness clouding my mind, as it had nearly every day since I woke up in the hospital. Every time my reactions were a little less *Nora* and a little more angry and irrational—a little more… something else. It lured me toward an edge that I wasn't sure was possible to come back from. I pushed back at it, clawing desperately for my normal. It was like standing on ice, hearing it crack, watching the pieces around me splinter, and knowing that one wrong breath was all it would take to plunge me to my death. So I held my breath and waited for the grin to go away, for winter to refreeze the ground beneath my feet. I closed my eyes and searched for bright white snow, but inside my head, it all seemed dark. So, so dark.

The Sandman brushed the hair from the back of my neck and placed a soft kiss on the skin there. "You're okay, Nora."

"Okay?" The word came out strained, and the ice gave out. I shoved the phone back in my purse and wrapped the strap around my hand. "Sure. I'm okay. I only have to learn how to keep myself alive in three weeks when the last five months have proved I'm incapable. It'll be fine. I'll just be the Lady of Nightmares who relies on the Lord of Dreams for the rest of eternity. The nightmares will *love* that."

"I didn't mean—"

"And stop reading my emotions," I snapped.

His jaw muscle twitched. "You know I can't help it."

"Whatever." I stormed back down the path to the parking lot.

"Nora, wait," the Sandman called. "I'm sorry."

I waved a hand through the air without turning around or breaking stride. He was sorry. *Sorry, sorry, sorry.* I'd heard it from him a million times, but it didn't change anything. Just like my being sorry wouldn't turn back time and make me listen to his warning about the balance between our worlds being maintained. I wrenched the car door open and hurled my bag into the passenger seat. *Sorry* was a hollow word, and regrets helped no one. I threw myself behind the wheel, pounded my palms on the steering wheel, and screamed.

The grin darkened, showing its cutting edges.

I jerked back and took a breath. Then another and another until my heart settled in my chest. The cloud lifted but the grin remained, a watermark on my vision, a living scar. It stayed longer and longer these days. My body trembled. *Go away. Please, please, go away.* But it didn't. I jammed the keys into the ignition and peeled out of the small parking lot for home.

Chapter Three

Nora

"Nora!" My mother bounced off the couch the moment I stepped through the door. She'd gained weight recently, her cheeks fuller from all the stress-eating, and her hair seemed to be a little greyer every day. "What took you so long? You were supposed to be back a half-hour ago."

I set my purse down on the console table just inside the door and took a deep breath. Be calm, I reminded myself. Be nice. "Ben and I were halfway up a mountain when you called," I said as neutrally as possible.

Her eyes narrowed. "I'm not sure how I feel about you disappearing like that with a boy you won't invite over to meet your family."

"You've met him."

"We say hello to each other when he comes knocking on the

door, Nora. I hardly think that counts."

"Colleen thinks it's a good idea," I lied with a shrug.

My mother grunted, clearly unhappy, but unwilling to go against my therapist. "Tell someone next time you decide to go hiking. I want the name of the trail and the time you think you'll be home in case anything happens to you."

Hello to you too, Mother. I chewed the corner of my lip and nodded. I wasn't going to truthfully divulge my entire itinerary, but I wasn't going to argue with her either. "So why did I have to rush home?"

As if on cue, the back-patio door slid open. "You're back!" Katie rushed in from the backyard and maneuvered around the counter. "I thought I heard a car pull up."

My sister's hair was still dyed darker than her natural color, her blond roots barely visible. Instead of the heavy makeup she wore before the Weaver tortured her or the bare face she wore after, her eyes were carefully lined, accented with perfectly blended shadow, and her lips coated in a nude gloss. She looked amazing and so unlike herself that I found myself unable to return her smile.

I cleared my throat. "Yep."

"Took you long enough." She gave me a quick hug that I didn't return. And was that…? *Pot.* She reeked of it. How did our mother not notice? Sure, my sister was hiding it behind a picture-perfect exterior, but I was about to get high just standing next to her. We sat through roughly twenty million *no recreational drug use* speeches, yet this was suddenly fine? But when I didn't mention the Sandman for years, I was still treated like a grenade.

"Come on," Katie said brightly. "I want you to meet someone."

"What are you doing home? Don't you have classes next week?" I asked, holding my breath against the strong odor.

Katie laughed. "Is that the first thing you have to say after not seeing me for three months? A 'Welcome home! I missed you!' would be nice."

"Oh, sister dearest, how I missed you," I said in a flat voice, but her words stung. Was I turning into my mother? *No.* I was turning into an evil overlord. *Some say potato.*

She *tsked* and motioned for me to follow her into the backyard. I hesitated, glancing at my mother for a clue about who was out there, but she was immersed in folding a mound of laundry that had taken over our couch. So, head bent with exhaustion and an utter lack of interest, I joined Katie on the cement patio. She had practically bolted out of Cedarbrook after I was released from the hospital. I could count the number of times she called home on one hand, and now she showed up a week early with someone for us to meet? I watched her carefully. If I didn't know better, I might think she was sleepwalking again instead of being wide awake.

Paul stood in front of the grill with a beer in one hand. He glanced up when he saw me and smiled. I was grateful my mother married him after she divorced my father, if not for how he treated me before, then definitely for how he did after. *The same.*

"I put a burger on for you in case you're hungry."

"Thanks." I folded my arms over my aching stomach. No matter how much I ate, the hunger never left these days. "I am."

"Nora, this is Kellan." Katie clung to a boy with shaggy brown hair, bloodshot eyes, and a cartoon character on his t-shirt. "Kellan, Nora."

"Hey," he said slowly, dragging out the word. "Nice sunglasses."

My mouth opened, but I wasn't sure what to say so I let the sound of sizzling meat fill the silence. Katie glared at me, imploring me with wide eyes to say something, anything, but I had nothing. A girl can only process so many surprises at once.

Kellan gave a low, uncomfortable chuckle followed by a lopsided grin.

"This is Katie's boyfriend," Paul supplied.

"I thought you were still dating Jen," I blurted.

Katie's eyes shot daggers at me. "She wanted something serious. I wanted… fun. You're only a college freshman once, right?"

Kellan laughed again. Katie and I turned to scowl at him in unison, but he was ignoring us completely in favor of his phone. I gave Katie a withering look and pointed at him. "*That's* what you call fun?"

She grimaced and gripped Kellan's arm. "Let's go set the table."

I gaped openly at them as they walked back to the kitchen. It was like watching a semi barrel down a one-way street at rush hour in the wrong direction, and I couldn't look away. "Did you know she was coming home early?" I asked Paul.

He took a long swig of beer. "Last I heard, she wouldn't be here until next weekend."

"Did I miss the memo that she was bringing someone with her?"

"Nope." He flipped the burgers. "But try to be nice, huh? Your sister's dealing with things in her own way."

I wasn't sure she was *dealing* with anything. More like

avoiding it. With drugs and… Kellan. I glared through the kitchen window where my mother chatted brightly with them and felt myself deflate. That's what she wanted from me—to pretend. To go to therapy, get whatever was troubling me off my chest, and come home with an easy spirit. But I tried doing that for years, and she never talked to me like she was talking to Katie now.

"You can bring Ben over for dinner too, you know." Paul scooped the burgers onto a plate. "We'd like to get to know him."

"Right," I said under my breath. Like I would bring the Sandman here after everything my mother did to make me forget him. Though I supposed if I *had* forgotten him, I wouldn't be in my current predicament. The dark grin prickled inside me. *Yes, you would*, it seemed to say. And it was right. Even if I forgot, I still would've been the Dream Keeper. The Weaver still would've come for me. Still would've taken Katie, killed my boss, my friends, my father—

"Coming, kiddo?" Paul asked, sliding the back door open with his foot. I nodded and followed him into the kitchen, where he leaned over to kiss my mother on top of the head. "Everybody hungry?"

"You know it," Kellan said, followed by another dull laugh.

The table was set with paper plates and cans of soda, a ring of condensation building on the plastic tablecloth around each one. Condiments, potato salad, and corn on the cob waited in the center of the table, while the buns and burger fixings lined the counter. Everyone except me crowded around the steaming meat. My stomach rumbled but I wasn't going to fight my way to the food, brushing against everyone with my aching skin.

"I'm going to wash up first," I said, though I doubted any of them were listening. I removed my sunglasses to avoid my mother's ire. I slipped into the downstairs bathroom and splashed water on my face, careful to avoid the reflection of a girl half-there. A girl that was only half a girl at all, really. I was a creature now—one that only appeared human on the outside. Behind my now-gold eyes laid molten veins and a creeping darkness brimming with untold magic. If a nightmare managed to kill me, would I become human again? Would I regain my green eyes? Or would I rot as I was? Was the original Weaver slowly decomposing? Or was he still sprawled out on the floor of the Keep where I last saw him like some sort of blood-soaked mannequin? I retched into the sink at the thought.

"Are you pregnant?" Katie whispered from the doorway.

"What?" I snagged a washcloth from the towel rack and dried my face. "No. Are *you*?"

"I'm not the one puking."

I snorted. "Right, because that's the only reason someone would be sick."

"Well, when you pair it with your attitude lately and—"

"*My* attitude? What do you know about my attitude? You haven't talked to me since you moved out." I forced my voice to stay low to avoid attracting the others, though I wanted to scream. "I walked through hell to save you but that wasn't enough, was it? No. *You* got to come back from that cave and pretend it never happened. *I* had to go back and make sure the Weaver never bothered us again. Did you ever once think to ask me what I had to do to accomplish that? Do you even care?"

"Shut up," she hissed. "You sound as crazy as Mom thinks you are."

"Maybe I am. But then so are you. You *saw*—"

"I didn't see anything. It was just a dream," she snapped.

"Keep telling yourself that." I tossed the washcloth onto the edge of the sink and moved to push past Katie, but she stepped forward, obstructing my way. "What, Katie?"

"Stop it. You have to move forward. Dwelling on what happened won't change anything. It's all in the past."

"Maybe it's in *your* past." I knew I should stop talking, should lower my voice, but the seal was broken. Each word that escaped was louder than the last. "Denying the truth will change just as much as my dwelling on it. And for the record, there is no moving on for me so why don't you—"

"Nora!" My mother forcefully pushed her way in between us, blocking me inside the bathroom and Katie in the hall. "What's wrong with you, talking to your sister like that?"

"Me?" I laughed bitterly. "What's wrong with *me*? I don't know, Mother. Why don't you drag me to a few more doctors to find out? It worked so well last time."

She gasped, eyes wide. "That's enough."

"No. It was enough when I was twelve." I shoved her arm out of the way and shot a look at my sister. "I thought someone would finally have my back."

"Go to your room." My mother's cheeks were a vibrant shade of red. "Now."

A smirk not my own played on my lips. "Gladly."

I ran to the stairs, but halfway up, Katie called out again, her voice angry yet hesitant. "Nora—"

"You're a coward," I said without turning around.

Kellan's slow laugh echoed in my ears. "Your sister's a savage."

I whirled around mid-step and leaned over the banister looking into the kitchen. "Excuse me?"

Paul's chair scraped the kitchen floor, and he stared at me, confused. "Go cool off."

I bit my tongue and stormed to my room, slamming the door. The string of tiny lights above my bed swayed from the force. I reached above the headboard and ripped them down before falling face first onto the mattress. I hated those lights. Hated them for reminding me every night of the one place I longed for more than any other. For burning my eyes with their taunting glow.

"Sandman." I sobbed angrily into the pillow. "Help me sleep."

But I knew he couldn't hear me. Not since I became the dark to his light.

I let out a long, hard breath and gave myself to the black place that found me every night. It pulled me under just as fast as the Sandman ever had—faster. The grin widened until it felt as if it swallowed me whole, and I opened my eyes to the dark abyss I'd grown accustomed to. At least here my body hurt less for an hour or two, until my mind jerked me awake. I closed my eyes and welcomed the oblivion.

***

I wasn't sure how long I floated in darkness before light passed in front of my eyelids. The quiet buzz of the emptiness suddenly roared as awareness crept through me, and I cracked my eyes open. Only, I wasn't awake, or, if I was, my body hadn't followed. It felt like waking from anesthesia, but the process halted right before consciousness took hold. This place was nowhere—it was nothing. Nothing except for a white fissure scarring the void. I pressed my eyes shut and opened them again, expecting it to disappear, but the crack didn't move. Nor did it bother my eyes. My body inched forward of its own accord until I stood right in front of it.

A shadow passed on the other side of the uneven opening. My breath hitched, panic bubbling beneath my skin. Maybe it was better to close my eyes and drift away again. But it seemed I was no longer in control of myself. Up close, the fissure was as wide as a window in some places, as narrow as my head in others, which I discovered when I pressed my face into the light. Grey and white layers of stone twisted and turned down a long passageway. The view moved as if I walked the path myself, but my feet were firmly planted. A ragged breath drifted from the scene, followed by a small, pained groan.

"Go," a voice called from behind. I threw a quick glance over my shoulder, but only the nothingness greeted me. "She's coming. We need to *go*."

The familiar voice struck a chord. *Sandman?* What the hell was going on? The scene moved up and down, and I realized I was looking through someone else's eyes. I held my breath, too afraid that if I blinked I would miss something important. This *whole thing* felt important on some instinctual level. My vision tilted and jerked as the person slammed into a wall, then slid down.

A pair of black boots shuffled forward. Knees slammed down on the hard stone. Tattooed arms reached out and shook the person. "Come on." The Sandman tapped the side of my vision and leaned closer. His violet eyes were vivid, the pupils blown wide. Dirt was smeared across his cheeks and chin, and blood trickled from somewhere near his temple. "Stay with me."

"I'm fine." The words sounded anything but fine. They sounded like the man's last. Weak. Broken.

A bloodied arm rose, trembling, to push the Sandman away, and my hands flew to my mouth. Black threads glimmering with gold shone on the man's wrist. *The Weaver.* The Sandman helped him to his feet, then crouched and ran around the next bend. My view clouded, then righted itself, moving in time with the Weaver's unsteady steps.

This was the Weaver's point-of-view. His memory. Was the Weaver so ingrained in the magic that it remembered too? A sour, metallic taste coated my tongue. Knowing some of the things the Weaver had done, I didn't think I could stomach seeing more. And what did it mean? The Sandman said he and the Weaver were friends once, but seeing the look of true fear on his face, the unfiltered terror that the Weaver wouldn't make it… With their combined power, it didn't make sense for them to run from anything.

The fissure snapped shut in my face, and I stumbled back. Icy pinpricks dotted my skin. Everything about this was wrong—the memory, what the memory held. Was it real? A fabrication? I tripped over my own feet, and the world spiraled around me.

Chapter Four

Nora

Waking was like dropping from the top of a roller coaster, only my cart wasn't connected to the tracks. My heart spasmed. I couldn't breathe. I was weightless, floating, and yet tethered to the instrument of my own death. Then I was suddenly on my bed. Safe. The familiar ache crept back into my bones, and my brain scrambled to reach that semi-peaceful place again. Though after what I saw, I wasn't sure peaceful was the right word. The Sandman and the Weaver were… I scowled. They were what? It all made perfect sense there, but now it seemed out of reach. Like a dream that ceased to exist upon waking. *A dream.* I always remembered mine before. Now, it felt like another person had seen the Weaver's memory. If that's what it was. Maybe I *was* dreaming. I groaned into the pillow.

Just what I needed. More problems and confusion.

My mother's laugh clawed through my door. The soft hum of other voices mingled with it, and I flipped onto my back. Dusk filtered orange light into my room through the open window. Had it been open when I fell asleep? It must have been—I would've woken up if anyone came in. My mother, most likely, had aired the room while I was out, probably as she searched for something incriminating.

I pushed myself up with a grunt. There was no way I was capable of going back downstairs tonight and *not* fighting with Katie. I didn't understand why she was acting like nothing happened. She admitted it was all real in the hospital and even asked a few questions after I woke up. I assumed she hadn't mentioned it again because she was sorting through it, but then she left for college without bringing it up. Even tonight, she more or less admitted she was pretending. Exasperated, I threw myself into my desk chair.

Ungrateful. All of them.

I slid open the top drawer of my desk and dug the tin pencil case out from the clutter at the back. The threads I stole from the Weaver that night in the storage unit thrashed inside, desperately hoping I would release them. How I wished I could. The only thing stopping me was myself, but that was more than enough. However much I longed to absorb their tiny scraps of power, the memory of the threads from the loom clinging violently to my arm was stronger. Sometimes I could still feel where they circled my wrist like a manacle. I pressed the cool metal of the tin against my chest and shut my eyes. *Soon,* I promised. *I'll take you home soon.*

Suddenly, the hair on the back of my neck stood on end.

Something was in the room with me, watching as it had on and off all day. Something familiar and right, but also perverse. *Painful.* My pulse thundered, but I was the Weaver now. Lady of Nightmares. The girl who was supposed to fear nothing. I forced myself to open my eyes, and every last cell in my body froze.

A girl in a threadbare white shift crouched on the desk in front of me. Her knobby knees bent up to her ears, her unusually long shins bare and covered in deep black veins. Chocolate brown eyes stared at me through horizontal pupils. "Hello, Lady." Her voice was a stilted, crackling thing as if she hadn't spoken in years. "Do they want to play?"

Don't be afraid, don't be afraid, don't be afraid. "W-what?" I croaked.

The creature reached out and gently scratched the pencil case with a long, jagged nail. I held my breath, not daring to move. Thick, fanned lashes rose and fell as she blinked. "Wicked, wicked Lady."

Sweat beaded on my forehead, and my knuckles turned white around the tin. What was she doing here? *How* was she here? The nightmares were supposed to be trapped in the Night World. That was the entire reason the Weaver did what he did—to get the secret to releasing his creatures into this world. If they could pop over whenever they wanted, it was all pointless. But it *couldn't* be pointless. People had *died* in the name of his failed mission. There had to be a logical explanation. I sat up straighter and squared my shoulders while my insides screamed to run. "What are you doing here?" I asked in my most authoritative voice. After all, if I couldn't face one of them in my own bedroom, there was no way I could face an entire realm.

She tapped her fingertips absently over her head of wild,

crimped hair. "I'm stuck."

"You're stuck?" I glared at her as the grin inside me turned into a deep frown, setting off tiny explosions of envy and anger. "How so?"

"Came before the walls." She sniffed. "Now I can't get back. So, I'm stuck, you see. Like you, Lady Nightmare. I can show you how to survive here. Would you like that? It's easy. You simply—"

"No," I blurted. "I'm going back, and you should too."

A smirk crept slowly over her face, not reaching her eyes. "Oh yes, Lady. I would like that very much. The last Weaver did not care to help a poor thing like me. Do you know how to take me with you? That's very simple too."

"I—" Heat rose in my cheeks. I didn't even know how to get myself back. "Who are you, exactly?"

"I have many names, Lady." She took a step across the desk, her knee bones shifting at odd angles beneath her skin to accommodate her crouched walk.

Don't back away. Don't give an inch. "Pick one."

The nightmare licked her parched, cracked lips. "Mara."

"It doesn't ring a bell. What are you the nightmare of, exactly?"

"I was never assigned a particular occupation, though I have my preferred methods of entertainment. Did the Weaver force nightmares to be one thing? It wasn't like that before the Night World became separate from the Day World, but, stuck as I am, I know very little about what home is like now."

Something inside me twisted in warning, but I ignored it. She said *before* the worlds were separate, which meant they weren't separate entities at one point. How long ago was that? Long enough that the Sandman didn't think to mention it—not that I should use that to gauge anything. It's not like we had time for intensive history lessons.

"Are there others trapped here?" I asked.

"We are solitary creatures."

I narrowed my eyes. "That's not an answer."

Her facial muscles spasmed, her smile strained. "The Sandman dealt with everyone the Weaver released a few years ago."

"I see." That wasn't an answer either. I stood and placed the pencil case back in the drawer. "I'm not leaving for a few weeks. Come back then."

"Why wait, Lady? You're growing weaker every day, just as I am. Your magic should have been completely absorbed within a week, and yet your arms look as if they've been dipped in paint."

Weaker? But I was training. Preparing. The Sandman wouldn't let me stay if it hurt my chances of protecting myself. The truth of her words hit home, though—I felt it in every ache. But the magic. How would she know the length of time it took to absorb it if the Weaver had always been the Weaver? *Focus, Nora.* I had to get rid of her before my thoughts spiraled.

"I have things to take care of first," I said. "Not that I need to explain myself to you."

Mara hummed. "As you say, Lady Nightmare. But if you want to go back sooner, I can help."

"You should leave." I crossed the room and pulled aside the curtains, then tucked my quaking hands behind me. There was no chance I was leaving her in the Day World to torment anyone. The mere thought of her touching me made me shiver—I could only imagine what she did to mortals. "I'll let you know when it's time to go.”

Mara leapt off the desk with surprising dexterity and crept toward me. She barely came up to my waist in her crouched stance. “Call for me, and I’ll hear you.” She jumped onto the sill and paused, balancing effortlessly. “Don’t forget.”

Then she shoved herself out the window. I stuck my head out after her, knowing she wouldn’t purposely splatter herself on the side lawn but needing to be sure. She landed gracefully beside the fence between my house and Natalie’s, then did a frog-like leap into the woods behind the backyard. I stared after her as sweat poured down my neck. The nightmares I’d met in the Nightmare Realm were terrible, but none of them had chilled my blood like Mara. There was something about her—an ancient, foreboding aura.

A light flicked on next door in Natalie’s room, and I slammed my window shut with a startled gasp. My back met the wall beside the curtains, and I wished—oh, how I wished—I could disappear into them. My best friend’s mother had a new nightly ritual that gutted me. Turn on the light. Sit on Natalie’s bed. Smell her pillow. There might have been more after that, but that was as much as I was able to watch. I gripped the fabric of my shirt over my heart and pressed down on the pain. It was my fault Natalie was dead. No matter what anyone told me, I knew it was. I slid down the wall and buried my head in my knees.

All I could do to avenge my friends, I had done.

All I could do to protect the people I was leaving behind, I would do.

Even if that meant taking Mara back with me despite the tiny voice in the back of my head screaming not to.

Chapter Five

The Sandman

Sneaking around to see Nora at night was a new experience, one I wasn't exactly fond of. Instead of her simply falling asleep—a perfectly normal human function—and arriving at the beach, I had to turn my gaze inward to her family's cords. Then I had to wait until they glowed brightly enough that there was no fear of anyone waking so I could follow one of them to Nora's house. As if voyeurism wasn't bad enough, creeping into Nora's room made me feel like a criminal.

I stood in the hallway at one a.m. with one hand pressed against Nora's closed door. Her anxiety pulsed through from the other side. I felt it constantly, sometimes mixed with other feelings—anger or fear, mostly, but always with the buzz of nerves. I sucked in a breath. Maybe tonight would help, even if it was only for a little while. Seeing her happy was worth everything. My stomach churned, and I slipped into the dark room, shutting the door with a quiet click.

"Hey." Nora didn't look up, her pencil scratching furiously over paper in the moonlight.

"Hi." Hope fluttered to life. She hadn't picked up her colored pencils since—since *before*. "You're drawing again?"

Her shoulders tensed. "No," she said after a moment.

Disappointment swept the hope away faster than it had come. "Are you busy then?" I asked when she continued to focus on the notebook.

"Not particularly." After a few seconds more, she set the pencil down and splayed her hands on the desk. A list ran the full length of the paper, more than half the notes crossed off. "I'm sorry about the way I treated you earlier. It wasn't right for me to overreact like that."

"You're under a lot of pressure right now," I said, taken slightly aback. She lost her temper more often these days, though not as badly as she had today, and we always pretended it didn't happen. I understood why she would be cranky trapped in the Day World, unable to sleep and in constant pain.

"That's not an excuse." Her shoulders relaxed, and she stood to face me. "It's been a hard day."

I knew. The spikes of hatred I felt earlier told me she'd had another incident with her mother. After the phone call during training, I half expected it, which was why tonight was even more important. I held out a hand with a sheepish smile. "Come with me."

Nora glanced over her shoulder at the window, then back at the paper. A flicker of doubt crossed her face. "Where?"

"It's a surprise," I said playfully. Her gold eyes stared, unblinking, as she chewed her bottom lip. The smile fell from my face. "Nora?"

"Sorry." She let out a quick breath. "I'm trying to figure out what I still need to do before I leave."

My eyes flicked back to the open notebook. Everything was already taken care of—a fake internship with her late father's company in New York, complete with a fake address and a working phone number where her mother could leave messages for us to return later. I estimated it would be at least two months before they suspected anything was amiss. All that was left was to pack a bag to keep up appearances, and even that wasn't completely necessary.

"Can I help?" I asked.

"No." A crease formed between her brows. "Maybe. I'll let you know when I'm done thinking it all through."

I took her hand and laced our fingers together. "Let me give you something in the meantime."

"Oh? The surprise is a present?" She perked up and squeezed my hand. "Tell me it's food, because I could eat a horse right now."

"You'll see," I teased.

She smiled and followed me quietly through the house. The excitement made it hard to move with any real stealth. Nora was going to love it. At least, I hoped so. As we turned toward the kitchen at the bottom of the stairs, something rustled in the living room, and I froze. The blue glow of the TV showed an unfamiliar boy slumped on the couch with Katie's head on his lap, asleep.

Nora bumped into my back, then followed my gaze and

groaned. "Just go," she whispered.

The boy laughed and clawed the air with one hand, mimicking an angry cat. "Careful with that one," the stranger warned benevolently.

I scowled, but Nora nudged me forward. I paused at the back door and pressed the code into the alarm system before swiping an open bag of potato chips from the counter. "I didn't know your sister was home."

"Yeah. You're not the only one with a surprise tonight," she said sarcastically.

I hadn't bothered to check Katie's cord while she was away at college. I doubted she would tell their parents if Nora snuck out, but it was better to play it safe. "Who's with her?"

"Don't ask."

I glanced back at the living room where the guy laughed quietly at something on the screen. Nora was right—I shouldn't ask. Nothing mattered tonight except her. Not the Night World, not magic, not training. Just us.

Nora slipped on a pair of flip-flops left on the patio, and we crossed the backyard to the small shed nestled against a pine tree. I lifted the ladder off the hooks screwed into the siding and propped it against the edge of the roof. "Wait here a minute. Hold these," I added, pressing the chips into her hand.

She wrinkled her nose. "Is this some sort of test?"

"No." Though I could see why she thought that. The last time I dragged her out in the middle of the night was to train after a rather grueling week in the Nightmare Realm. I grazed her cheek with my thumb. "Trust me."

I hurried onto the roof and emptied handfuls of sand onto the shingles, forming it into the perfect nest. A thick, down-filled comforter to lay on with an array of pillows and another heavy blanket, big enough to cover us both. There was only one thing missing, but first… "Close your eyes," I said, peeking down at Nora.

"What?" Her gaze darted to the woods, then back at me. "Why?"

My chest panged. She was still afraid of shadows, and who could blame her? But there was nothing to fear now. Not tonight. "Please?"

She hesitated before complying. I stared at her a moment, taking in each freckle. Warmth radiated through my body, flushing my cheeks. Did anyone in the world love a girl more than I loved her? It didn't seem possible. If someone told me years ago that the Dream Keeper and I would have feelings for each other, I would've laughed at them. She was only meant to serve a purpose, not become the most important thing in my personal life. We became friends one night at a time, despite my attempts to keep distance between us, and then it happened. One night I looked at her, smiling and laughing as she told me about something that happened at school, and new emotions bulldozed me. It took half a second, and I was done for without even knowing I was in danger. But what a wonderful danger to be in.

A warm grin spread across my face as I emptied the rest of the sand onto the blankets. With one upward motion, it soared into the sky and hovered, waiting.

"You can come up now," I called softly.

The ladder creaked almost instantly. It took all my self-control not to rush her, and when her blond hair popped up over the edge, my heart did somersaults. Her lips parted in a wary smile. "What's this?" she asked, patting the blankets.

I held out my hand to help her off the last rung. Once she was on the roof, I lowered myself onto the blankets. She eased down beside me and immediately snuggled into my side. A small groan sounded in my throat before I could stop it. No matter how many times she was close to me, the heat of her skin meeting the heat of mine felt like the first time. It was the most precious feeling in the world to have her pressed into me like I was her anchor. I pulled the top blanket up around us before settling down and loosening a breath. Nora stared at me in the way I always wished she would, but the gold of her eyes was an unwelcome reminder that her feelings might not survive her reign.

When she closed the distance between our lips, I drank her in as if she was the last oasis in the desert. Her hands wound around my neck, and I cupped her face. I kissed her until I was drunk from it. Until everything else fell away, and all I knew was the feel of her. Until the moment a kiss wasn't all I wanted. I pulled back then, because a kiss was all I could allow myself until our relationship stood on undeniably solid ground. If Nora regretted things later, it would crush me a thousand times worse than a thousand kisses ever could.

I pressed my forehead to hers. When my pulse slowed and my breath calmed, I nudged my magic toward the sand hovering overhead and brought my lips to her ear. "Nora?"

"Hmm?" she answered, content.

"I brought you the stars."

She twisted in my arms and gasped. Above us danced a million glimmering stars as bright and brilliant as the ones above the Dream Realm. Hot tears rolled down her cheeks, dripping on my hand where I propped myself up. "Thank you," she breathed.

I kissed her tears away, catching the ones that escaped with my thumbs. Then I kissed her nose, her mouth, her neck, until it felt as if we were glowing just as brightly under our blanket.

"Tell me something," she said when I finally put some space between us again. "Something I don't know yet that isn't about dreams or nightmares or magic."

Those three things took up my entire life. What could I tell her that was new? Not that George Washington dreamed of cheese almost every night or that children used to call to me for more than sleep. They wanted stories and, for a while, I would agree to short ones on the beach, spinning tales before sending them into blissful slumber. Centuries had passed since, but those were other tales of dreams and magic.

"Before you, I never felt real," I admitted reverently. "I was simply a legend. Even when people believed in my existence, that was all people thought of me—that I brought good dreams. They didn't see me as an individual. As a *person*, like you do."

"Of course you're a person," she said defensively. "Different, maybe, but in the ways that count, you're more human than a lot of us are."

Nora's hair slipped between my fingers, smooth as silk, and I lifted another lock. Hopefully she was right. Everything seemed so much heavier than the burdens placed on a mortal. Balancing the Day and Night Worlds wasn't easy to do alone. Nora snuggled into my side, and peace flowed through me. I wasn't alone. Not anymore.

"Stay here with me tonight?" she asked. "Like old times."

I lifted her hand and kissed her knuckles. "I wouldn't leave for anything in the world."

***

Dawn broke much too soon. I released the magic holding the stars and eased my arm out from beneath Nora's head. "I have to get back." I kissed her, slow and lingering. "And you have to get inside before anyone wakes up."

She stretched out on the blankets with a sleepy grin. "I don't *have* to."

"We have training later," I reminded her, tracing a line down her side. She jerked away, laughing, when I brushed against the ticklish spot above her hip. "I won't be gone long."

She stuck her tongue out at me and sat up. "Thank you. For this."

I kissed her again, cupping her neck, and sighed against her lips. "I miss you."

"I miss you too." She reached up and plucked at one of my curls. "It feels like we haven't talked in a long time."

It was true, but I hated hearing it. Talking was what brought us together. Lately, our conversations centered around rogue nightmares, training, and all the problems in between. I still hadn't told her about the attack on the Dream Realm for fear of overwhelming her. It was over and done with, and soon they would have their Lady to set things right.

"I—I met someone last night," she said quietly.

I reared back as if she had slapped me. There was no way she meant another guy—Nora was a lot of things, but unfaithful wasn't one of them. "Someone?" I asked, my head tilted.

"A nightmare," she clarified.

The blood drained from my face. "That's impossible. I killed everyone the Weaver let out before I bound him."

"She told me that, but I don't think she's technically one of his. She felt… different." She rubbed her forehead as if she had a headache. "She claims to be stuck here because she came before the Day and Night Worlds were separate."

"Before…" My hands shook. "*Mare* was here?"

"She said her name was Mara, but—"

"What did she say to you? Did she do anything? Did she hurt you?" I asked in a rush.

"I'm fine. A little surprised, obviously."

So was I. Mare was banished so long ago that she should've withered away under the stress of the Day World by now. Or, at the very least, been too weak to do any damage. If she tracked Nora down from halfway across the world where the Weaver and I left her, she had to be in minimally decent condition. Unless she had drifted this way without my noticing.

"What did she want?" I asked carefully.

"To go back home." Nora touched my fists thoughtfully. "It'll be okay. We'll take her back with us before she—"

I took Nora's hands, squeezing them hard to make sure she knew I was serious. Enough horrible things had happened because she took my warnings too lightly. "Stay away from her. Promise me."

She frowned. "I don't think we should leave her here. What if she hurts someone? Katie's still here. Paul, my mom—"

"She's been relatively harmless for ages while there's been nothing and no one here to stop her." At least, I thought so. Belief in Mare faded away so long ago that it had to be true. Even her myth wasn't well-known anymore, but I wasn't sure Nora would forgive me for setting Mare loose in the Day World to protect myself. *Ourselves.* The Weaver and I banished her together to protect everything we'd built, though we had no way of knowing the consequences then. Cleaving our worlds in two is what eventually turned us against each other. That set the scales. Light and dark. Dream and nightmare. Good and bad. We each became what we had to become after that.

But at least we existed.

In the Day World, Mare was worn down and nearly powerless, killing Dreamers by sitting on their chest while they slept. She was different in the Night World—a ferocious creature that delighted in tearing things apart with her bare hands and using their bones to pick their flesh from her teeth. People, places. Nightmares. If the Weaver and I hadn't expelled her, there wouldn't be any world at all.

"She's not stuck," I reluctantly told Nora. "The Weaver and I banished her here. If Mare goes back, she'll destroy the Night World, and the Day World will die along with it."

She cringed away from me. "Again with the balance."

"Yes. Always." Fury curled unbidden from my center. "Was becoming the Weaver not proof enough for you?"

"Obviously the balance exists," she snapped back. "But I don't think the consequence of destroying one world will be the destruction of another. The Weaver's death didn't kill you."

"Yes, it did," I shouted. Heat licked up my neck, scalding me with shock. "It *almost* did," I corrected myself, softer. I never wanted her to know what happened to me that day, but maybe it was wrong to keep it a secret. Still, meeting her eyes as I spoke the truth tempered my anger and crushed my soul. "I felt as if I broke into a thousand pieces outside the Weaver's keep that day. I was a single breath away from death. I'm not sure what stopped it, but Nora… We can't take that kind of risk. Mare's not worth it."

"You—" Nora's voice stuck. The color drained from her face until she was as white as snow beneath her freckles. She clutched at her stomach and swayed. "I—" She lunged for the ladder but overshot.

I looped an arm around her waist before she fell from the roof. "I'm sorry."

"For what?" She shook beneath my arm. "What could you possibly be sorry for? I almost *killed* you. And you spent the last five months pretending I didn't."

I winced. "I don't blame you, Nora."

"You *should* blame me." She shoved my arm away and slid down the ladder.

I fought the urge to run after her and tell her that I forgave her, but it wasn't entirely true. She didn't fully trust me—that's what hurt the most. She trusted Rowan and Kail, two strangers, two *nightmares*, more than she trusted me to rebind the Weaver. So, while I understood her actions, the ache they caused still lingered. Hopefully digesting the information would dissuade her from wanting to bring Mare back, not that I would ever allow it.

The Weaver and I had given up too much to get Mare here. Our friendship was destroyed when we bled white and black from grey. *We* were destroyed. And still, it killed me to know that Nora was hurting. I slammed a hand down on the roof, dissolving our nest of blankets. She was the leader of nightmares now, and if she was going to survive, I had to stop coddling her. She needed to understand. But the look of intense pain on her face as I spoke the truth would never fade from my memory.

My lungs struggled to expand, my muscles to move. It was

as if my very existence was weighed down by the growing mound of trouble. First, the Weaver killed Nora's loved ones, then Nora killed him, *then* Rowan took the Keep. Inside, the loom—Nora's source of power—was held hostage. Now Mare. I groaned and gave into the magic, letting it pull me home to the Dream Realm. The quiet serenity of the beach swallowed my thoughts and projected them back tenfold. If I stayed here with my warring feelings of love and hate, anger and understanding, I knew which emotions would win. So, instead of grappling with the desire to make peace with Nora, I forced myself to cross into the Nightmare Realm without looking back.

***

A narrow path led away from a landscape of open graves, some stacked with rotting corpses, others empty and waiting. I followed where the packed dirt twisted through a crooked cemetery gate with the wails of unseen mourners following at my heel. Before me, tall, skeletal trees lined the walkway as far as the eye could see, reaching into the sky where the tops disappeared in a thin red mist. Red berries lay scattered at their roots. It was silent here. I strained my ears in hopes of hearing a Dreamer in need of saving. Not that I wanted someone to be in danger, but I needed to let off some steam.

"Sandman."

I froze and squinted ahead of me. A figure sat at the very edge of the hazy path. I stepped closer, one hand sliding into my satchel. "Show yourself," I demanded.

"You don't recognize me?" the voice answered, taunting. "I'm wounded."

"You've got to be kidding me." I groaned to myself and took another three steps forward. It wasn't the voice itself that I recognized but the attitude behind it.

Kail perched on a jagged stump, the only tree not identical to the rest. His white pointed mask gleamed in the shadows. An easy smirk played on his lips beneath the curved beak as he picked at his embroidered sleeve, and I closed a fist around my sand. If it wasn't for him, Nora would've gone along with my plan and everything would've gone back to normal. I took a breath, preparing to throw every weapon I could think of at him, but then I paused. This wasn't right. I was looking for a fight, but not this one. At least not until I could get confirmation from my spies if he was still working with Rowan or not. And if he was, I couldn't touch him because Nora needed to avenge herself. I turned and began walking away.

"You'll want to hear what I have to say."

"Doubtful," I said with ire.

"All right, all right. You win. I'll give you a free swing at me first." When I didn't stop walking away, he added, "I know how to help her."

"Help her?" I spun and stormed back down the path before I could stop myself, each step reverberating through my core. "If it wasn't for you and Rowan, Nora wouldn't *need* help." I gripped the collar of his black jacket. "How did you get the knife?"

"I don't know how Rowan got it." He studied his fingernails, seemingly unfazed by my unspoken threats. "But speaking of Rowan—" He brushed my hands away. The tip of his mask skimmed his chest as he smoothed out the wrinkles my clenched fists had left behind. "This used to be her."

I opened my mouth to demand the truth about the blade, but

curiosity won out instead. "What used to be who?"

"Rowan. As in the tree." Kail kicked the jagged stump with the toe of his boot. "The Weaver liked to recycle things on occasion. Seems irrelevant, I know."

"Completely irrelevant," I agreed. "What am I supposed to do with that information?"

Kail shrugged. "Just planting a bug in your ear."

"You said you could help Nora," I snarled. It didn't matter if Rowan started as a tree or a speck of dirt. She was what she was now, and she would pay for what she did. "Why would you want to?"

One blue eye bored into mine while the other flickered through various colors. A small seed of satisfaction grew inside me, knowing that the steady iris was Nora's handiwork.

"When Nora comes back, I think it's only fair she has a fighting chance." Kail shrugged.

"You don't care about her."

"Who said I cared?" Kail laughed. "Maybe I'm just curious what she'll do, given the chance. As an outsider. As a Dreamer."

I swung a fist into his jaw. He stumbled back and looked up at me from behind his mask. "Stay away from her," I warned.

Kail rolled his eyes. "Her magic is too different from yours. You can't help her with this."

"Don't tell me what I can or cannot do. She—"

"But I can," he shouted over me, then stormed away before I could punch him again.

I wanted to run after him and rage. Hit him. Break him. Instead, I shouted wordlessly at the empty space he'd occupied a moment ago, spittle flying. Kail would pay for everything he was part of from the moment Nora fell into the Nightmare

Realm.

Him and Rowan.

I glowered at the jagged stump and imagined it as the woman herself. Imagined white hot flames licking up the sides, crackling the bark. And then they were. My sand fed the conjured blaze, urging it higher and higher, until the exact moment I realized I had lost control of my thoughts. The sand acted on instinct, enacting my will. I pressed the heels of my hands against the throbbing in my temples. *Calm down.* I had to calm down.

After a handful of long, deep breaths, the fire flickered out of existence, and I turned for the Dream World without looking back.

Chapter Six

Nora

The whirlwind of the mall nearly swept me away. People moved in currents, brushing past me where I stood as if I were a boulder in their river. Some grumbled at me to move, but most moved with silent purpose. My body shook in response to the sensory overload. The people, the lights, the crushing noise. My skin felt raw beneath my layers of clothing. But I was almost done. With this place and this world. If I could just hang on a little longer.

I slid my sunglasses up my nose and clutched the list in my hand. All three presents were checked off. A picture frame for my mother with a family photo inside and an engraved flask for Paul—he would need it after I left. For Katie, I found a pair of black tassel earrings with gold caps. Perhaps gifting my sister a reminder of the Weaver's threads was a bit petty, especially since I braved the same shop where we had watched the cashier stab herself to death to buy them, but she *deserved* petty. She *should* remember, her eyes *should* stay open, so she could look out for herself if she ever needed to.

"Nora?"

My back tightened at the familiar voice. The last time I saw Detective Bell, he was asking my mother for a chance to apologize while I was in the hospital. Her vehement *no* was a relief. I never expected to run into him again, but there he was, cutting through the crowd until he stood in front of me. Instead of his usual shirt and tie, he wore a black hoodie with a jaguar head screen-printed on the front. His silver-framed glasses were missing but had left seemingly permanent divots in the sides of his nose, and his jaw was sprinkled with faint grey stubble.

I forced a small smile and held up my bags. "I'm just on my way out."

"Wait." He cleared his throat. "Please. I only need a minute."

"I'm sort of in a rush so…" I glanced around him to my final stop—a dollar store where I planned on grabbing something colorful to wrap everything in, but the white tissue paper we had at home would serve the same purpose if it meant avoiding the detective. "See you."

He reached out to stop me but dropped his arm at the last moment. "I want to apologize for everything."

"Are you referring to the interrogations, the threats, or just suspecting me in general?" I cringed at my own tone and for opening the door to a conversation by asking the question. I wanted to get away from him, not hear him out. Besides, he wasn't wrong in thinking I was involved. I pressed my arms to my sides and inched further into the flow of the crowd.

"I should never have focused on you," he admitted without hesitation. "You weren't capable of most of those things and obviously had nothing to do with the death you witnessed firsthand, but you were the only link to all the murders. The graphic nature of the crimes affected me more than I'd like to admit. I was exhausted and seeing things by the time everything ended." He paused to draw a long breath.

Exhausted. Seeing things. The internal grin curled in amusement at the words, and I shifted my shopping bags to my other hand. "What kind of things were you seeing?"

"It's not important. I only wanted you to know how sorry I am." He hunched his shoulders, shaking his head as if to clear it, and turned away.

The grin continued to spread, smug. It was almost like the dark part of me recognized something in him. Almost like—*More than one sleepwalker,* the Weaver told me once. It would've been just like him to use the police as another way to pressure me into giving him the dream. It was more than enough that people around me were dying and my sister was missing, but not to him. To the Weaver, it wasn't working. I was still resisting. If life in prison loomed over my head as well… It made sense. Everything the Weaver did made sense.

"Detective Bell?" I called.

He stopped. "I'm not a detective anymore. I resigned."

I scowled, deflating a bit. Another life ruined. "Did anything you imagined actually happen?"

"How did you—" He rubbed a hand over his bald head. "Take care of yourself, Miss Gallagher."

I watched him walk away a different man than I knew over

the summer. Gone was his confidence, his anger, but something else had taken their place. Confusion. Guilt. It wafted off him like bad cologne. *He locked Katie in the storage unit.* The thought came and went so fast it barely had time to register. The residue it left was sticky with truth. He did it.

"Hey," the Sandman whispered.

My heart jumped, one hand flying to my chest, and I spun toward the Sandman while keeping my eyes on Bell. "You scared the crap out of me."

"Sorry." He took my bags and wove his fingers between mine.

I stared at his hand, felt the warmth of him, and fought the urge to rip myself free. To run back home and hide under the covers. How could he dare to touch me after I went behind his back to kill the Weaver? After my brash act nearly killed him? The tell-tale pressure of tears began behind my eyes, and here I thought I had cried them all out in the shower this morning after leaving him on the roof.

His grip tightened as if he sensed my thoughts. "Wasn't that the detective that covered all the murders? He isn't still bothering you, is he?"

I nodded, then realized that only answered one of his questions honestly. With a deep steadying breath, I said, "That's him, but he wasn't bothering me. I think the Weaver used him."

"Used him how?"

"He—" I swallowed hard and looked up into the Sandman's earnest face. He didn't know about the grin I carted around. Mainly because I didn't know how to explain it, but also because I didn't want him to stop looking at me the way he did. There was precisely one person in the entire world—in both worlds—

that put me first in their heart, and I selfishly didn't want that to go away. Each breath became hard won, and the crowd felt as if it was closing in on us. I'd done enough to give him reason to hate me—how much more would it take until he did?

"I can't explain how I know," I said carefully. "But the Weaver made him sleepwalk. He's the one who locked Katie in the storage unit and did who knows what else."

"What do you mean you can't explain it?" the Sandman asked, his voice sounding uncertain.

"It's just something I *know*." I shifted on my feet, desperate for him to drop it and focus on the more pressing revelation: that Bell had been the one to lock Katie up.

"Right." His scowl deepened. "Anyway, we need to talk about something important."

More important than the Weaver using Bell against me? Though I supposed that was a moot point now. "What happened?" I asked warily.

"Come with me."

He pulled me close, tucking me beneath his arm, and we snuck through one of the back exits. Cobwebs filled every corner of the dim hallway, and the beige tiles were stained black from years of wear. Each door had a sign taped haphazardly below a peephole with the name of the store for receiving deliveries. The exits didn't open to any of the customer parking lots, so they were rarely used by anyone other than employees, making them perfect for a private conversation. I leaned against the tiled wall and welcomed the coolness of it seeping through my shirt.

"Okay." I held my breath, knowing this couldn't be good. "Go ahead."

The Sandman ran both hands through his hair and licked his

lips. "Rowan's going to be a bigger problem than we expected."

Anger flared in me, hot enough that the wall would surely have scorch marks afterwards. *Of course she was.* She set me up to kill the Weaver so she could kill me. Then she stole my Keep, loom included, and riled up my nightmares. "What did she do now?" I asked through my teeth.

"The other day when I told you that Baku and I killed a nightmare?" He waited until I nodded to continue. "After, when we went back to the Dream Realm, we found it under attack."

"*What?*"

"Nothing I couldn't handle. A single giant beating at the barrier and some talking mushrooms," he said, hands raised. "I didn't want to say anything until my spies confirmed Rowan sent them, and then today I saw Kail."

"*Kail?*" I screeched.

The Sandman's eyes widened as the sound echoed down the hall, and he shot a look over his shoulder. "He offered his help."

"His help?" I barked a laugh. "He's helped enough, wouldn't you say?"

"Regardless, we can't trust him."

"You think?" I agreed. The grin flickered to life. *Calm down,* I thought to myself. *Don't lose yourself.* The Sandman and I both knew what Kail had done, and neither of us would forget that.

The Sandman paced away from me. "The timing is off. Why would he wait until right before your return?"

"Does it matter? He obviously wants to set me up again."

I rapped my fingers on my thighs in contemplation. Why wasn't Kail in the Keep with Rowan? Did she send him to find the Sandman? They could've had a falling out and delivering me was his way back into her good graces. Or maybe he wanted to be the one to find me first. The one to kill me and take the Weaver's power.

"I think…" The Sandman drew in a deep breath and stared at the exit sign over my head. "I think we should move the date back."

Sweat broke out across my body, and I shoved away from the wall. "I knew this would happen. Are you out of your mind?"

"Not by much," he said in a rush. "An extra week so there's time to find out what their plan is."

"You have eighteen days to figure that out." I scowled, and the grin mirrored the sentiment. Enough was enough. Rowan wasn't going to make claiming my realm easy no matter when I returned. If anything, giving her more time was the worse option. Why let her get any stronger than she already was? We would have the element of surprise if I went back now, but I needed the Sandman to take me. And apparently, he wouldn't. "Is this because you don't want me to go back? You'd rather let Rowan rule in my place?"

He blanched. "Why would I want someone else running the Nightmare Realm? Especially Rowan? As much as I hate admitting it, it's yours. Besides, the nightmares are too unstable to rule each other—they need you."

"*I'm* unstable," I shouted. I doubted I'd be any good at ruling, but anything I did there had to be better than the nothing I was doing here.

"I believe in you, Nora," He said simply.

"Then take me back. Now, not later." I tore off my sunglasses. "Look at me. I don't belong here anymore. Keeping me here is doing more harm than good. If Rowan and Kail are setting a trap for me, we'll deal with it together."

He lifted a hand to my face and ran his thumb over my cheekbone. "Let me get more information before we decide."

"We decided a long time ago."

He hesitated before leaning down to kiss me on the corner of my mouth. I wanted not to react, to let him know I couldn't be sweet-talked into changing my mind, but I leaned into it instead. There was no telling how many more kisses we would have or what would change between us once I got back. I would be busy claiming the Keep and learning how to use the loom in order to cement my authority. And he would be… What would he do? He couldn't be seen helping or the nightmares would never respect me.

"Give me today to see what I can find, and we'll talk about it again tonight," he murmured in my ear.

I turned my head so my lips matched his perfectly and kissed him gently. He could have today to do whatever he wanted, but I wasn't staying. If Rowan was planning something, it was even more reason to go back and snatch everything away from her. Everything she had given me.

I'd been gone too long already.

Chapter Seven

Nora

The glue of the envelope was bitter against my tongue. I pressed the flap down and clicked my pen, doubting myself for the hundredth time. *I won't be home for a while*, I explained in the letter. *I'm safe. Don't look for me.* I would hide it in the bottom of my closet along with their gifts for them to find after they realized the internship was a lie. But what if my mother never found the letter? Or worse, what if she found it before I left? She snooped regularly in both my room and Katie's—mostly mine. It was entirely possible she would happen across it even if I locked it in a box and bricked it up inside a wall. I could only imagine how my last moments here would go then. Still, I had to leave *something* for them.

I tossed the pen down without writing *Mom* across the front and tucked the blank envelope inside a study guide that a certain someone passive-aggressively left on my desk. They wouldn't believe a word of the letter anyway, but what else could I tell them? *Gone to kick a nightmare off my proverbial throne. Back eventually. I hope.* That would be monumentally worse, but Katie would suspect the truth, even if she didn't want to speak it out loud. No one would believe her if she did—a fact I knew all too well.

Coming back to visit after I learned how to Day Walk would be interesting. Who knew how long it would take for me to secure my position? What if they were all dead before I managed it? Being eternal, the only nightmare in a rush was likely Rowan. There were four quarters left on the board and the clock was eternally stalled. I shoved away from the desk, my heart fluttering in my chest. Goodbye was different than *goodbye*.

I lifted my hands and stared at the stained skin. At the gold pulsing beneath. The internal grin cracked its lips, darkness spilling out. It circled my thoughts, twisting them until they almost broke. I strained to hold it back. *I would come home. I would see them again.* I drew a ragged breath.

Then, just as fast as the darkness had spread, a sense of calm washed over me. The Sandman's emotions brushed against mine, and the grin faded. I scrambled to shutter my own feelings. To hide the terrifying thing residing in me from him, but it was pointless. Even if I was an expert at it, the Sandman already felt the desperate fear. That's why he cracked his door open—to offer me the only comfort he could. What would he do if he knew the reason? The truth pressed down on me, begging to come out, but who could I tell if not the Sandman? Definitely not Colleen. I glanced at the wall I shared with my sister and twisted my hands together. It was worth a shot.

I crept from my room and up to her open door. Should I tell her? Katie wanted to forget, but maybe she would stop pretending if we were alone. Five minutes. That's all I needed from her. I leaned against the door frame and watched as she lounged on her bed with one of the random catalogs we got in the mail. She was probably thinking about buying something since more than a few corners were dog-eared, the folds fanning the top of the pages out. My mother always made sure to toss them in the garbage before my sister had a chance to see them, but she'd clearly grown lax while Katie was away at college. I'd never forget the time Katie ordered whoopee cushions in bulk, their purpose still a mystery. Simpler times. Carefree. A pang of longing left me slouching into the wood.

"Where's Kellan?" I asked when she didn't notice me.

Katie jumped, snapping the catalog shut. "Natalie's parents went to California for Thanksgiving, so he offered to walk their dog."

"Dog? When did they get a dog?"

Katie shot me a withering look. "You can talk to them, you know. They miss you."

The blood drained from my face. They had tried more than once to get in touch with me, but I couldn't. Not when I was the reason their daughter was dead. At least Emery's parents gave me a wide berth the few times I had seen them out and about. I was a reminder to them of what they lost, Colleen suggested, but I didn't need a reason. I deserved to be avoided—not hugged like Natalie's mother wanted to do every time she saw me. They should all hate me.

"I thought you said you were done running from your problems," Katie said. "Isn't that what you told me when I was in the hospital?"

"Didn't you admit the Sandman was real in the same conversation?" I countered, all sense of nostalgia flying out the window.

"It's not healthy to believe in fairy tales." Her voice dropped at the end, her face contorting. "It's easier to live in the here and now."

"Easier?" I echoed, giving her an icy stare. "Easy isn't always right. Easy is blind. It's spineless and weak and accomplishes nothing."

"It accomplishes giving me a normal life. What does believing do?" she asked. "Does it help you? Are you happy, Nora?"

"Are *you*?" I dug my nails into my palms. My happiness was forfeit—the price I paid for everyone's safety. This was a mistake. Katie favored her fantasy world over the truth, and hearing that I was about to become a permanent part of the Dream World wouldn't change that. "You will never have a normal life, Katie. You've seen the Night World, and its stain will always be a part of you."

"No." She stood and stormed to her closet. "*I* get to decide what's a part of me. Not you. Not *them*."

I rolled my eyes. "You can't choose it any more than I can."

She ripped an old sweater from a hanger and slammed the closet shut. "This is your fault, Nora. If you hadn't welcomed the Sandman into your life, he never would've been a part of mine. So, no. You're right. I can't change what happened, but I can live with it in my own way."

She wasn't wrong. How different would things be now if I had told the Sandman *no* when he first asked to hide a secret in my dreams? A secret that I still carried in my head like a tumor. Its presence wasn't painful, but I knew it was there, a fading light among the darkness. I unwittingly brought this reign of terror down on my family. On my boss, Randy, and Natalie and Emery. Even Detective Bell. But I also saved countless others. Something a different Dream Keeper might have been too weak to do.

Katie *tsk*ed at my silence and brushed past me, careful not to make physical contact. I stood in her doorway until I heard the front door slam shut behind her.

Fine. Just… fine.

I ran back to my room and tore my note from the study guide. If she didn't want to hear it now, she wouldn't want to hear it later. I shredded the note into tiny pieces and threw them in the trash. Reality hid behind all kinds of masks. Katie didn't want to recognize the Night World? Then let her believe I was still in this world. At an internship, in a crack house, dead. They lost their right to know. I was the Lady of Nightmares now, and I had to do what was best for me. No one else would. Right now, that meant getting back to my rightful place.

Not in three weeks.

Not in four.

Now.

The Weaver's magic swelled inside of me, black smoke coiling, consuming. My anger at Katie, at everything, fed it. The promise of leaving calmed it.

"Mara," I called, my voice strangely authoritative. Nothing. I rapped my fingers on my thighs and tried again, standing taller. "Mara!"

"Lady," she croaked from behind me. A gentle breeze

brushed through the now open window, and I turned to find her perched on the edge of my mattress. Thin lines crinkled around her dark eyes, and she bobbed her head once. "How may I be of service?"

The rational part of my brain screamed at me to send her away. The Sandman had warned me not to interact with her, yet here I was, inviting her into my bedroom. *Don't be stupid.* The thought echoed against my skull, but I was committed. "Do you know the way back?"

She blinked her wide eyes. "If I did, would I be here?"

"Don't play with me. You said you could help." My tone was sharp enough to cut. "Do you know or not?"

"I cannot travel it," she said carefully.

I folded my arms across my chest to cool my temper. "Knowing how and being able to travel it are different things."

"Indeed, indeed." Mara's face twitched. "If you are asking how *you* can get back, I do know a way."

I leaned forward on the balls of my feet. "Tell me."

She grinned. "First, we must come to terms."

"Terms? I already said I would take you back to the Nightmare Realm."

"How do I know you aren't lying?" she asked.

"You don't." *Because I was.* I didn't like leaving Mara in the Day World, but I'd ignored the Sandman's warnings once before. Asking for advice was one thing; bringing her with me was another. "If I have to wait for the Sandman, what do you think your odds will be? He banished you, so something tells me he won't let you just waltz back in."

Mara's thick tongue darted from between her teeth and licked her thin lips. "There's no guarantee he'll ever take you back. He already wants to delay your return by another week."

"He—" I went still while my heart kicked into overdrive. "Have you been *spying* on me?"

"Following. Not spying. How else was I to know when you were ready for me?"

My mouth fell open. *How? Where?* I should've noticed. Should have somehow sensed her lurking. A cold chill prickled my skin. *I had.* That was her I felt watching me the other day during training, and again in my room. There had to be other times, too. What else had she seen? Sweat trickled down my spine. My mind raced over conversations between the Sandman and me. If she knew he warned me about her… No wonder her promise of help was laced with disbelief. Still, there was no guarantee she was near the shed that morning, so I had to play it cool.

"The Sandman will take me back as promised," I said with conviction. "Unless you help me get back sooner."

"*Me?*"

I glared at her. "You what?"

Mara tilted her head. "You said help *me* get back. Not us."

Crap. I schooled my expression into one of indifference. "I'm the best chance you have, and it's now or never. Make a choice."

She was quiet for a moment, her gaze sweeping over my arms. "You might not be strong enough to carry us both back," Mara said at last. "It seems to take a great deal of focus."

The probability was high that she was right. I *was* weak, and, more importantly, my magic was untrained. There was no way to test it here outside of shuttering my emotions, and that continued to be an epic fail. I needed to be in the Nightmare Realm to learn. To test my limits. To reach my full potential. I drew a sharp breath. "Then why are we having this discussion?"

Mara crept along the edge of my room. "You still carry the Sandman's dream which might help... buffer things."

"You know what?" I snapped as my unease grew. "Nevermind. I'll figure it out on my own."

"I'll help, Lady. If you give me your word that I'll go with you."

I had lied to the Weaver, tricked him into leading me to my sister. This would be no different, but if she had heard—if she *did* suspect...The Sandman said she was too weak to do any harm while still in the Day World, but she was strong enough to continue following me undetected. "And if I can't carry you back?"

"Promise to *try*," she seethed.

"I make promises to no one."

Mara's scowl darkened her entire face. The dark veins beneath her skin spread like wildfire, creating a map of twisted lines.

"But," I added, "if you tell me how to get to the Nightmare Realm, and *if* I decide to use that way instead of having the Sandman help me, I will consider it."

"That's not enough."

I nonchalantly shrugged one shoulder. "It has to be."

She hissed. "Let the Dream Lord take you then."

"All right." I waved a hand dismissively. "Leave."

Mara leapt out the window without another word, and I flopped down on the bed, staring at the ceiling. *Double crap.* The Sandman wouldn't leave me here forever, that much I was sure of. He loved me, and it would kill him to watch me completely wither in the Day World. But three weeks was too long to wait.

I closed my eyes and exhaled slowly to calm myself. In and out. Two times. Three. On the fourth inhale, something bore down hard enough to make me wheeze. My eyes flew open to find Mara leering down at me.

"Lady," she said in a grave voice.

Her feet rested on either side of my head as she sat on my chest. I pushed at her knobby knees and attempted to twist my way out from beneath her, but she was like a slab of granite. Hard, heavy, and immovable. She blinked, callous, and a flash of heat raced through me. The taste of sulfur burned up the back of my throat, the grin widening into an angry snarl on my face.

If I couldn't handle one weakened nightmare, the Sandman was right: I wasn't ready to go back. I let instinct focus my energy, let the grin guide it with pinpoint accuracy. Magic built and built, a flooded lake held back by the flimsiest of dams.

Seeming to sense I was about to burst, Mara lifted herself slightly. "Use the threads to take you home. And dare not forget me."

Then she was gone a second time.

I stared at the empty space above me and lifted my head from the pillow. She would not be forgotten; leaving her behind would be a conscious decision. If she thought she could threaten me— *me*—into taking her back, she would learn a hard lesson. One nightmare that thought they were better than their Lady was one nightmare too many, and I already had Rowan. Possibly Kail. There were undoubtedly others too. There was no way I was bringing Mara into the mix.

But she gave me what I needed. The threads I kept locked away were the key all along, and tomorrow I would use them. I would go to the only place I belonged and make my mark on it.

A quietness filled me, my thoughts drifting into silence, save one.

I'm ready.

Chapter Eight

The Sandman

Cool water and mud plastered my pants to my legs. My knees sunk deeper into the riverbed as I wrestled a nightmare covered in a smooth, pod-like shell. It vibrated beneath my bare hands, but I refused to release it. The nightmare's crab legs clawed at the air, the tiny, piercing tips barely missing my forearms. It had followed me since I crossed into the Nightmare Realm—spying, no doubt. Just like I was. If Rowan wanted to know what I was doing, she didn't need to resort to using lesser nightmares as spies. I passed numerous nightmares every time I was here that could easily report back.

If she had to send a nightmare to follow me that meant one of two things: the pod was a decoy meant to distract me from another nightmare tracking my movements, or, more likely,

Rowan wasn't as strong as she wanted us to believe. Either way, it irked me when the thing dove into the water to avoid capture.

I slipped, falling forward, and landed on the shell. It shredded through my vest, but its legs weren't quite sharp enough to go through my tunic and into the flesh underneath. "Enough," I groaned, and I called sand from the satchel at my hip. It spun together in a tight line and dove beneath the nightmare's shell, stealing its mind. A handful of seconds later, the lobster-sized creature stilled. I heaved myself up, tossed it to the shore, and flung mud from my fingertips. It splattered against the nightmare's metallic underbelly, where its legs were now neatly folded.

"Do you speak?" I asked, climbing from the river.

The creature didn't move so I flipped it over with my boot. The shell clicked open into ten even sections, revealing dozens of tiny, open mouths with dull teeth. A bit of black blood dripped from one of them. The lesser nightmares with black blood weren't intelligent; most of them didn't even speak. They simply followed their instincts or direct orders from the Weaver. I winced. *Nora.* They would follow orders from Nora. And, as it appeared, Rowan, because dominance mattered here.

"Let Rowan know Nora is offering a peaceful transition. She can return to leading the Blood Army alongside Kail without retaliation from us," I instructed. A vicious lie, of course. Nora and I both knew she would have to kill Rowan eventually.

The nightmare's legs snapped out, and it scurried over the grassy hill toward the Keep. Something told me I already knew Rowan's answer. Why would she give up such power without a fight after all she'd done to obtain it?

I wasn't sure how Nora would feel about the deal—real or

not—but it was best to delay the fight, especially if she still insisted on coming back sooner than planned. Rowan couldn't be trusted, but if Nora had time to orient herself first… I let out a careful breath and followed the shell's path. It was already out of sight by the time I reached the top of the hill, but I knew the way on my own.

Without my power being pulled in a million directions, it was possible to waltz into the Keep and destroy everything in a single afternoon, but I couldn't simply wipe the Nightmare Realm clean. The balance would be thrown off again, not to mention Rowan would put up a good fight, as would whatever followers she'd gathered.

Besides, I was the Dream Lord. Unfortunately, that meant I couldn't win Nora's power for her. If I tried, if they thought Nora wasn't strong enough to do it on her own, she wouldn't last a day. She would be seen as a puppet—*my* puppet—and no nightmare would allow me to have that kind of power over their Lady. It was bad enough they all knew about our relationship, and worse that there would be creatures coming for her regardless. Nora *was* power, and they would either bow to her or try to seize it as their own.

Anxiety nibbled at my insides, but I pushed it down. There wasn't time to worry, only time to do what had to be done. I crouched in the same patch of cattails Nora and I had hidden in the last time we came to the Keep. Except this time, instead of hiding from me, nightmares covered the entire yard. Large and small, feathered and scaled, hairy and bald. The variety wasn't lacking, but they all had one thing in common: not a single high-minded nightmare graced the lawn. Either Rowan had none willing to stand with her or they found themselves too good to stay outside with the rabble.

The increased number of nightmares wasn't the only change in the last few months. The skeleton of the Weaver's palace—the one destroyed the night I bound him—was no longer in ruins. The stone foundation no longer peeked from the grass, but rose two feet, three in some places, the new stones carefully laid. It followed the same pathways as the old structure, then extended outward on all sides. I scoffed quietly. Rowan wasn't wasting any time.

I quickly and quietly wound my way around the outer wall to get closer to the Keep. It hadn't changed—black marble, veined gold, half-capped with a dome and the other side consisting of open-aired arches. The spy I stole was nowhere in sight, but red mist leaked from the basement windows, which meant Rowan retained at least some of the Blood Army. Probably all of it, as they operated like a hive mind rather than as individuals, but there were too many for them all to fit in the Keep. It begged the question: *Where* was *the rest of the army?*

A door slammed open, and Rowan appeared on the terrace. Her red dress was a bright wound between two pillars. The black, skeletal wings jutting from her back were hidden in shadow, her skin so pale it nearly glowed. My pulse quickened. There she was. The biggest threat standing in Nora's way stood before me, and I couldn't touch her. It was foolish to even offer a truce, especially without consulting Nora first. Rowan had everything, and my offer gave her nothing. Nora didn't exactly strike fear into anyone yet, nor was she likely to for a while.

A familiar set of clicks rang through the air. My eyes darted across the yard, searching for the spine and bulbous skull that was Despina. The last time I saw her, she was trying her best to defend the Weaver while he worked more threads through his loom. If it weren't for her, maybe things would've ended differently. I could've finished off the other nightmares fast enough to stop Nora from killing the Weaver.

The ivory skull darted down the side of the building, dark hair flowing over her exposed spine. The vertebrae glided back and forth like a snake, and her two-fingered hands guided the way. My hands twitched at my sides, eager to grab sand. *Focus.*

An unseen nightmare chirped behind me, and the cattails rustled as it raced away. I cringed. Despina swiveled toward me, her empty eye sockets locked on their target. There was no hesitation in her approach. She flew toward me as I stood, gathering handfuls of sand. I didn't want to destroy her with more pressing issues at hand, but I would if I had to. My sand circled me, protecting me.

But Despina came to a screeching halt a yard away and tossed the pod-creature at my feet before retreating just as fast. I focused on her until she started back up the wall of the Keep, then turned to the cracked shell at my feet. Carved into the smooth surface was Rowan's answer.

Never.

I kicked the dead nightmare away and glared up at Rowan. She met my eyes from the top of the Keep, the crown of raven's beaks atop her head catching the dull light, and raised her hands as if to say, *Come and get me.* I lifted my chin. If there wouldn't be a peaceful transition, there would be a bloody one. It would just take longer.

I turned on my heel, the sand returning to the satchel, and strode back the way I came. Every nightmare lurking amongst the foundation stared at me. Their gazes followed my face, my hands, my back, but none of them noticed the small line of sand I directed down my leg. They didn't see it glide among the grass and split in three different directions toward their comrades.

One spy for the air: a giant hairy spider with four large, paper-thin wings and legs covered in eyes.

One for the ground: a deer with two heads and the ears of a rabbit.

One for water: a seal without skin.

The sand inched inside each of them, wrapping around their minds like a vice. My magic would kill them eventually, just as it had the others I'd turned over the last few months, but hopefully not before I learned something of importance. I released my grip on the sand so they wouldn't act differently by stilling or focusing too eagerly on me, giving away my secret. Later, when I reclaimed it, everything they knew, I would know too.

But for now, Nora was expecting me.

I only wished I had better news.

Chapter Nine

Perhaps I should've been a bit more hesitant when I found a new fissure waiting when I fell asleep, but I went straight for the glowing memory. The Weaver's ragged breath filled my ears. Anger painted the hiss of every inhale as he stormed over jagged marble and rock. Black dust coated everything in sight, and fire smoldered beneath pieces of rubble. The Weaver trailed a hand over the walls of his Keep, his arm bare of thread minus a single strand circling his wrist. One last nightmare at his disposal. I squinted, not daring to get any closer to the memory. Dead things littered the yard, many of them half buried and torn apart.

"That bastard," the Weaver shouted. A wave of anguish shuddered through him—through me.

He pounded up the same outer staircase I used the day I

killed him. The image blurred in and out along with his vision, though I wasn't sure why. Was he hurt? He seemed to be moving fine. At the top, he shouldered his way through a door, and the image froze completely. It was like looking at a photograph of the loom, filtered red with rage. The *broken* loom. Treadles were scattered across the floor, the beater snapped in half, the roller missing. There was no reason I should know what those things were called, let alone where they went, but it all felt as obvious as my own name. Was that part of the magic too? Like the memories? Maybe there was more I would simply know once I returned to the Nightmare Realm.

The Weaver fell to his knees at the sight of his loom, and a heart-wrenching cry echoed through the room. His movements were slow, his hands shaking as they collected the treadles. The image quivered with his terror, his hurt. The loom was fixable, but it would take time—time he didn't have. There was a frantic edge to his thoughts, though I did not know what the thoughts were exactly.

I shouldn't know them at all.

The door slammed open behind him. The Weaver spun, clutching the splintered wood to his chest. The Sandman stood in the doorway. His clothes were torn and soggy with blood. Scratches ran along his cheek. My body jolted. I remembered that tear on his chest, the way it seemed to follow the upward curve of the moon tattooed beneath. This was the night we met, only I hadn't seen his face then. I was glad for that now. If it looked anything like it did now with the unspoken threat swirling in his eyes, I would have run in the other direction.

"What have you done?" the Weaver shouted.

The Sandman's gaze flicked down to the loom's broken

pieces, and surprise flashed across his face. "I did not do this," he said carefully.

"Oh?" The Weaver tossed the wood to the floor in a chorus of hollow clanks. "Then who did?"

The Sandman lifted his eyes and looked directly at the Weaver. At me. It felt like I was looking at a stranger. "I swear it, Weaver. This wasn't me."

The Weaver leapt at him, fingers extended toward his throat. There was a quick flick of the Sandman's hand, and something fell from his sleeve. A needle-straight piece of the Weaver's thread, embossed with silver, not gold. Like it was when he used the thread to find Katie. The rest happened in the blink of an eye. The Weaver gripped the Sandman's throat. The Sandman lifted a hand to his chest and shoved the stolen thread into the Nightmare Lord's heart. The Weaver stumbled back with a soft cry.

"I tried talking sense into you." The Sandman winced, his expression clearly pained. "But you wouldn't listen."

The Weaver ripped open his shirt and clawed at a red pinprick on his skin. The picture blurred and cleared and blurred and cleared. His breath was a hoarse wheeze. "What—" He gasped. "What is this?"

There was a short pause before the Sandman answered. "I've bound you to the Nightmare Realm."

"You—you can't do that. Not with so little thread," he said in shocked disbelief.

"I had more," the Sandman replied quietly, sounding almost sorry. "It won't last forever."

"I'll kill you," the Weaver spat. "I'll—"

"Nora." The Sandman's voice drifted in from the dark

nothing outside the glowing memory. It sounded different—the hard edge gone, replaced with the loving concern I was so used to hearing. "Nora, wake up."

I cracked my eyelids open to find his violet pupils inches away and flinched. The way he looked at the Weaver was branded in my mind. Would he look at me like that one day too? They were friends once, after all. I saw them together, as close then as we were now. It was only a matter of time. My stomach churned.

"Let me up." The words came out too high, too panicked.

"Sorry. I didn't mean—" He leaned back, surprised, and ran a finger over my knuckles. They were white where I clenched the sheets. "Are you okay?"

"I was—" I wasn't sure if I should tell him what I saw, but I didn't want to keep anything from him either. *Anything else.* "I think I found some of the Weaver's memories."

He sat down on the edge of the bed. "You said there was nothing there when you slept."

I nodded. "There still is most of the time."

"Most of the time?" A hurt look crossed his face. "How many times have you seen things?"

"Only once before tonight." I rubbed my eyes, pressing a little too hard. "I didn't mention it because I didn't know what to make of it or if I imagined it."

The Sandman tugged at the air near his temple like he used to do with his hood when he felt self-conscious. I didn't have to feel his emotions to understand. That I kept this from him made him miss the security of his hood. He had never known someone like me before, so not only did he lack answers to a lot of my questions, but I held things back from him. Dealt with them on my own. That was new for him—for us. Sometimes I wondered if he doubted my feelings for him too.

"I suppose it's possible," the Sandman started. "Some of his memories could've transferred with the magic, especially since he generated it himself instead of relying on an outward force." He rubbed his thumbs over his navy-blue fingertips, and for the briefest second, I swore it looked like he was jealous. "What did you see?"

"The first time, you helped the Weaver because *she* was coming." I paused to study his face, hoping that rang a bell, but he gave nothing new away. "You said you were friends with the Weaver once."

"A very long time ago," he answered quietly.

"What changed?"

The Sandman shifted uncomfortably. "Things changed for us both after we built the wall to keep Mare out of the Night World. Everything became more black and white." He sighed. "The Weaver became restless, which made him reckless. At the time, I thought he spiraled down his path to darkness rather quickly, but looking back, he was taking steps toward it for a while. It—*we*—"

There it was. A hurt so deep he apparently couldn't finish the sentence, and that's when I knew what I saw was real. The Weaver's magic hadn't conjured up something to make me sympathetic, nor had my own mind put the ideas there. The longing I saw on the Sandman's face today was something that would only exist if the friendship I saw in that first memory was true.

"You never told me the worlds—" Searing pain streaked across my forehead suddenly. I cried out and fell forward into the Sandman. Stars winked behind my eyelids. My head was going to explode. *Oh God.* This was it. The end. "Sandman," I gasped.

His hands were all over me, searching for an explanation. A wound maybe, though he wouldn't find one. This was something else, something dark and biting, and it came from inside.

Then, just as quickly, it was gone, and I took a tentative breath. An echo of it remained, throbbing in my temples, but I could see again. Move again. My stomach settled slowly. Had it been upset? I hadn't noticed.

"It's gone," I whispered.

"What is? What happened?" The Sandman pulled me close, squeezing me as if I would disappear otherwise. "Are you okay?"

"Just a headache." Darkness throbbed in a hollow pocket in my brain. I latched onto the Sandman's arm, forcing him to keep still so I could lean on him a minute more.

"A headache?" he echoed with concern.

"I've been getting them lately, just not this bad." Which was true. Only, I didn't think this was *just* anything. It felt like the Day World's way of saying *get out*, and I had no intention of ignoring its warning. "Did you find what you were looking for in the Nightmare Realm today?"

I felt his muscles twitch. "I created a few spies, and Baku is still trying to get a rough tally of Rowan's followers, but…"

I braced myself and met his gaze. "But what?"

"I offered Rowan a peaceful transition of power."

It felt like he dumped ice water over me. All the pain washed away, only to leave sparks of shock in its wake. Rowan didn't deserve anything less than death for turning me into this—all so she could kill me. I had trusted her, though I knew I shouldn't have, because the nonsense about maintaining a balance had seemed to be exactly that: nonsense. But Rowan knew it was real, and for that she needed her head ripped from her body.

Shh, the darkness cautioned, and I took my first full breath since the Sandman spoke. It was right. The Sandman wanted peace, not war, and I needed him on my side. More than needed. I *wanted* him there the same way I wanted him in my dreams every night, and that counted for more than anything else could.

I took another slow breath to ease the hard edge of anger and asked, "What was her answer?"

He pressed his lips into a straight line and shook his head.

"Of course," I grumbled.

"We have time before you go back. I can draw her out and finish this before then, if it's what you want."

"No." I broke away from him. "The nightmares have to respect me. *Fear* me. If you win this for me, they won't do either, and you know that." He knew it *well* because I shared the same thought months ago only for it to be shot down by his sound logic.

"Nora—"

"This isn't something either of us wanted, but it is what it is. *I'm* what I am." I pushed back at the grin, widening as if it had claim to that sentiment. "How many are going to suffer because of this? How many Dreamers have you saved, and how many more needed to be saved and weren't? I have to take responsibility for what I did to the Weaver, so you can either take me back tomorrow or I'll find my own way."

"We won't know much more than we do now," he argued.

"A lot can happen in twenty-four hours." A lot could happen in twenty-four seconds. A choice. A swing of a blade. A transfer of magic.

"It's too soon," the Sandman said softly.

No. I sighed. *Tomorrow is too late.*

I found myself once again on the eve of betrayal. Only this time, I wasn't uncertain like I had been when we left the Dream Realm for the Weaver's Keep. There was a chance that I wouldn't use the knife then; there was no chance that I wouldn't try to leave now, with or without the Sandman. My chest ached at the thought. How had we managed to get to this place? We were so close for five years. Was five months all it took to change that?

When he stood to leave, I grabbed his arm. My heart pumped, panic racing through me like blood in my veins. I loved him more than anyone or anything, and I was about to risk it all. Again. There was only so much a person could forgive, and I'd already nearly killed him. It wasn't intentional, but if I listened to him, it wouldn't have happened at all. For anyone else, it would've been the final straw. To do this, to go behind his back without ignorance as an excuse—I swallowed hard.

"Don't leave me," I whispered, my voice cracking.

He stared down at me, confused.

Don't abandon me, I wanted to clarify. *Don't hate me.* But I couldn't without giving myself away, so I scooted over and patted the bed instead. He sat without a word and draped an arm over my shoulders. I breathed in his scent. Soaked up his warmth. Reveled in the feel of his skin. "What you did with the stars the other night was amazing. I miss them." I snuggled closer. "I miss you. *Us.*"

His hand tightened on my shoulder. "I'm right here. I'll always be right here."

Not always.

I tilted my head up to kiss the spot beneath his ear. His breath hitched, and I smirked against him. Then I did it again. His fingers drifted from my shoulder up the side of my neck before he lowered his lips to mine. It was a soft reminder that, at least for this moment, he was mine and I was his. Just like we promised. Even if he couldn't forgive me, even if I couldn't forgive *myself*, I knew I would never stop loving him. There was no Nora without the Sandman. I moved closer and leaned in to deepen the kiss. His fingers found the back of my head, weaving into my hair.

I felt each of his movements with every part of me. The sureness in the way he cradled my head, the gentle way he moved against me. The bed shifted, and he knelt in front of me without breaking contact. His free hand dug into my lower back, holding me closer, and in return, I gripped the sides of his vest.

Now, with the Sandman close, the darkness felt far away. It was as if I was *me* again, and I took and took until I wanted more than his kisses. My hands slipped down to his waist. My fingers found the hem of his shirt and slipped beneath it. He shivered as my fingers ran over the sensitive skin just above his pants, and a small moan escaped my throat. I loved that I had this effect on him. My palms flattened against his stomach, and his mouth fell to my cheek, my jaw, my neck. I tilted my head to give him easier access and tugged on his bunched shirt.

The Sandman broke away long enough to let me pull his shirt and vest over his head. The crescent moon tattooed on his chest glowed faintly in the darkness of my room, lifting and falling with each of his rapid breaths. The sight sparked something inside me, and another small groan escaped my lips as he kissed my neck again. His grip tightened on my arms at the sound, almost as if he were forcing himself to keep them in place. But I didn't want him to. I wanted to feel them on me. I needed to—so I wiggled beneath him until I finally managed to remove my shirt too.

The Sandman stared at me, pupils blown wide. "Nora—" I held my breath and waited. Waited for him to tell me again that we should stop. Instead, his eyes trailed down my body before coming back up to my face. I watched as the internal struggle vanished from behind his eyes. "We don't have to do this."

"I want to," I assured him.

His throat bobbed. "Are you sure?"

"I'm more than sure," I whispered and gave the fabric around his hips a little tug, begging him to stop talking and start touching.

Still, he hesitated a moment longer, and then a small trail of sand rose from the pouch around his neck. It floated across the room and disappeared into the crack around the doorknob. There was a faint click of the lock.

I turned back to the Sandman with a playful smile. "Smooth."

"I try." His voice was deeper than I'd ever heard it before.

He kissed me again, slowly. Reverently. My heart hammered in my chest, and my hands shook as I worked the ties at the front of his pants. He lowered himself back over me and nudged my ear with his nose. "I love you."

"I love you too." And I meant it with all that I was.

Chapter Ten

Nora

The pen slid smoothly across the envelope. I took my time with each cursive letter, feeling the finality of the words inside. Now that I'd cooled down a bit, I knew I had to leave them something. The explanation of my whereabouts was still vague, but a little more elaborate in that I gave a general idea of where I was going-but-not-really-going. I would scope out New York, live it up a little before the internship started. *Better to ask forgiveness than permission,* I wrote at the end of the letter. So what if it wasn't completely logical to manage such a feat? After not working for months, the money I made from working at Howell's Furniture and Decor wasn't enough to travel for so long in such an expensive place. Most of my savings went into the small arsenal hidden beneath GED books in my bookbag.

I clicked the pen twice and set it carefully on the desk. The letter should probably go to my mother, but I couldn't bring myself to scrawl those three little letters. Instead, Katie's name stared up at me. My sister wouldn't know exactly what happened or where I was, but she *would* know I hadn't hopped the first bus out of town, even if she pretended otherwise.

This was it. I drew a deep breath and placed the envelope at the center of my desk. It was the lone object on the surface, the study guides now in the trash and everything else swept into drawers. If this worked, there would be no going back.

I set my head on the wood and squeezed my eyes shut against the prickle of tears. *Don't cry.* Strength. Fearlessness. Fortitude. *Don't cry.* I couldn't stay. *Do. Not. Cry.* I didn't want to go to that horrible place. *No tears allowed when I can only blame myself.*

My gaze shifted to the bed. The sheets were still rumpled from my time with the Sandman. When he left at dawn, I spent a long time lying there, wrapped up in his scent, before showering. I wondered if the pillow, which still had an indent from his head, would smell like him after so many hours. I bet it would. My heart twisted around itself.

Truly, I was a horrible, selfish person. I knew what being together meant to him. Even though I felt desperate, even though I *wanted* to be with the Sandman—had wanted it for so long—it wasn't right. And the night before I snuck back into the Nightmare Realm? Self-loathing foamed in my throat, threatening to choke me.

I leapt from the chair, fluffed the pillows, and flung the sheets into place so there was no trace of what we did. If only it were that easy to erase my impending betrayal. The grin faded in, spewing its darkness in what felt like impatience. Maybe eagerness. Both.

I felt the same way.

With twitchy movements, I lifted my bookbag from the floor and eased my arms through the straps. Carefully packed inside were a few changes of clothes, necessary toiletries, and a variety of weapons: my Swiss army knife, a Taser, pepper spray, and, most notably, Paul's handgun I pilfered while he was in the bathroom this morning. With luck, I wouldn't have to use any of it, but this was the Nightmare Realm. A place where an unknown percentage of creatures wanted me dead. Who was I kidding? Luck had nothing to do with it.

I removed the pencil box and felt the threads' desperation through the tin. My hands shook as I opened the lid. Gold filament glimmered weakly around the black threads. I stopped breathing as I stared down at the squirming, unborn nightmares. An ache bloomed inside me. Starved. Angry. I picked up one of the threads and closed the pencil box before I could change my mind. A coil of darkness swirled from the grin the moment I shut it back in the drawer, but I held it back. This wasn't something to rush into when I'd never used my magic before. For anything. At all. I gnawed my bottom lip.

With a deep breath, I stared at the thread. My vision blurred, and suddenly I saw—not with my eyes, but some new part of me—exactly what it held. Or, part of the nightmare it would become if given the chance. Off-white skin with pointed thistles along a thick arm, part of a torso, and two nondescript legs. I hadn't exactly been precise when I'd ripped the thread off the Weaver's arm, but it felt like something that could be fixed with a working loom.

"Okay." I held it up in front of me and thought back to the

one time I saw the Weaver turn a strand into a nightmare. He flicked his wrist and it straightened; the Sandman warned him not to create a nightmare in the Dream Realm, and then—then there was that horrifying *thing*, but I didn't want to bring the nightmare to life. I swallowed hard.

"Let it in."

I jumped at the sound of Mara's voice. She crouched in the corner of my room, staring out at me from behind a curtain of coarse hair. "What?" I snapped.

"The Night World. Let it in. The thread is your tether."

Let it in? Wasn't it *already* in? "Have you been spying on me again?"

"You gave me no choice. If I hadn't, you would leave me here." She rocked side-to-side. "Besides, it seemed like you needed further guidance."

"And you think I'll take you now just because you're here?" I clutched the thread to my chest, hiding it from her steady gaze. "I told you I make promises to no one, and you creeping around me twenty-four-seven doesn't exactly make me feel charitable."

"You make promises to the Sandman," she crooned and eyed the bed. "With words and without them."

My face became blistering hot. She was here? She… "You *watched* us?" I shrieked. "What the hell is wrong with you? Are you—"

"Relax, Lady. I didn't stay." Her tongue flicked out in disgust. "I left when he locked the door."

"Oh. My. God." I gaped at her. Enough had happened by that point. "Get out right now."

She parted her hair with her long nails. "There's no need to be embarrassed."

"I'm not embarrassed," I lied. "I'm pissed off."

Mara flicked a look at the fist I still held to my chest. "Are you going to try or not?"

"Not," I growled.

Mara tutted, then vanished.

I slumped in my chair and ran a hand over my face. Did she have to say anything? I could've lived the rest of my hopefully-very-long life without knowing she'd seen us kissing. Shirtless. The memory of what followed sparked through me, and I bit my lip. I was still sore despite how gentle the Sandman had been, but it was a good pain. A reminder of what we shared. It also made the guilt a million times worse. We cemented a bond that was already there, and now—

No.

I couldn't second guess myself. I had to go before the entire Nightmare Realm bowed at Rowan's feet. Before the Day World whittled me down any more than it already had. I swiveled my chair back toward the desk and took a deep breath.

Right. I exhaled slowly. Just let it in…

I willed the dark, muted sense of the Nightmare Realm forward, the grin more than eager to assist, but nothing happened. I huffed and slammed the thread down on top of the envelope. The grin sneered. *Quitter,* it taunted as more wisps caressed its lips. I lifted the thread again.

And stared.

And stared.

I stared at that perfect, watermarked smile. At those curls of black smoke.

The gold filaments on the thread brightened, the impression of the nightmare fading to nothing. The Nightmare Realm rushed toward me in a flurry of chaos. It called to me, a siren song, beckoning me back into its fold. Begging me. I rose from my seat. "Yes," I whispered to its unasked question.

My stomach bottomed out. I careened toward a black shroud, feeling as if I was still and moving all at once. The air burned my eyes, but I kept them wide open out of fear. Fear I would miss something. An obstacle. A danger. The terror of the endless falling sensation gave way to horrified excitement.

Then pain sliced across my shoulders. The pull slowed, held back by something heavy now attached to my back, and I scrambled to lean forward again. The stabbing pain doubled as whatever held me gripped harder. The movement sent my body careening out of control. I flailed, trying desperately to shake it off. My nails scraped against hard, calloused skin, but whatever it was didn't let up. If anything, it held even tighter. A scream burned its way out of my throat.

A thin veil of silver fibers cast a soft glow ahead. I tried to aim for it, but the faster I spun, the harder it became. My stomach clenched, threatening to spew its contents as the spinning continued to intensify. I screamed again, a low, pitiful sound, and black hair whipped into my mouth. I ripped it out and held the coarse locks in my palm. Even with the universe twirling around me, I knew what I was looking at.

Mara.

"No!" I pulled at the shank of hair. Reached back for her head. Tried to bite at her hands. All to no avail. I was too dizzy. Too disoriented. "No!" I cried again. Not Mara. She couldn't be in the Night World. *No, no, no!* She would destroy everything. The Sandman would think—

A silver veil snagged us like a net, stretching around my body like a cocoon. It wrapped tight, cutting off my airway, and stars burst across my eyes. It felt like I was stuck there for ages before it gave way with a loud rip. I gasped for air as the fall suddenly resumed. The spinning, thankfully, did not. But even more concerning was the hard ground rising to meet me at an alarming speed. I twisted myself around in the air to let Mara meet the ground first.

Her body crunched beneath mine, her nails pulling from my shoulders with sickening pops. The world slowed around me. My ears picked up on every little sound my body made, all set to the backdrop of the ringing in my ears. I rolled off Mara, bones grinding, and wheezed. My sneakers scraped against the dirt to find purchase, but it was no use. Jell-O. I was Jell-O.

Mara leapt to her feet and shook her limbs out. "Thank you, Lady," she croaked with a knowing stare.

"Mara," I squeezed out. "Wait."

Instead, she raced away in her loping gait. I shoved myself up to follow, but my knees buckled. My cheek scraped against the rock and dirt, and I groaned. Exhaustion bore down on me with its full weight. I struggled to keep my eyes open, but after five months without any real rest, it was a beast of a thing.

***

Consciousness hit me like a freight train. I flew up into a sitting position and instantly regretted the movement. My head swam through murky water, my muscles ached. I squinted down at my body, a hiss leaking from between my teeth as my neck throbbed. Everything looked intact, albeit filthy. I wiggled my toes. *All in working order.* It was more than I expected after dropping out of the sky into… My pulse quickened. This was decidedly not the place where I collapsed. When I fell on Mara, it was…I wasn't exactly sure. The whole thing happened so fast—the falling, the landing—but the brown dirt on my clothes proved the overwhelmingly green landscape around me was different.

Green buttons, to be exact. Stacked from largest to smallest to make a forest of pines.

I blinked the last bits of fuzziness from my eyes to find a dozen shapes hidden among them, watching me. I froze and stared back at the woodland nightmares. Rabbits, squirrels, deer, a single raccoon, and tiny birds. Their eyes, made of black buttons, seemed lifeless, but they were undoubtedly alive. Their bodies, made of more stacked buttons of varying colors and shades, clicked gently with every slight movement.

"What the hell is this?" I staggered to my feet.

As I did, the nightmares bowed their heads. The string holding the buttons together peeked through each tiny crack. I gave a quiet, surprised gasp. That was a good sign, but there was no way any of them could have dragged me here, so who did? I reached for the straps of my bookbag to get a weapon, only to find it missing. "No." I spun, searching the carpet of brown and green buttons beneath my feet and slammed my palms over my shoulders as if finding them bare was a mistake.

A rapid burst of pain splintered beneath my hands and sent me reeling back a step. *Mara.* I slid the neck of my shirt over my left shoulder to examine the wounds from her long nails. Black thread dipped in and out of my skin, holding the holes together with a slight pucker. My heart thudded in my chest. Who—

"Lady!" A high, feminine voice cut the air. "You're awake. Splendid."

A female nightmare bustled through the trees. She appeared human in every aspect, though she was clearly modeled after someone's eccentric aunt on an acid trip. Dozens of spools of thread were affixed to her short jacket and strands full of buttons clicked around her neck like pearls. White tights ran down to her floral Mary Janes and her skirt was a rainbow of neon tulle. Her blond hair was divided down the middle in two French braids, and a tiny top hat, no bigger than my thumb, sat cockeyed on her head. She blinked large, owlish eyes and smiled. "Join us, join us!"

"I'm—" I cleared my throat in hopes of sounding more in control. "I'm in a hurry."

"Oh, I'm sure you are," the nightmare said. "You've been asleep so long." She stepped around the button creatures and tucked my arm through hers. "I was just starting a new project, but it can wait. It's not every day the Lady of Nightmares pays a visit."

Project?

She led me through rows of trees into a clearing. Mounds of buttons nearly twice my height were sorted by color on the far side, but it was what sat in the center that stopped me: an elderly woman strapped to the surface of a dinner table by large red ribbons, each bow expertly tied.

"Don't pay her any attention," the nightmare chirped. "The beginning stage is always a bit messy, but she'll be beautiful in no time."

The Dreamer turned her head and large blue buttons stared in our direction, sewed over her eyelids. "Help me, please," she begged, her voice raw.

I wrenched my arm from the nightmare and bit my tongue.

The Weaver wouldn't let this bother him. I needed to win the nightmares to my side, and that wouldn't happen if I outwardly judged and chastised them for doing what they did. I had to be diplomatic. For now. Once I cemented myself as their leader, I could change the rules.

"Who are you?" I asked.

"Oh, goodness. How rude of me." The woman straightened her jacket. "I'm the Doll Maker."

"Ah." I put on the face I wore so often: the calm, unbothered expression my own mother bought for so many years. "Well, don't kill her. We don't need to give the Sandman reason to put the barrier back up."

She bowed slightly. "Of course, Lady, but I would never hurt my dolls."

I watched a bead of blood travel down the old woman's face and held back a cringe. We apparently had very different opinions of what *hurt* meant. My fingers skimmed over the stitches on my shoulder. "Did you do this?"

"Yes, Lady." She tapped her fingers together in front of her and rocked on her heels. "I hope you don't mind. I know you heal quickly, but when I found you, the wounds were bleeding quite badly."

I shook my head. "I appreciate it."

The Doll Maker beamed. "Don't hesitate to come back next time you need stitching. You won't find another nightmare with as light a touch as mine."

Next time. She didn't have to sound so sure about my needing to be mended again. It stood to reason I would, but still, let a girl find her feet before knocking them out from under her.

"How long was I out?" I asked.

"Six hours or so."

Six hours? My family would know I was missing by now. So much for not ruining Thanksgiving. I rubbed at the guilt rolling through my upper abdomen. The Sandman probably knew too. Would he also know about Mara? I had to warn him before Mara hurt anyone else.

"Where's my bag?" I asked.

The Doll Maker flung her hands up and scurried around the table. A moment later, she stood in front of me and gingerly held the black bookbag out as if it were a baby. "I had to remove it to get to your injuries, but it's all there. I didn't even peek."

I nodded slowly as I eased the straps over my shoulders. It hadn't occurred to me that she would steal anything, but now that she brought it up, I would be checking as soon as I got a moment alone. Doing so now would be insulting, and she seemed to like me, which was both lucky and invaluable.

"So." I looked around the button forest. "Which way would the Keep be?"

"Terrible Rowan. Terrible, terrible," the Doll Maker spat. "Taking what's not hers. It would be one thing if the nightmares following her were only doing it because they craved a powerful leader. A majority are, mind you, but there are a few that she's spent decades wooing to her side. Ah—" She cut herself off sheepishly. "Forgive me. That was not your question, Lady. If you head—"

A gloved hand materialized on the Doll Maker's shoulder, followed by a man nearly seven feet tall. I swallowed a scream as he loomed over her with a wide red hat swooping low over his features. People didn't just *appear* like that. But he wasn't a person. He was more dangerous than that, which made staying silent all the harder. When he brought his chin up, a black Venetian mask covered his entire face. Red painted lips swooped up into a cold smirk, and red looping scallops were painted around each eye—or where his eyes should've been if the mask offered holes to see from. The black and red color scheme from his mask continued into the rest of his clothing, from the high, puffed collar to the matte shoes on his feet.

"Halven! My goodness," the Doll Maker chattered. "Two visitors today! Aren't we lucky?" she called to the woman on the table. "Though you did give me a bit of a fright."

Halven gave her a soft squeeze before removing his hand, then stepped toward me. *Don't move* .My legs quaked from the effort to stay still. He extended a hand covered in a black silk glove, and I flinched. He seemed to contemplate the reaction, his head tilted. I could feel him staring, though there was no outward proof of it.

Then Halven bowed deeply.

"Umm…" I glanced between him and the Doll Maker. "Hey."

"Such good timing." The Doll Maker shifted closer to me, almost as if she sensed my discomfort. "There's no one better than Halven to guide you where you're going."

Doubtful. Besides, I was sure his timing was anything but a coincidence. "But he doesn't know where I'm going," I said as neutrally as possible.

"Of course he does." She patted Halven's forearm as if she were a proud mother. "He knows where everyone is, where they've been, and where they're going. Sometimes even before they do, isn't that right?"

Halven, still in his bow, dipped his head lower.

"He can take you right where you're going, my Lady. Don't you doubt that!"

Halven lifted his head, and it felt as if he stitched me to the buttons beneath my feet. "Do you know where I'm going?" I asked, somehow sure he did, though I sure as heck didn't know my destination. Heading straight for Rowan before I got my footing was foolish, and I would need to get in touch with the Sandman before making a move. For his help, and, more importantly, for his forgiveness. If the worst happened, I didn't want to die without apologizing first.

Halven nodded.

"And is it the Keep?" I asked curiously.

He shook his head, and I fidgeted with the straps of my bookbag. "I'll need some things before I face Rowan. Supplies. An army—?" I said carefully, testing their reactions to gauge how bad things really were. I really, *really* didn't want to raise an army. Or lead one. But if Rowan had the Blood Army at her service...

"Army?" The Doll Maker pressed a hand to her chest and glanced quickly over her shoulder toward the woman on the table. She shuffled closer and lowered her voice. "My Lady, you don't need an army to defeat the usurper. All you need is—"

Halven shot up straight and snatched my hand with his. Before the Doll Maker could say another word, we were halfway through the button forest with every step feeling like ten. The darkness inside me reveled in it. Unfortunately, I couldn't share the sentiment.

"Stop," I whispered, trying to shake away the disorientation. When he didn't, I sucked in a breath. "Stop!" The voice was half mine, half something else. A commanding thing. Halven came to an abrupt halt and released me. "I didn't give you permission to touch me."

He bowed low.

"What was she going to tell me?" I snapped. "All I need is what?"

"Your power, my Lady." His voice was deep and forced from behind the mask, as if it took all of him to speak a single word.

I waited for him to continue, but he remained silent. An innocent enough answer, so why rip me out of there? But now wouldn't be the best time to call him on it. We were alone, for one. I took in the desolate landscape. "Where are we?" A fiery geyser blasted up from the ground, and a wave of heat brushed against my face. *Oh, cool.* Death by fire. My favorite. "Nevermind," I muttered.

"I will not betray you," Halven vowed. "Trust me."

"Trust has to be earned."

I had given it too freely before when I took the dagger from Rowan and Kail. I wouldn't make the same mistake twice, but the truth was I didn't have much choice. Not unless I wanted to wander aimlessly and hope the next nightmare I ran across wasn't an enemy. I'd only seen a small amount of my own realm: the cave Katie was tortured in, the Barren, the Blood Tower, and a few other random places on the way to the Keep. Nothing that would offer me shelter.

The straps of my bookbag dug painfully into my shredded shoulders, but I did my best to ignore it in favor of the very real, very big problem in front of me. I stared at the black spaces where Halven's eyes should've been. *Don't do it.* But the grin, half formed and unsure, nudged me forward.

"So earn it," I dared. "And keep your hands to yourself."

Halven gracefully swept an arm out, and I edged past him.

I can do this. I can rule here.

Not that I had much choice.

Chapter Eleven

The Sandman

Snow crunched beneath my boots, my breath clouding in front of my face, but not even the frigid temperature could wipe away my smile. My heart was quieter than it had been in a long time, and my body felt more alive. I could still feel every line Nora traced on my skin. The taste of her lips lingered on mine, along with the memory of her breath on my neck. The shiver that ran over me had nothing to do with the nightmare landscape surrounding me.

Pay attention.

I had a job to do. The three nightmares I took control of on the lawn of the Keep waited at the top of the mountain overlooking the ruined palace. I ignored the booted footprints, large enough for me to lie down in, that lead in the same direction. Either an enormous nightmare lurked nearby, or they were there for the fear factor. That I left no prints of my own did not escape me. It was likely designed to confuse Dreamers when they couldn't retrace their steps, but it benefited me in a way that would've irked the Weaver into altering the entire cliff side.

My smile did waver then. The Weaver was dead, and—Nora's situation aside—I should've been glad of it. Part of me was, but not *every* part. It was strange to know I would never fight him again. There was something like comfort in an enemy one knew and something like grief in the ghost of our friendship. Having both ripped away left me disoriented. Maybe it was a good thing I was too busy to process that aspect; maybe the uncertainty of it would fade away with time.

The two-headed deer trotted toward me, its eyes glazed over with my magic. I laid a palm on its forehead and closed my eyes. My magic skated to the surface just below his fur. An image grew slowly. It warbled and faded, but the message was clear. At least two-thirds of the Blood Army lurked in the swamp near the Keep, biding their time, hidden from view. Their usual near-constant moaning had ceased, likely on Rowan's order. Their black cloaks blended in well with the dark trees. The hiss of the red mist coiling around their ankles could be attributed to the tears of children hitting the scalding swamp water or the cry of the witch dwelling at its center. All-in-all, the swamp was well chosen. I tried not to think about how many of the remaining third were in the basement because even a fraction of the Blood Army was more than enough to pose a threat.

Other images came and went but showed nothing I hadn't already seen with my own eyes. My hand fell to my side, and I willed my magic to fade back into the deer's subconscious. The nightmare's pupils constricted as the creature regained itself, and a moment later it raced back down the mountain with its tail in the air. I had hoped to learn something more. One of Rowan's weaknesses, maybe, or if a more advanced nightmare was helping her. I couldn't take out Rowan, but that didn't mean I couldn't weed out other powerful enemies. Unless the other two spies had anything we could use as a springboard, I didn't see how I could justify bringing Nora back earlier than planned.

There's time, I told myself continuously over the last few months. We would figure it out one step at a time, but now that time was almost up, and we had figured out precisely nothing. The thought of Nora coming here, staying here, ruling here, made my blood run cold.

A quiet buzz of wings zipped down the mountain. The spider's black form cut a line through the stark white horizon. It veered left, then right, as if it were unsure which way to go. *Here*, I called to my magic, but a stone spear whizzed overhead, straight through the spider's wings. The arachnid flipped through the air, legs flailing, and stopped only when its abdomen became impaled on a broken branch. I froze. Between us, the bright white handle of the spear stuck straight into the sky like an icicle. My heart thumped, heavy. A spear that size would need a nightmare even bigger to throw it. The footprints—

The spider's legs quivered and black blood oozed from the base of its missing wings. I scanned the direction the spear sailed from but saw nothing. The obvious thing to do was leave. The spider was dying, and there was no need to pit myself against anything that could help Nora later. But if it learned something, *anything*, it could make the risk worth it. There was a world of possibilities left unaligned. Baku and I hadn't killed so many nightmares saving Dreamers that it would affect—

A cutting gasp of Nora's fear rippled through my veins, yet it was the excitement mixed into that caught me up. It was a dark thrill woven with magic I knew all too well, and it left me with a warm, pooling sense of accomplishment. Nora wouldn't, would she? *Could* she? I rubbed my chest as it grew closer. *No.* Nora had barely mastered basic combat. There was no way she could make it to the Nightmare Realm without help. Then my lungs deflated as every other sensation gave way to blinding terror. I zeroed in on the pain, nearly bright enough to blind me, and reached out desperately for something solid to grab onto. For a cord no longer there. But there were others. I latched onto the closest one and held on to the dull cord as if it were my sole lifeline.

By the time I could see straight again, I stood in Nora's bedroom. I gripped the edge of her dresser, panting, but when I raised my eyes, it wasn't Nora that stood in front of me. Katie faced the desk, and her hand shook as she clutched a piece of paper, her knuckles white. Pieces fell into place. The note. Nora's absence. The emotions.

"No." The word fell from my tongue so quietly I barely heard myself speak, but Katie did. She spun toward me, banging into the desk, and her eyes locked onto me with something between recognition and fear. "Where is she?" I asked from beneath my hood. Katie opened her mouth, either to answer or scream, but nothing came out. I stepped forward and plucked the paper from between her slackened fingers. "She's safe?" I asked, reading over the letter. The page crumpled in my grip. "Taking time to enjoy the city?"

"Why don't *you* tell *me* where she is?" Katie asked in a wavering voice.

The Nightmare Realm. She was in the Nightmare Realm. My body felt numb, my brain scrambling to find answers. How? I glanced at Katie. At least I had an answer for why. Her mother and sister—the only two close blood relatives she had—made her feel like she was out of her mind, and she was starting to believe it.

I flung my hood back and stared Katie right in the eyes. "Are you sure you want to know?"

She slammed one hand over her mouth. "Ben?"

I held the note out for her to take back, waiting for her answer. Katie did everything in her power to pretend nothing happened five months ago, including lying to Nora's face. Why would she want to know now, now that it was too late?

Something hard flickered through her eyes, her expression shuttering. "Or should I call you Sandman?"

"Call me whatever you like," I said, harsher than intended.

When Katie didn't take the note, I set it down on the desk. Dusk had barely settled outside, casting the room in cool light. Already it felt cold and empty, the four walls missing their heart. The sentiment echoed in my chest. Nora asked me to take her back to the Night World, and I failed to give her the answer she wanted last night. So she went anyway. Because she didn't believe in me. I searched out her emotions but found a black wall as hard as granite. I fell onto the edge of her bed. The same bed we… She knew what being together meant to me. I wanted to take things slow and make sure our relationship had a firm foundation so there was no chance for regrets. But still she… Had she planned on leaving with or without me even then? I should've known. The night she found me in the Dream Realm with the knife Rowan gave her, she wanted the same thing from me. It was all to distract me from her lies.

"You won't find her," I said softly to Katie. I covered my face with my hands and fought to breathe. "What have you done, Nora?"

Katie made a disgusted sound in the back of her throat. "It's happening again, isn't it? What did you rope her into this time?"

I pressed the heels of my palms against my eyes. "I can explain."

"No," she said in a low, angry voice. "I don't want to hear your sorry excuses. Get out of my house."

"I—"

The door slammed. When I looked up, I was alone in Nora's room, and my heart tore. *Gone.* Nora was gone. What more could I have done to make her believe in me? When had she stopped? There was a time not so long ago that we were inseparable and had leaned on each other. She told me she trusted me, *loved* me, as I loved her, but she had taken the knife from Rowan. She killed the Weaver, nearly killed me, because she hadn't believed what I said about the balance. And now… She didn't believe me when I told her what she was about to walk into. And yes, part of me selfishly wanted to keep her from the Nightmare Realm to protect her, but I wouldn't have. What I wanted was nothing compared to what she needed. It never was.

And yet—

And yet, I couldn't stop myself from running a hand over the dark wall between me and Nora. "Let me in," I begged softly.

To my surprise, something pulsed in response. A glimmer of silver fractured the stone. My power—the dream Nora carried—

cried out to me, and my chest twisted. *The dream.* Nora got herself back to the Nightmare Realm and, before that, found some of the Weaver's memories. Why hadn't I noticed she was already capable of it? What was to say she couldn't find the dream too?

I followed that small, hopeless piece of magic to the Nightmare Realm and braced myself for the worst.

***

Though Nora's magic read loud and clear, it seemed no matter which entrance into the Nightmare Realm I used, she seemed just as far away. The center of the realm seemed a logical place for the barrier to spit her out, as that was where the Keep was, but I hoped she was anywhere else. I tried to stuff the hysteria down as the magic lured me into the Doll Maker's domain and focused on Nora. The possibility of Rowan having her—*no.* She couldn't. If Rowan had Nora, she wouldn't waste time killing her.

There.

Just ahead. A massive concentration of Nora's magic. I broke into a run, my boots clattering against a blanket of buttons covering the ground. I wove around trees of the same material, and a smattering of creatures raced further into the forest to distance themselves from me. I slid to a stop at the edge of the clearing, and my chest exploded.

She was there, alive and seemingly safe, flanked by two nightmares. I squinted across a table occupied by a strapped-down elderly Dreamer and past the Doll Maker to the masked nightmare standing beside Nora. One graze of Halven's hand and he could whisk Nora away to anywhere within the Nightmare Realm. Worse, I wouldn't be able to find her, magic or no magic. Not if the nightmare of lost things maintained contact with her. He knew exactly where someone wanted to go and exactly how to take them as far from that place as possible. If he saw me, Nora would be gone in an instant, but I couldn't let her take his offered hand. I held my breath, searching frantically for a solution to get them away from each other, but then Nora spoke.

"I'll need some things before I face Rowan. Supplies. An army—"

An army? My eyes widened. What was she talking about? She didn't need an army. She had *me*. She had someone she could trust.

But she didn't.

After everything, Nora didn't trust me. She couldn't—not if she did this. Ice shrouded my heart as it slipped from its place in my chest and shattered.

"Army?" the Doll Maker exclaimed, then twisted to stare at me across the clearing.

I shifted into the shadows, my mind repeating *Nora doesn't trust me* over and over. My lungs ached, unable to take in air, and I flipped my hood over my head. I leaned into one of the tall button trees. What could I do now? What should I do? I could barge over there and protect her, or I could stand here and do nothing. We were beyond talking now. Nora made it clear she didn't want to listen.

"You can come out, Dream Lord. She's gone," the Doll Maker called in a sour tone after some time. "I haven't hurt her, so I trust you won't hurt me."

I stepped out of my hiding place and forced my shoulders back. Halven was nowhere to be seen, and I nearly crumbled when I saw Nora wasn't either. Had she taken his hand of her own free will? Did he force her to go with him?

"Are you so sure about that?" I asked.

"She's safe with Halven." The Doll Maker plucked a large needle from her hair and circled the table where the old woman thrashed. "Like I was about to tell her, there's no need to build an army. It will only take one person with the right skills to kill the usurper."

I bared my teeth. If it were that easy, I would've brought Nora back a long time ago. "If that's true, if you're so loyal, why don't you kill Rowan yourself?"

The Doll Maker laughed and bent over the Dreamer. "Do I terrify you, Dream Lord? No. I terrify only these precious souls." She ran a hand lovingly over the woman's hair. "Given that, do you think I've survived this long by entwining myself in power struggles?"

"There would be no struggle with Rowan dead."

"Does a snake not still have venom after it's dead? She has those loyal to her." The Doll Maker tied a knot at the end of a string. "Besides, Lady Nightmare has many weaknesses. There will be struggle after struggle until she learns to snuff the rebellion, and when that time comes, Sandman, she will no longer be the girl you knew."

"She will always be Nora," I insisted.

The Doll Maker began stitching the Dreamer's mouth shut, muffling her screams, and my jaw tightened. "Oh, don't look so perturbed. She'll be fine when she wakes up." The Doll Maker rolled her eyes. "And as for the Lady always being Nora, maybe you're right. Or maybe she already isn't. What do I know?"

She *was* Nora. True, she was changing—growing into her

new self—but everyone did that over the course of their life. The Weaver had. I had. Long before the worlds were separate, he wasn't so dark, and I wasn't so light, but we became what we needed to become for things to work. Nora was a new entity though. There were no established rules, no baseline. She could become what she wanted to become, and I wouldn't let her lose herself completely without a fight.

"Where did Halven take her?"

"How should I know?" The Doll Maker tugged thick black thread up in front of her with a small frown. "I'd venture to guess he's going to his twin. They've been more open about their meetings now that Rowan's no longer at the Blood Tower. Don't you fret: Lady Nightmare will be safe for now—unlike the rest of us, now that Mara's back."

The world spiraled out from under me. *No.* Nora wouldn't… I told her who Mare was, *what* she was. She would never… Mare was the worst kind of nightmare. Not even a nightmare, if I was being particular. Mare was something else—an Ancient, like Baku—and they played by no one's rules. That was why the Weaver and I locked them in the Ever Safe not long after we were made. They killed without reason, destroyed things just to feel the despair it caused. And what better place for primal beasts than a world filled with mortals? If Mare had her way, she would take us back to the dark days when danger roamed without borders. Gone were the creatures of legend from the Day World because the Weaver and I took them from it. Lured them into a cage and bolted it shut. Only two ever made it out again. We'd gotten lucky with Baku, who was content as long as his stomach was full. Mare on the other hand would've spent every day of her eternal life trying to break down the doors to the Ever Safe.

Oh, Nora…

I never imagined she would kill the Weaver and destroy the balance, but I hadn't known better then. Now I did. I stared at the place she stood moments ago. There was no catching up to her now that she'd gone with Halven, but even if there was, I didn't have time to follow. With Mare back, I had to reinforce every ward around the Dream Realm. And more. I had to add more. And then—then I would find Nora. Because, if nothing else, I deserved answers.

Chapter Twelve

Halven's outfit looked more ridiculous the longer I stared at it. His black jacket, piped with red, was covered in an illogical pattern of embossed lines. The collar rose high enough to cover any exposed skin, and the hat shadowed the entirety of his head not hidden behind the mask. From the laces on his boot hung a small key, rusted with age. He oozed a gentlemanly air, while his appearance made him seem more like he belonged in a theatrical group performing satire.

"What are you the nightmare of, exactly?" I asked.

His chest rose with a deep breath, and he forced out an answer. "Being lost."

"What?" My steps slowed. "But the Doll Maker said—and we've been—"

I was duped right off the bat. *Stupid, stupid, stupid.* Even the darkness inside me had hesitated to follow Halven. And the worst part was that this wasn't even the first trick I'd fallen for. Mara fooled me as well, though to my own credit, I never trusted her. And I hadn't purposely brought her back, but she was here nonetheless. Somewhere. Doing who knows what. While I was—*oh, no.* Where was I? I was so busy staring at Halven's ridiculous clothes that I hadn't paid attention to anything else. I whirled around. The button forest was nowhere in sight. Instead, a mountain rose in the distance, pricking at a bad memory, and an orange pond swirled into a whirlpool on our left. How long had we been walking?

Halven patted his chest with a flat hand. "I know where someone is going bec—" His voice cracked. "If not—" He rubbed at his throat through the ruffles. "If I don't know where they *want* to go, I cannot make them lost."

Right. Of course. *Of course.* I was putting my fate in the hands of a nightmare that excelled in getting people lost. Was I too lost for the Sandman to find me? I winced. As if he would even try after what I did. I was on my own now. A weight pressed down on my chest, my heart fluttering, bordering on panic. *Stay calm.* I inhaled slowly and let it out through my mouth. *Calm.* I was the Weaver. This was fine. I would be fine.

Halven motioned me forward with another dramatic sweep of his hand.

Fine, I chanted in my head. I walked alongside him, this time keeping my eyes on my surroundings. Something about them felt familiar, but I hadn't seen this golden prairie before. Small, tan, rodent-like nightmares popped up from the tall grass. They blinked red eyes once, twice, then bobbed their heads in our direction and scurried away, whispering excitedly among themselves.

"Should I be worried about where they're running off to?" I asked.

Halven shook his head.

Still, I watched the grass move as what had to be dozens of them fled from our path. The animals in the button forest had stayed and bowed. Head-bobs could've meant anything. A signal to each other that I was here. That they should rush off and tell Rowan where I was. Or even a signal to Halven that his heinous plan to trap me was ready.

I reached slowly for the small pocket on the side of my bag while keeping one eye on Halven and another on the grass. The zipper made a small sound, and my hand froze. Halven cocked his head toward me and shifted closer. I took a step away from him, my mouth dry. His shoulders rose and fell before he turned to face me fully. He seemed to study me through his mask for a moment, then was behind me in two lightning-fast steps. I leapt away, whirling on him at the sound of my bag's zipper.

Halven held my Swiss Army knife on his palm. "Here," he rasped and held his arm out for me to take it.

I narrowed my eyes at him and carefully plucked the weapon from his hand. So much for keeping my distrust on the down low. "How much farther?"

He held his index finger and thumb a half inch from each other indicating it wouldn't be much longer.

"And where are we going exactly?" I was proud of myself for keeping the fear from my voice, but I doubted it escaped his notice.

"There." He pointed to a tiny black structure past the prairie, an expanse of sand, and a rocky outcrop.

"That looks pretty far to me," I said in a flat voice.

Halven held his hand out for me to take again. "Faster."

"Pass." I gripped the knife harder and let my hands fall to my sides.

He shrugged and led the way out of the dry grass. White sand filled my sneakers as we zig-zagged toward the building. I ignored the grains working their way through my socks to irritate my toes and focused on breathing. The grin inside me, so quiet during the entirety of my journey, now balked. I felt it twisting as if it were my own expression. I touched my mouth with my free hand, but it maintained the neutral mask it was trained to keep. *I am not afraid.* I flicked open the knife just in case.

Halven left more than an arm's length worth of space between us the rest of the trip, coming closer only when the local geography made it necessary. I refused to take his hand again but did allow him to guide me carefully around jagged rocks. The climb was just steep enough to cramp my calves. What I wouldn't give for a bottle of water. Too bad I hadn't packed one. There were probably a lot of things I should've brought that I wouldn't realize until it was too late, but I wasn't up for carting around a fifty-pound bag either.

When Halven paused at the edge of our destination, my body burned with shock. The reality of what stood before me slammed down like a blacksmith's hammer on hot metal, chinking away at my last bit of patience.

Blood flowed between the dark stones of the Blood Tower instead of mortar. The towering double doors and arched windows were all too familiar. My vision blurred, fury gripping me tightly. I snagged the front of Halven's shirt and held my knife to his throat in a movement so smooth even the Sandman would've been impressed. "You lying, traitorous piece of—"

The tower door flew open and banged against the outer wall. Kail braced himself in the doorway, leaning into the stones as if it were the only thing keeping him on his feet. His chest rose and fell quickly beneath the embroidered overlay on his jacket. Behind his white hooked mask, Kail's eye—the one I hadn't stabbed with the corkscrew attachment on my knife—flashed rapidly between colors. I shoved Halven away and pointed the knife at him, my pulse thundering in my ears.

"You," Kail wheezed.

"*You,*" I repeated, my words poison. "I'm going to kill you for what you did."

"I didn't do anything." He straightened, completely unfazed, and scanned the landscape behind us. "Did anyone see you? Where's the Sandman?"

"You didn't do anything?" The knife shook in my hand. My skin was hot enough to blister. "You gave me that damn knife and sent me after the Weaver."

He leveled a glare at me. "Problem solved. No? Your family is safe."

I launched myself at him, screaming, and swung at his chest with the knife. His hand circled my wrist and held fast before I could even nick him. "*I hate you.*"

Kail rolled his eyes. "Were you seen, Halven?" he asked again.

Halven made a movement with his hands that seemed to say we were but not to worry.

"Good." Kail glared, not daring to release my arm. "The Sandman sent you? Did he tell you we spoke?"

"Don't worry about the Sandman. Worry about me." I attempted to twist free of his grip, but it was made of iron.

"Yes, yes. You're terrifying." He sighed. "So he didn't tell you I offered to help? Obviously not, I suppose, or you wouldn't look so surprised to see me."

I laughed, the sound bitter. "Just like you wanted to help me last time?"

"I didn't *want* to help you then. Rowan did, and what reason did I have not to go along with it? Other than your failure meaning my impending doom, which was reason enough itself. I'll have you know, my death meant just as much to Rowan as yours did." He eyed the sky. "Let's finish chatting inside."

"Better plan." I finally broke free and strode past him into the tower. A metallic smell swallowed me, and I held my breath against it. "I'll go inside." I whirled around, and Kail nearly bumped into me as I braced myself in the door frame. "And you scurry off to whatever hellhole you crawled out of."

His changing eye slowed. "Are you evicting me?"

"Consider this a hostile takeover." I smiled coldly. "I'm sure Rowan will have a room for you at the Keep. Just make sure you don't get too comfortable, because I'll be taking that too."

"Not without help, you won't," he said matter-of-factly.

I slammed the door in his face and slid a heavy bolt in place with a shaking hand. Tarantulas wallpapered the hallway, and black goop secreted from the floorboards. My stomach rolled. I had locked myself in a torture chamber. *Smart.* It wasn't too late to run out the back door. The grin took on a disgusted edge. *No.* The Weaver did not run. I dug my nails into my palm and strode down the main corridor. I was here. Alone—sort of—and alive, which was an achievement in itself. Now I just had to settle in and make a plan. Easier said than done.

"Face it." I jumped at Kail's voice behind me. He strode down the opposite end of the hallway, hands held out to his sides, smug. "You need me."

"How did you—"

"Did you think I wouldn't know more than one way into my own house?" He *tsk*ed and stalked around me. "Stop worrying, *Lady Nightmare*. If I wanted you dead, you would be."

"Oh geez. What a comfort."

"Let's see it then." He nodded to the bookbag. "What have you brought to exact your revenge?"

My arsenal consisted of the weapons in my bag and the gold in my veins. I couldn't rely on the Sandman to fight this with me, though I was certain he wouldn't fight with Rowan under any circumstance. I puffed my chest out. "The Weaver doesn't need an arsenal."

"*The Weaver* did not. But you—" He gave me a sly grin.

"*I* am the Weaver now. Get used to it."

"No. You are something *else*." He gave a mock bow. "Regardless, I am at your service, and if you'd like to stay alive, I suggest you take me up on the offer. Only a third of the nightmares are in favor of you. The rest are either for Rowan or too stupid to make a conscious decision."

A third? That was less than promising. Hopefully a majority of the others were neutral, though based on the victorious glint in Kail's eyes, I couldn't place stock in it. "And you belong to that last group, I assume," I quipped to cover my uncertainty.

"I am anything but stupid," he said easily.

No, he was not. "So you're for Rowan."

"How many times am I going to have to say it?"

A thousand times wouldn't be enough. Words were nothing more than puffs of air. He could claim loyalty now, but when the wind blew in another direction, his support would go with it. "Oh, Kail," I drawled. "*I* would be the stupid one if I trusted you. You're turning on the woman you spent forever with for one that stabbed you in the eye. What does that say about you?"

He bent to my level and leaned forward until the curve of his beaked mask skimmed my nose, but I refused to yield an inch. "It's *because* you stabbed me that I want to help."

"Okay. You're clearly deranged." I placed my palm against the cool mask and shoved his face away. I raised my knife between us. "I wonder what taking out the other one would get me."

His laugh was short. "I admit to ulterior motives. One being that you fix my eye."

"One," I said pointedly. Another being the chance to stab me in the back. I strode around him and down the hallway, doing my best not to look at the arachnids on the walls. The hair on my arms stood on end at the thought of accidentally brushing against them.

"The Weaver can alter nightmares even after they're born," he called after me.

"So?"

He dashed in front of me and cut off my path. "I'm relying on the human part of you to have a bit of compassion."

The honesty in his eyes shook me. He was a nightmare—the nightmare of the unknown. More importantly, he had tricked me into becoming the Weaver so Rowan could slaughter me. Why would he give me actual answers now? Why be truthful when he clearly had a knack for lying?

"I have compassion for the Dreamers," I said slowly. "Not for you."

His eye flashed faster. "Consider it compensation for my assistance then."

"You're barking up the wrong tree." I turned down another hall, searching for another door to lock myself behind. *Aha!* There was one just ahead.

He followed close on my heels. "Where are you going?"

"I'm trying to get away from you," I hissed.

"Good luck with that." His arm snapped across a doorway, stopping me again. "Unless you're able to make me leave?"

I scowled at him, but he didn't move. Didn't speak. He just let the question hang there. We both knew the answer was a resounding *no*, and I wasn't about to give him the satisfaction of hearing it. My fingers flexed, aching to land a punch, but a second before I could swing, he leaned away.

"I didn't think so." He straightened his jacket. "Might I offer you Rowan's old room? We can begin your training tomorrow— the important things the Sandman wasn't able to teach you. Meaning we start from scratch, really."

"How about the room I stayed in last time instead?" I asked, ignoring the part about training—not only because he was right that I learned nothing useful, but because there was no way I was going to train with *him* instead. Besides, the idea of sleeping in Rowan's bed gave me the heebie-jeebies.

"That's my room," Kail countered.

I did hit him then: a solid punch to his ribs that produced a satisfying *oof.* He stared at me and, without looking away, kicked his heel against the opposite wall, revealing a hidden room.

Kail said nothing as he stepped away from the entrance.

Inside, soft lights flickered to life, revealing a bed carved into the wide trunk of a low tree. Plush black blankets were piled at the center. Vine-like branches hung from the ceiling with ribbons and small dried flowers dotting the grey-green foliage. It was beautiful and eerie and strangely fitting for Rowan.

"Why don't I just sleep outside?" I asked.

"If you want to, go ahead." He shrugged one shoulder. "The important thing is that *I'm* not out there where something might use me as their midnight snack."

"If that's a possibility, maybe I'll leave the front door open and hope for the best."

He leaned closer and whispered, "What if they find your room first?"

"They wouldn't dare," I said, unsure.

"Wouldn't they? You haven't proven yourself to anyone, and no one fears you nor respects you, though I say we aim for fear in the future." He flicked a piece of hair beside my face. "I hope you're ready to get your hands dirty, *Lady Nightmare*."

"Get out of my tower," I demanded.

"I'll be upstairs in *my* tower if you need anything. You remember the way, don't you?" Kail cracked his knuckles, his face hardening. "Until tomorrow."

"I hate you," I told Kail again.

"So you've said." He sauntered away, tossing a wave over his shoulder.

Chapter Thirteen

Nora

"Focus," Kail drawled from behind me.

I glared at him over my shoulder and ground my teeth. "I'm so glad you're here to remind me of that every two minutes."

He stood, arms folded, watching me carefully just as he had the last six days, and I instantly regretted ever giving in to *training* with him. To be fair, no one was better than Kail at being annoying. He was my own personal amoeba. For four days he woke me up at regular intervals while my body tried desperately to sleep through whatever adjustments were happening. Then for two days he followed my every zombie-like step while I explored the tower, sometimes never saying anything, sometimes never shutting up. He drained my energy, sending my patience level far into the negatives until I caved.

So there I sat with a pile of the Weaver's thread on the table in front of me. The gold fibers flickered against the black cords as it tried desperately to snake up my arm. My skin ached to let it circle my wrist as it had that day five months ago.

Inside, the grin widened, impossibly cruel, at my denial. The threads were the Weaver's power—my power. I understood that. I *needed* these threads, and they needed me too. But it was exactly because of how much I needed them that I pushed them away. When I ripped them from the Weaver's arm in that storage unit, it took time for him to regain strength. I didn't want the threads to be a crutch for me like they were for him. Darkness poured from the grin, clouding my doubts, pushing me to extend a hand.

"Remember what I said about personal space?" I asked when Kail inched closer.

"I do," he said, unbothered, and his arm brushed against mine.

I gritted my teeth. "What's the point of this anyway? I told you I can see the nightmares inside. Just give me a pair of scissors."

Kail winced. "You can't *cut* them apart. They don't end just like that." He snapped his fingers. "Think of them like holding hands. If you will one of them out, they'll let go."

The image of the disfigured nightmare that brought me to the Night World flashed through my mind, and I wrinkled my nose. "Sure. It's one big pile of comfort and joy."

"It's one big pile of loyalty and respect. Even Rowan wouldn't go hacking her army into pieces," he said with a sharp edge. "Stop whining and try again."

I stared at the threads. At the bits of gold catching the light.

At the rust-colored blood staining nearly half of it. The Weaver's blood, Kail informed me, from the floor of the Keep where he liberated the bundle of thread before Rowan noticed. I glanced down at the gold veins pulsing beneath my stained hands and wondered how true that was. Not that it mattered—the threads were real enough—but I thought all of it hitched a ride when the Sandman took me back to the Dream Realm. It was already established that Kail was a liar, but I couldn't think how else he would have this thread.

"You were the one who said I needed to be feared. Did you think I'd accomplish that by being thoughtful?" I asked.

The beak of his mask skimmed my cheek. "Without those threads, you're nothing."

"I'm the Lady of Nightmares," I ground out. *Like that makes a difference,* my inner voice balked. One day I would be able to utter that title without feeling like I bit into a lemon, but today was not that day.

"A leader without power isn't a leader at all." He set his hands down in the middle of the threads and dragged them across the table to me. I tucked my hands under the table to protect them. "The Weaver understood that, so if you truly want to be the Lady of Nightmares, take them."

I snatched Kail's mask where it touched me and shoved his face hard enough that he stumbled sideways. He studied me from the corners of his eyes with a grim set to his mouth. The air in the room thickened, sparking between us, but I was in charge. If anyone was going to back down, it would be him. And, after what felt like a lifetime, he did.

"You can change it, you know," he said in a careful voice.

"Change what?" I pinned both ends of the threads to the

table with a finger and poked at them with my other hand.

"The mask." When I glanced up at Kail, he tapped the hard, bone-like surface covering his forehead. "You can change it. Remove it even."

"Ah." I rubbed my temples, suddenly tired. "But then where would your mystique go?"

He smirked and resumed his perch behind me. "Try again."

This time it didn't sound like an order. It was more like a friend urging me toward greatness, and I knew that's what these threads were. Greatness. I took a deep breath and closed my eyes. When I reached for the threads again, one end snapped around my finger in a tight coil. "Hold still," I said under my breath. The mass stilled. I cracked my eyes open. *Interesting.* I closed them again and ran a finger down the length of it, pinching where it felt right. A shaggy dog with bulging eyes and steaming drool looked out from the darkness. Its jowls shook in anticipation. Not the most ideal choice for my first nightmare, but I was ready to be finished and that's what I found so—

I focused on his end like Kail told me to. Coaxed it away from the others. Something kicked inside me, the growing darkness throbbing. The grin relaxed, satisfied. I pulled gently at the dog until it frayed, then hesitated. Was this right? Was I hurting it? I scoffed at the concern and resumed the task. *Let it hurt.* But another part of me slapped the thought away, and the thread split, pulling apart fiber by fiber.

I opened one eye at a time to find a six-inch thread between my fingers. The rest of the pile was halfway up my arm, heading straight for the edge of my sleeve. I watched it creep higher with growing fascination. The grin eased forward. Eager. Nervous. Waiting for me to rip it away. The darkness seemed to hold its breath while I decided what to do.

The decision swam slowly from the depths of my thoughts and hovered just out of reach. Suddenly, the darkness wasn't the only one not breathing as I waited for it to take the final step. I held my breath so long my lungs ached. Then, when I exhaled, it was as if I blew the dark cloud away.

Yes. I wanted the threads—and their power—as much as they wanted me.

My body reveled in the sense of completion as the threads fused with the sleeve of my grey t-shirt. The thing I was missing while stuck in the Day World: this was it. One of the things, at least. The power washed over me. Filled me. It radiated with every beat of my heart. I felt larger, bigger than the world. I was Atlas. Nothing could touch me here.

"What is it?" Kail asked, breaking through my euphoria.

"What?" I breathed.

"The nightmare." Kail stared hungrily at the single thread. "What is it? Will it fit in here?"

I held it up and blinked myself fully back to the present. "I think so."

"Good. Then do it."

"Do what?"

"Bring it out." He waved his hands impatiently.

Bring it out. I thought back to the Weaver on the Sandman's beach when he created one of the first nightmares I'd seen. With a flick of his wrist, the thread went straight and stiff. Then there was a burst, followed by the presence of a newly created nightmare. That didn't seem so hard. I wrinkled my nose and flicked. Nothing happened.

"You have to mean it," Kail admonished.

I stared at the thread, at the dog, and flicked it again. It hardened slightly but fell limp. Again and again I tried. Again and again I failed.

"Do what you did last time," Kail suggested, pressing closer until I shot him a death stare. "Just… more."

"Personal. Space." I jabbed a finger into his upper arm. "Do you even know how to do this, or are you guessing?"

"I… don't. But I know what it felt like from the other side."

So they *could* feel it. I twirled the thread between my fingers and looked Kail up and down, marveling at how something so complex could come from something so simple. His mind, his body, his clothing—his abilities, whatever they were, exactly. All of them were once contained in something that wouldn't have been thick enough to sew on a button.

"Enjoying the view?" he purred.

I rolled my eyes. "Don't flatter yourself." He opened his mouth, but I cut him off before he could make a sound. "Are you going to tell me what it felt like or not?"

He was quiet for a long while, staring at the threads on my arm, and just when I thought he wouldn't, he let out a short breath. "Before, it's like—like you exist and don't. It's peaceful, but you desperately want to come out because peace isn't what you were made for. Only you don't know that, so you're trapped in a mild state of constant panic. There are others beside you keeping you from floating away into the nothingness, and you're doing the same for them. Then suddenly there's a pulse of magic and you wake up for the first time. The world becomes so clear. There's this person in front of you—someone you know you want to be closer to—and he's calling you forward so you let go." He cocked his head. "And then you're real."

I rubbed the threads circling my wrist. "They know me then? That I'm the Weaver? Or will I have to assert some sort of dominance the second I give each one life?"

"Anything you make will be loyal to you until you give it a reason not to be." Kail shrugged. "The Weaver gave a lot of us reasons, and most still remained true. It's a sickness, really, but there it is. We don't have time to convince every existing nightmare to believe you're up to par, so if you want to turn the tides—"

An army. Right here on my arm and all I had to do was call it into being. I bit the inside of my cheek and met the fire dancing in Kail's eyes. The grin spread, pleased. I spun back to the table. The thread hung loose between my fingers, taunting me. I pushed my thoughts toward it—*wake up, let go, come this way.* Nothing. So, for the first time, I stared straight at those haunting pearly whites haunting my vision. *A little help?*

The grin brightened as it grew. Coils of darkness spread through me like another set of veins and didn't stop until it felt as if there was nothing left inside me but that sardonic mouth. I winced against it but didn't fight. The Weaver was a being of dark things. If I was going to rule them, create them, I had to let the same darkness in. As long as I kept hold of the key, I could lock it away when I was finished. The thread straightened, and I bolted up in my chair.

Heat zipped from my hand into the thread. It exploded, knocking my chair backward. My head thwacked against the hard floor, and the smell of sulfur nearly choked me as I scrambled to my feet. The table was a pile of splinters, but in front of me was the same brown dog I saw in the thread, only *better.* He was nearly as tall as me with two rows of needle-sharp teeth and silver blades for nails. His green eyes met mine, and he licked the drool from his jowls.

Kail's slow clap filled the room.

"I did it." I laughed. "I did it!"

"Yes." Kail skirted around the room, keeping an eye on the watchful new nightmare. "Though you did say it would fit in here."

"I said I *thought* so." I leaned closer to the nightmare, admiring the hard muscles beneath the fur. With a pack of these, I could do practically anything. "And he does fit. Technically."

Kail leveled me with a hard stare. "He's nearly three times wider than the doorway. How are you going to get him out?"

"You will be loyal to me," I addressed the dog, ignoring Kail's valid point, though the words didn't feel like they were truly mine. "Me and no other." Kail cleared his throat behind me. "And don't eat him—yet," I added.

"Yet?" Kail scoffed. "All I have to do is step into the hallway, and he won't be able to eat me at all."

"If you can make it to the door before he does." I touched the dog's muzzle. Coarse hair followed my hand as if it were a static balloon. "Should we test his speed?"

Kail's eyes widened, not in fear, but with something that almost resembled humor. "Get this giant, frothing thing out of my tower."

"Why?" I asked, enjoying his agitation.

"*Why?* You've got to be—"

The tower walls shook so hard, paintings clattered from their nails. I gasped and gripped the back of the chair for balance. The dog growled, the blades on his feet digging into the area rug, and Kail braced himself in the corner. His warm brown skin paled.

"Was that supposed to happen?" I asked slowly, fearing I already knew the answer.

Kail swore and raced to the window. His knuckles turned white where he gripped the sill. "We're leaving."

I leapt to the second window just as a ball of fire soared toward the tower. I flattened myself against the nearest wall as the impact shook the building again. Black spots danced in my vision. "What the hell is that?" I screeched.

"Not what. *Who.*" Kail grabbed my wrist and yanked me into the hallway. "There's no time to explain."

"Wait," I commanded. The giant dog reached a paw out after us, whimpering. "We can't leave him."

"Worry about *us*," Kail shouted over the impact of a third fireball.

My chest twisted. I wasn't sure if it was the human part of me or part of the magic, but I couldn't leave the dog to die. He was a nightmare. He was *my* nightmare. The only thing here I created. Proof that I was capable. A reminder that I was powerful.

"Break the walls down," I ordered him, and his nails ripped through the nearest floorboards in response to my demand. "Escape and find me later."

"In," Kail instructed as he shoved me through another secret door before I could get another word out.

My eyes adjusted quickly to the dark room. Too quickly to be considered normal. Behind us, the inner walls creaked and snapped, while the outer walls continued to shake. Kail kicked aside a woven rug and bent to lift a large trap door. Red and black flecks of dust rained down from the ceiling.

"What are you doing?" I asked.

"Escaping."

He shoved me forward, and I stumbled into the opening, slamming my chin against the edge before falling six feet. The landing sent a bolt of pain up my tailbone. It had to be broken. Could a tailbone break? It was fractured and bruised, at least. My wrists throbbed from catching part of my weight. Kail leapt down beside me, landing perfectly on his feet. A soft thump told me he replaced the trapdoor, though without the rug to hide it, I didn't know why he bothered. I dabbed a finger against my chin and hissed. Blood dripped onto my chest.

"What the hell, Kail?" I cried.

"Would you have jumped if I told you to?" he snapped.

No. Because I would've needed to trust him to jump into a black pit.

"Exactly," he said at my silence and hauled me up by my armpits. "Let's move."

"My bag—"

"It's not worth it."

"I beg to differ," I said, unyielding. My weapons were in there. My clothes. Everything I owned was inside that bag. I jumped, trying to reach the overhead door, but didn't even graze the wood. "I'm not leaving without it."

"The Hours will eat you alive." Kail lifted me up and threw me over his shoulder.

I pounded my fists against his back. "I'd like to see them try."

But he was already racing down a dirt tunnel. Roots reached out for us, and worms snapped tiny mouths when he disturbed their hornet-like nests, but Kail didn't slow. Didn't stop.

"Kail! Put me down."

"Sorry, Lady. You're my only chance at getting fixed." He

swatted the back of my thigh. "Stop squirming before I drop you."

"*Drop me*," I demanded. Then I fell on my already bruised butt with a groan. *Broken.* Definitely a broken tailbone. "You're such a jerk."

Kail crouched down in front of me. "Keep talking the big talk. See what happens. But Rowan sent the Hours after you, which means she's not planning to wait for you to learn how to walk the walk."

"I'd rather face them than take your advice again." I eased myself to my feet, wincing against the ache in my backside. At least my Swiss Army knife was still in my pocket.

He huffed and stood, looking down at me. "You're a horrible liar."

Dirt rained down on us as another fireball hit the tower, and I wondered how many it would take to bring the whole thing crashing down on our heads. I sobered, anger dissolving under the weight of my survival instincts. "Please tell me there's a way out of here."

"I *did* say we were escaping, didn't I?" Kail held out his hand the same way Halven did, and I narrowed my eyes at the gesture. "Just take it. It's easy to get lost down here, and we have to get to the safe house."

I reluctantly took his hand. "What are the Hours?"

"Twelve nightmares you're nowhere near ready to face," Kail said, stoic.

I swallowed hard and ran beside him, taking turns I didn't see until they were upon us. Not knowing our final destination was anxiety-inducing, but I understood why he wouldn't vocalize it any of the times I asked. Ears were everywhere. I had to wonder if it mattered though, seeing as Rowan had been his partner for so long. Surely she knew the location of Kail's safe house. "Maybe we should go somewhere Rowan doesn't know about so she can't send her minions after us," I suggested.

"Rowan clearly doesn't know or we'd go somewhere else," he replied, guarded.

"Keeping secrets from your bestie?" I asked bitterly. It didn't bode well for me considering I was far from being considered his friend.

Kail's laugh held no humor. "Who do you think I needed safety from, *Lady?*"

Chapter Fourteen

The Sandman

Don't do it. I stalked away from the sand-made sunflower I'd created beneath the brightest star in the Dream Realm. The place Nora and I met every night until we no longer could. *Don't go.*

Nora walked into the Blood Tower of her own free will a week ago. If she wanted to talk, she would've sent a nightmare with a message or let her walls down so I could feel her—her what? Guilt? Remorse? Longing? What did I expect her to feel? I'd done nothing but ask her for more time even though she constantly told me she didn't have more to give. It had to seem like I didn't care, or at the very least, like I didn't take her feelings seriously. And now she no longer trusted me to do what was best. She hadn't even tried to send word that she was okay, though she must've known how worried I would be. That hurt the most—that she would allow me to think the worst.

Well, *almost* the worst.

Everything was upended, my soul ripped apart, but there were bigger things to deal with. If we were to survive long enough to fix this new rift between us, Nora first had to take control of the Nightmare Realm. Then we had to deal with Mara before both the Day and Night Worlds ceased to exist.

I wanted to rage, to break something, to shake some sense into Nora. Instead, I sent a surge of power into the sand, and the perfect likeness of the Weaver swirled together before me. I punched the stupid grin off his face. Then I formed him again. And again and again until I was short of breath and my arm muscles ached.

I ran a hand through my hair, feeling marginally better. *Okay.* Anger later, life-or-death problems now. Both Nora and I had an eternity ahead of us, and I needed to remember that she didn't have the same life experiences I did. She made a choice—a stupid, horrible choice—but it didn't define her. I knew who Nora was, and I would stand beside her so that she would survive, with me or without me.

Stars. I was a lovesick fool. How many betrayals would it take for me to forsake her? The answer was carved in my heart: never. I would never give up loving her. Just as my friendship with the Weaver never stopped haunting me, I would live with this devotion for the rest of my life.

And so I put one foot in front of the other until the sea of glimmering sand disappeared and the muted colors of the Nightmare Realm surrounded me. My chest filled with dread at leaving the beach with Mare loose, but the Dream Realm was as secure as I could make it. It was better protected now than it was when I warded it against the Weaver, and I couldn't stay forever. Ignoring the creatures that scuttled into hiding as I passed, I made straight for the Blood Tower.

Only to find it smoldering.

My heart slammed into my chest hard enough to bruise. *Rowan.* It had to be her. Who else would burn down the tower? *Anyone that wanted to be the next Weaver.* The acrid scent of smoke burned my nostrils as I picked my way through the rubble. Kail wouldn't let anyone else harm Nora. Whatever game he was playing, it had to be for Rowan's benefit. Unless—unless he wanted to rule the Nightmare Realm himself. But he wouldn't need to burn down his own house when he had every opportunity to kill her.

I reached inward, searching for a hint of Nora's magic. Just a scrap. Something to tell me she was safe.

There.

Not in the rubble, but to the far north. I let out a breath, nearly falling to my knees. I had to see her, even if she didn't want to see me. Sand circled my boots, pushing my feet to move faster, faster, faster. The dream Nora held called to my magic, pulling me like a magnet. I wasn't sure how long I had walked before I saw two figures trekking through rows of billowing sheets clipped to clotheslines. I saw only flashes of them between the white linens before they became silhouettes behind it. Red handprints stained some of the fabric, while others were splattered with blood, and the rope they hung from was made of stretched intestines.

I wove my way between the gaps until I found the same row Nora and Kail walked. Seeing her now felt like taking my first breath in a week. I wanted to run to her, to lift her into a tight embrace and tell her how much I loved her in between kisses, but the uncertainty of her reaction shackled my legs. Each of my steps were measured and careful, taking me forward when I suddenly wanted to go in any other direction. I flipped my hood up and swallowed hard.

As I neared, still undetected, I noticed the dirt on her pants and a slight limp, and what was left of my excitement fizzled. Blonde hair clung to her cheeks, bright red from heat and exhaustion, and her shoulders slumped.

Kail slowed when he finally saw me and motioned ahead with one hand. Nora's head snapped up, and her eyes went wide, her body stiff. She said something to Kail, but they were still too far away for me to hear the hushed conversation. They exchanged a few more words while I stood rooted, and then Nora came forward alone.

I waited, not daring to breathe, until she was out of Kail's earshot. She stared up at me, her eyes the brightest gold without any trace of green remaining. There was no apology in her expression, only wary anticipation. "Hi," I forced myself to say.

She blinked a few times and the glow in her eyes faded. She stood with rigid and wiped the sweat from her forehead. A bruise colored her chin. "What are you doing here, Sandman?"

"Did you think I would never come?" My voice scratched its way from deep inside. "That I would find out you left and say *oh well?*"

She blushed, a feat considering how red she was already. "No, but—"

I was vaguely aware of Kail watching us a few sheets away, but with one look from Nora, he trudged further ahead, giving us the illusion of privacy. I stepped closer to Nora anyway. "Why?" I breathed. "I asked you to give me one day. If you insisted on coming after that, I would've brought you here and helped you find safety."

"Would you have?" She winced. "You knew what being in the Day World was doing to me. I told you I couldn't wait anymore."

"You promised me one day, but you barely waited five hours. And we—" I couldn't finish that sentence. Coming back to the Nightmare Realm wasn't the only thing I wanted to wait for, but I stupidly thought that night meant something for both of us. Something good—not the goodbye she intended it as.

"I know." It came out as a reverent whisper. "I'm sorry."

"Why?" I asked again.

"I had to." Her voice was soft but not timid, apologetic but determined.

A lump formed in my throat. "Because you don't trust me anymore."

"No." She gripped my upper arms, meeting my gaze again. "Of course I do. I just needed to take my fate into my own hands instead of waiting around for permission. The Day World was destroying me."

"I only ever wanted you to be safe. This is all so new to you, and you don't understand—"

"I will, Sandman. I'm learning." She lifted her arm to show me the circling threads. "I can see them—the nightmares. When I touch different parts of the thread, I see what each piece will become, and I'm working on bringing them to life. I already did it once. How could I have learned that at home?"

How could she learn that from me? She didn't say it, but she didn't have to. I plucked something white from her hair—a tooth. A human incisor, complete with the root. I flicked it to the side and turned a horrified look to Nora.

"Our escape from the Blood Tower ended in a field of teeth," she explained, shaking her hair out. "I thought I got them all out."

I ran a hand down my face. "You can't trust Kail. Not only has he been with Rowan forever, but there's no incentive for him to turn on her."

"I know I can't trust him." She sighed and pressed the heels of her hands to her eyes. "But this isn't me versus Rowan for him. He admitted he has ulterior motives, but what does that matter? I'm figuring this whole thing out, and soon I won't need him."

"*What does it matter?*" I gripped her face gently with both hands. "Do you really believe that, Nora? Because the last time Kail tried to *help* you get what you wanted, you killed the Weaver. Even if he is telling the truth about helping you take the Nightmare Realm, what then? At what cost?"

She leaned up on her tiptoes and slid my hood off, looking into my eyes, willing me to understand something. Then she kissed me. It lasted only long enough to make me stop talking, but the softness of her broke me. *Please don't let this be the last time.* My heart was hers. My realm was hers. My life. As long as she was okay, I would give any of it freely, but that was dangerous. There were millions of lives unknowingly depending on what we did. Giving the Dream Realm to the darkness would be catastrophic, but that didn't stop my mind from warring between what I *needed* to do versus what I *wanted* to do.

"I need time to figure out who I am," Nora said as gently as she had kissed me.

"You're Nora," I rasped.

"I *was* Nora." She chewed her lip. "Now I'm something more—or less. Maybe I'm someone completely different. That's what I need to figure out, and I can't do that if you're helping me every step of the way."

"You have all the time in the world to figure it out."

"Look at me." She spoke firmly, but her tone remained kind. "*Look at me*. When will I be safe? *When?*"

"After we take care of Rowan and—"

"Stop." She squeezed her eyes shut. "Please, please, stop. I feel this place inside me. I've felt it every moment since I woke up covered in the Weaver's blood, and now that I'm here, it's worse. I need to learn to walk with it, so it doesn't knock me off my feet. But with you, it's like I'm on life support. And Rowan is just one problem. One nightmare. She's who we need to deal with right now, but she's far from the last. I have to embrace the new me in order to be as safe as the Weaver was—if you could ever call him safe. I don't know how much of me will be left." Her eyes fell at the final statement, the words choked.

I reached out to hug her, but Kail's hand landed on my shoulder. "She asked for some time."

In one movement, I flipped him so he landed on his back on the ground. It was more a reflex than anything, but I wasn't sorry it happened. He should've known better than to touch me.

"Unnecessary," he grunted.

"See what happens if you dare lay a hand on Nora," I seethed. He wouldn't have hands left if he tried it again. He wouldn't have *anything* left.

"This is what I mean." Nora touched my arm and sighed

heavily before turning to Kail. "Were you listening?"

"Forgive me, Lady." He stood and brushed himself off with an annoying amount of composure. "The acoustics here don't serve privacy well."

She gave him a pointed look.

"Well, then," he blurted before she could say a word. "Time to be off before we're spotted."

Not yet. It could be days—weeks—before I saw her again. How much time did she want? How much space was too much? But Kail was right. They had to go before the wrong nightmare saw them. It didn't make saying goodbye any easier though. "Nora, I—"

She kissed my cheek, imploring me not to make this harder by allowing her emotions, her aching resolve, to brush through me. "I'll see you soon, okay?"

"Okay," I said reluctantly.

When she left with Kail without so much as a backward glance, she took a piece of me with her. A limb. A lung. A heart. But I would get them back. She just needed time, and I needed to respect that. Nora was the Weaver, and, if she was to survive, she was right. She had to become her new self. That didn't mean I was going to walk away. It only meant I needed to protect her from the sidelines.

Chapter Fifteen

"Are you listening to me?" Kail asked, clapping his hands in front of my face.

I swatted at him and kept walking. Of course I wasn't listening. He hadn't stopped naming different nightmares and their specialties since we'd walked away from the Sandman over two hours ago. It was like my life had become the worst infomercial ever. *Can't remove the rust from your sink? You need a bunch of extra slimy sucker fish. Starve them of Dreamer blood for a couple days and voila! In a few short minutes, they'll eat your problem away.*

It was an information overload, for one, and I currently didn't care. Also, I *really* needed to stop hearing Kail's voice, so I could replay the entire conversation I had with the Sandman. Every word. The tones. Facial expressions. I wished I removed his hood earlier, but I was too scared to see what was underneath. It would've been better if he looked at me like the traitor I was than the girl I wasn't. Had I made my reasons clear? Maybe I said something wrong. I tried my best, but there was so much left unsaid. He couldn't be expected to forgive me. Not yet. Not ever, maybe.

Kail palmed the top of my head and turned my face toward him. "You're *still* not listening."

"Tell me something I want to hear then," I quipped. Anything—anything *else*—that got my mind off the Sandman and the fracture in my chest.

Kail looked up at the sky and shook his head in disbelief. "How I wish I could kill you without becoming you."

"Yes, well." I shrugged. "Not everyone enjoys self-improvement. You do you."

He glowered at me and spoke in a droning voice. "We're here."

A chain link fence towered over us. On the other side, a long concrete building stretched between two rows of glowing signs. They faced away from the fence, as if intended for someone fleeing whatever dwelled inside, and each was more ominous than the last. My personal favorite was *Danger Lies Beyond*, but I couldn't read them all from this angle. Curling letters decorated the face of the building itself, but I couldn't make those out either.

I laughed. "You're kidding, right?"

"Why would I be kidding?" he asked with a raised brow.

I waved my hands frantically at the yard. "This is *literally* putting a neon sign on your hideout."

"Do any of them mention me? No." Kail pried a piece of

chain link fence away from a post. "In you go."

"No way."

He stared incredulously down at me. "Why not?"

"This is all reverse psychology, right? Don't go out *there* because it's *dangerous*, but what you really have to worry about is what's inside." I crossed my arms, waiting for him to deny it, but he didn't. "What's Plan B?"

Kail rolled his eyes. "It's just a wax museum, *Lady*. Why would I drag you all the way out here if I didn't know we would be safe?"

I grimaced. Why would he? Because he was a cat, and I was a mouse. "Was that supposed to make me change my mind? Because you obviously haven't seen wax figures with their creepy smiles and—"

"Look." He huffed, obviously agitated but trying to control himself. "You can't be afraid of your own nightmares."

"I'm not afraid. I just don't like them," I grumbled, not wanting to admit that he had a point. Besides, my feet were killing me and there was sweat in places I didn't know I could sweat. I grunted and slipped through the hole in the fence.

Kail followed, and the fence clanged perfectly back into place. "Ladies first," he said with sarcastic enthusiasm.

I ground my teeth together and strode past the signs. One was nothing more than a neon red skull, a dozen more were in languages I didn't know, and one was a blank headstone.

"That one adds the Dreamer's name and personal information," Kail whispered conspiratorially when he saw me looking at the carved stone.

Of course it did. I raked a hand over my face and waltzed up to the red door. It opened without a single touch to reveal a grand

foyer with black silk wallpaper and a crystal chandelier. A long
banquet table sat against the far wall, the entire surface covered
with a long, metallic gold tablecloth. A book lay open at its center
beside an ink pot and quill. On either side were trays of grapes
and cheeses.

"I thought this was a wax museum," I said from the corner
of my mouth.

"It is." He stepped across the threshold. "A very *refined* one.
Care to sign the guest book?"

I sucked in a breath, ready to explode, while Kail plopped a
grape in his mouth before disappearing into a side room. I
continued to stand in the doorway. What was I doing? I
should've gone with the Sandman. He would never drag me into
a place like this. But where else could I go? Not the beach. There
was nowhere for the Sandman to take me that guaranteed my
wellbeing.

"Keep up," Kail called from the other room.

I scowled. Why did I have to be stuck with *him* though? The
moment I stepped fully inside the foyer, the door creaked shut
behind me. I stared at the red-painted iron as if it were a living
thing. In a way, it was, but… Panic burned its way into my throat.
Where was the handle? "Uh, Kail," I shouted. "We can get out
of here, right?"

"Worried, Lady?" he asked, leaning out of the other room
before vanishing again. "Come on."

I would kill him when this was over. Stab out his other eye
and feed it to whatever happened to be nearby. But for now, I
followed his voice into a room with several wax figures. No one
famous—just a family of four in a seemingly innocent setup: the
father in a suit by the fireplace, the mother in a hoop skirt in a

chair beside him, and two young girls playing with a puppy on the rug at her feet. I met the mother's glassy stare as I moved toward another door. Her eyes tracked me through the room and her full lips broke into a big smile. Fear drove a spike through my forehead only to meet the dark, steely grin inside and shatter. The grin seemed to recognize the woman. The room. All of it. It softened into something proud and content.

Kail's beak grazed my shoulder, and I nearly fell over. "What part of *keep up* confused you?"

"Something is about to be up," I said in a raised voice. "My foot up your—"

"Now, now. Watch your language around the children." He put a finger to his mouth, shushing me, and winked at the two little girls. The one facing our direction looked up and giggled.

"Holy fudgsicles." I accidentally used the curse my friends and I used around Emery's little brother. *Had* used. When my friends were alive. The memory was sobering. "You're in such a hurry, so move."

"Testy," Kail sang.

In the next room, a cell door stood between us and three wax figures. The inmates wore black and white striped jumpers straight out of the movies. Two of them played cards on a moldy straw mattress and the other clanged his tin cup on the bars. I itched under their gazes and shuffled closer to Kail. The rooms got worse the deeper he led me into the museum. A flailing pig on a hook, a woman crawling from her own grave, and a shipwreck in a sea that swallowed the passengers, even though it appeared as nothing more than a puddle. I shut my eyes against the guillotine setup but still heard the metallic whir of the blade falling toward a man's neck. The thwack of it hitting its mark.

The thump as the head fell into the waiting wicker basket.

When I stepped into the next room and lifted my gaze, I wished I hadn't. A small group of men and women gathered in front of a large, raised platform. The women all wore white caps on their heads, and the men wore top hats. Their clothes were moth-eaten, their skin grimy, but they weren't what stopped me in my tracks. It was a girl no older than me balancing on a stool atop the platform with a noose around her neck.

Kail skipped up the side steps to stand beside her. "Don't just stand there," he said, motioning me forward.

"What are you doing?" I asked, suspicion seeping out.

"This relationship isn't going to go anywhere if you don't learn to trust me a *teensy* bit." He held his fingers up with the slightest space between them.

"I should've gone with the Sandman," I grumbled, regretting my choice yet again, and eased around the wax figures to stand beside him. "For the record, *this* isn't a relationship. It's survival."

Kail gasped dramatically. "Are you breaking up with me?"

I pulled the Swiss Army knife from my pocket and flicked open the corkscrew, twisting it so it caught the harsh lighting.

"No sense of humor, that one," he whispered to the girl on the stool.

"Kail," I warned.

"Excuse me, dear," he said nonchalantly to the girl. Then he kicked the stool out from under her.

"Kail!" I shrieked.

He ignored me in favor of lifting a trap door beneath her swaying feet. I gaped at him. "What?" He flicked a piece of hair from the forehead of his mask. "The longer you stand there, the longer she'll suffer. Once we're gone, the display will reset itself.

So…"

I stared at him, halfway sure he lost whatever sense he had. "What?"

He pointed into the darkness below the platform. "Secret bunker. Geez. Did you land on your head or your butt back at the tower?"

"Is this your thing?" I hissed, ignoring the still swinging wax figure. "Trap doors?"

He glowered. "That's a bit judgmental coming from someone that was *saved* by the fact that I have them."

My blood warmed. *You know what, ya jerk…* I shoved Kail toward the hole the same way he had shoved me into the first one. His knees banged against the edge of the opening, then his beak smacked against the opposite side before he fell in. A soft glow filled the hiding space. I smirked to myself, pleased I was able to catch him off guard. More than pleased. I peered over the edge to find Kail flat on his back and waved at him.

"I'm fine. Thanks for asking," he said, breathless.

I leapt down beside him, not caring that it was nowhere near the graceful landing he managed back at the Blood Tower. The important thing was that *he* was the one on the ground and *I* was the one on my feet. "Keep talking the big talk. See what happens," I repeated the words he'd said to me.

"Touché." He stood slowly and reached up to shut the hatch. "Don't pretend this isn't an ingenious hiding spot." The sound of wood scraping against wood came from above my head, and the creak of the rope ceased. "See?" he added. "Wax Girl is all better."

Pick my battles. Pick. My. Battles.

I turned, taking in the supposed safe house, though it was

more of a safe *box*. A sleeping bag was rolled up in the corner beside a wooden chest, and one of four lanterns was lit with small floating orbs. That was it. Where were the weapons? The food? *Food.* When did I eat last? Not since I arrived in the Nightmare Realm. So why wasn't I hungry? In fact, I felt pleasantly full. But still, what kind of safe house didn't have even basic supplies?

"Kail." I took a breath to center myself. "There's nothing here."

He kicked the trunk with his boot. "What do you call this?"

"That depends on what's inside it."

He lifted the lid to reveal a variety of items. A few coins, a map, and what appeared to be an extra set of the same clothes he was currently wearing, plus a cape. And he made fun of *me* when I wrapped a sheet around myself so the Blood Army wouldn't boil me alive. Not that it would've worked. "Did you raid a five-year-old's toy box?" I asked, my voice high with disbelief. "All you need now is a stuffed parrot and a plastic sword. Where are the weapons? Supplies?"

He huffed. "*We* are your weapons. And what other supplies would I need? Gold in case I need to bribe any nightmares that like to play human, a map of the Nightmare Realm—albeit extremely outdated at this point—and clean clothes."

I lifted the cape with two fingers. "This is a joke, right?" He snatched the fabric from me, and I rolled my eyes, reaching for the map instead. Crudely drawn lines covered the yellowed parchment. "You *did* steal this from a child, didn't you? Is this even accurate? Look at the size of this tree compared to the mountain over here. Is there a giant forest I should know about?"

"Okay, you know what." He snapped the paper from me.

"You can sleep on the floor tonight."

"As opposed to the feather bed?" I asked, crossing my arms. His eyes flared murderously, and I reminded myself that I did, in fact, need to sleep near him. I tugged my t-shirt off, and the threads whipped away from the sleeve in favor of my razorback tank. I wadded the fabric up to use as a pillow. "Forget it. Where's the food?"

"We feed on fear, not food." He snagged the sleeping roll for himself. "Which in turn feeds you. The whole thing where the Sandman banned Dreamers left most of us starved, so you have him to thank if you're feeling a bit peckish."

My stomach growled in protest, as if it missed the food it no longer needed. "You ate a grape when we came in."

"I didn't say we *couldn't* eat. It's instinctual sometimes, especially with the mindless brutes, but there's no reason for me to meal plan for emergencies." He grinned, almost too satisfied with my discomfort. "You'll live."

True enough. If it took me nearly a week to realize I hadn't eaten, there was no point in lugging food across the realm with us. I eased back on the hard cement floor and shoved my shirt beneath my head, too tired to argue with Kail. "See you tomorrow." I said through a yawn.

The last thing that passed through my mind before I fell into a fitful slumber wasn't that he would kill me. He could've done that a hundred times by now. No, the last thought I had was much worse. It was the look of pain on the Sandman's face. A hammer to my chest. I treated him horribly. More than horribly. And, honestly, I wasn't sure there was a way to truly come back from that.

***

When I saw another fissure waiting for me in my slumber, I hesitated. They had only given me more questions so far, and I didn't have the energy for that tonight. There were enough unanswered things in my life. Why was Kail helping me? How long until this was over? Did Rowan really have no idea where this safe house was? *Real* issues. Not something that I already had a general answer to. The Sandman and the Weaver survived whatever they were running from the first time, and I knew all too well how the Weaver's binding ended.

But, as they say—whoever *they* are—curiosity killed the cat. So I looked anyway.

A woman with long, crimped hair stood with her back to me, surrounded by thick metal bars. The breeze blew a snow-white shift around her body as she hummed.

"A new tune, Mare?" the Weaver asked.

Mare. Wasn't that what the Sandman called Mara? And, true enough, when the woman turned to gaze at the Weaver, it was with the same horizontal pupils as the nightmare in my bedroom. Her knobby knees were visible through the shift, though she stood tall. Nearly eight feet, I would guess, which was extreme compared to the posture I was familiar with.

"Weaver," Mara crooned. "Come again, have you?"

"Tell us how you escaped the Ever Safe," the Weaver demanded.

Mara wrapped her hands around the bars, iron dipped nails clinking against them. "Ask Baku. He followed."

"Baku doesn't speak, and the path is too dark for his dreams to reveal anything useful."

154

She sneered. "And yet, he is out there while I am in here."

"Because he doesn't want to rip the world out from beneath our feet," the Weaver said with an edge of impatience.

"Weak-minded," she spat.

"Smart," the Weaver corrected.

The breeze around Mara ceased, her clothes and hair utterly still as if she commanded it. Her eyes, on the other hand, were a tempest. "I am caged because I let you cage me." To prove her point, she pried the bars apart and stepped through the opening. "I think, dear one, I will no longer allow it."

The Weaver ran then, screaming for the Sandman, before the memory snapped shut. My sleep was pitch black again, and I let out an aggravated huff. *Every time.* Each memory stopped just before anything important happened. But maybe I'd seen what I had to. Mara as the Sandman knew her.

Mara as Mare.

Chapter Sixteen

Nora

"Wakey, wakey," Kail droned.

I rolled over and refused to give him the satisfaction of a groan. It felt as if I aged fifty years the way my joints had stiffened after a night sleeping on the hard floor. "What time is it?" I asked, my words thick with the remnants of sleep.

"Time for task number two," he said.

"What was task number one?" I eased up off the floor, stretching my sore muscles, and yanked the dirty t-shirt back over my head. The glowing orbs still floated around inside their lanterns, and Kail's belongings were gone—probably back in the chest.

"The dog." Kail gripped me by the shoulders and spun me around to face a stained cloth draped over something square.

"That's task number two."

I blinked the sleep from my eyes. Where did that come from? It was probably better not to ask or to think about how he got it in here without waking me up. "How long have you been awake?"

"Aren't you going to ask me what's inside?" he asked, sounding far too excited.

"Nope," I quipped, but couldn't stop staring. It was too small to be the loom—not that he could've broken into the Keep and dragged it here—and that was all that mattered right now. Well, that and killing Rowan, which was really the same thing. "We have more important things to deal with." Whatever was underneath the cloth rattled the bars. Hard. I jumped, my back slamming into Kail's chest, and quickly shoved away from him. "Get rid of it."

"You don't even know what it is," he admonished.

"I don't care what it is, Kail. We need to figure out a way to defeat Rowan, not mess around with…*that.*"

Kail whipped the sheet off with a dramatic flair to reveal a small cage. Inside, a monkey—or what resembled a monkey—less than a foot tall with dark matted fur bared its tiny fangs. A white moustache curled away from its face like an Emperor tamarin, but in true nightmare fashion, it was deformed. Its arms were short with small hands where elbows should've been, and a bare, rat-like tail twitched behind it. Pointed ears flicked at the edge of a scaled face with black eyes. It had no nose, and its pointed canines hung over its bottom lip.

"Do you know how hard this thing was to catch?" Kail said in a hard voice. "It bit me. Twice. *And* it peed on me."

I smirked at that. "Smart nightmare."

"You're welcome." He crumpled the cloth into a ball and flung it at me.

"What am I supposed to do with it?" I asked, dodging his throw.

"Practice. Obviously."

"Oh, obviously." I rolled my eyes. "Take it outside and let it go."

Kail laughed. "No."

"Yes."

"You seem to have some sort of moral objection to testing on animals, but you need to get over it. We agreed you need to be feared, and that won't happen if you don't want to hurt one of us." He banged on the cage, and the monkey squawked, outraged. "You need to master us before we master you."

He wasn't wrong, but it felt wrong. The monkey hadn't done anything against me, so what good would it do to hurt it? I could be feared and fair at the same time. *No, you can't,* the grin seemed to say with its sarcastic curl. The sentiment filtered through my logic, but I fought against it. I could try.

And fail, the grin implied.

"What exactly do you want me to do?" I asked, weary of my own warring thoughts.

"Change him. You can alter nightmares with almost no effort."

"But…" The monkey's eyes darted between Kail and me, pupils wide. Did it understand what he was saying? I cringed. "It's already alive."

"So?" Kail watched me carefully. "You draw, don't you? Once you finish a picture, is it impossible to tweak anything?"

I narrowed my eyes. "How do you know about that?"

"Rowan," he said dismissively.

For some reason, that made it worse. I ground my teeth together. "How does Rowan know?"

He sighed. "Look, I don't know, okay? Let's not get off topic."

"I don't know how to change nightmares," I admitted. "Besides, it looks fine to me."

He scoffed. "Watch."

Before I could stop him, Kail pressed my hand against his chest. I struggled to escape his grasp, but he cut me a bored, irritated look, and I stilled. Through the fabric of his jacket and the somewhat thicker material of whatever was beneath, I felt it. The thread. It was balled, tightly knotted, and pulsing as if it were a heart. But something about it was off. One end was untucked, dangling, frayed. "What—"

"It's not hard." He shoved my hand away as if the touch had disgusted him and smoothed his clothing. "All you have to do is unknot its thread and coax it into something else."

"I thought the threads were predetermined."

"You're the Weaver. We are whatever you want us to be. A lot about us is decided at the loom, but you can change details. Split us in two even."

"Split you in two? But how? Why?"

"One step at a time, huh?" Kail lifted the cage. "Try it. Turn it blue or give it a mohawk. Something small."

"I'm not touching that thing," I said incredulously.

"Don't be ridiculous."

"You just told me it bites." I scowled, and Kail held the cage closer to my face. He wasn't going to give up, and maybe that's what I needed. To be pushed past my comfort zone. Nothing in this realm was okay with me, but I was here to rule. I had a choice to make: become the Lady of Nightmares or become… dead. I took a deep breath and nodded. "Okay, okay. Just—set it down."

Kail smiled, pleased, and did as I told him.

I knelt and stuck a finger inside the cage. The monkey hissed at me. "Can't we try this with something a little less…?" I motioned to the entire nightmare.

"Where's the challenge in that?" Kail winked, and I almost punched him. He shoved the trap door open. The stool slammed to the floor, and the rope creaked again, the shadow of the girl swaying on the wall outside. "I'm going out for a little bit. Stay in the museum while I'm gone."

My mouth dropped. "You can't leave me here."

"If you want to leave, change it." His expression was more serious than I'd ever seen it. "Learn to control your magic. Until then, you're a liability."

He grabbed the edge of the platform and hauled himself deftly out of our hiding place. "Actually, you know what?" His masked face popped back over the opening. "On second thought, you're right. Maybe this isn't the best nightmare to start on. Hand me the cage."

My heart sang in relief, but somewhere in the back of my mind, a warning bell rang. I pulled the cage protectively toward me. "What's with the sudden change of heart?"

"Just give it to me," he insisted.

I glared at him, but he gave nothing away. No twitch of his lips, no devious gleam in his eyes. His forte, of course, but it was unnerving all the same. The monkey clawed at my fingertips where I held the cage, drawing blood. "Here." I threw the cage up at his face. "Bring something a little less pointy back."

Kail caught the cage and set it next to him. "Actually, that sounds like an awful lot of work." His voice took on a false edge, his eye sparkling for the briefest moment. "On third thought…"

"Kail," I warned slowly. "Whatever you're thinking, don't."

"I'm just giving you a little more incentive."

My eyes widened, my pulse speeding up. "What does that mean?"

He maintained eye contact as he slid the cage to the ledge. And opened it. The monkey fell straight down, landing at my feet with a high-pitched shriek. The door slammed shut overhead.

"Kail, you asshole!" I screamed, dancing away from the nightmare. "Get back here!"

His laugh rumbled overhead, his footsteps receding. The monkey launched itself from wall to ceiling to floor and back up again like a furry bouncy ball. I jumped up to shove open the hatch but couldn't quite reach. Covering my head, I darted over to the chest and kicked it to the center of the room. The monkey whizzed past and grabbed a handful of my hair. It swung around my head, strands wrapping around my mouth. I gave a muffled scream and smacked at the creature until it let go. I leapt onto the chest, heaved the door open, and bolted.

Unfortunately, so did the nightmare.

I shrieked and hurdled off the platform, the mob of wax figures tumbling around me.

***

There was no telling how long I avoided the ping-ponging nightmare as it followed me from set to set, but the whole debacle ended with us in the foyer, gasping for breath. Bits and pieces of the crystal chandelier were scattered across the floor, and the chandelier itself hung precariously overhead. Each one of the rooms endured different levels of destruction—some more than once after they reset themselves. I was bruised and covered in scrapes from a dozen different props.

And the stupid monkey. It wasn't as funny when it threw waste at me as it was when it peed on Kail. At least it had bad aim, though the mother in front of the fireplace wasn't so lucky. I hadn't gotten close enough to get bitten, but I couldn't complain. Who knew what nasty germs it was carting around? I'd probably end up with some deadly nightmare virus.

"Are you done now?" I rasped and brushed the hair from my sweaty face.

The monkey scowled at me from its place on the overturned banquet table.

"Look, let's just get this over with." I used my softest voice and leaned up onto my knees, but it still stiffened, ready to run. *Not again.* I threw myself forward. It tried to dodge, but its movements were slowed by fatigue, and I caught it by the scruff of its neck. "Just hold still," I urged.

It narrowed its eyes at me and tried to squirm away. After a minute, it sagged, defeated. I hesitated. What should I change? It really did seem fine as it was, but I had to do something. Without a handle on the door, there was no way out unless Kail opened it.

The door.

Kail wanted me to change a nightmare to leave? Fine. I grinned at the monkey. "Want to get out of here?" It perked up, and I set it carefully on the floor. When it didn't try to bolt, I released my hold. "Be good."

I set my palm against the door and closed my eyes, feeling, searching, prodding. The ball of thread writhed at the intrusion, but I held firm. There was no visible end like with Kail's. I didn't know how to pinpoint the door inside the massive knot that made up not only the entire building, but everything inside. I poked at it with my mind, pushed at it, but nothing happened. I clenched my jaw. This was stupid. There was no changing it.

But the grin surfaced, burning bright behind my eyes. One side lifted, smug, and the scent of sulfur hit my nose.

The monkey chirped behind me, and my eyes flew open. Pride swelled at the sight of a round knob in the middle of the door. "I did it," I said breathlessly. "I did it!"

But how? I stared down at my hand in wonder. It just seemed to happen. I didn't really *do* anything. To be honest, it didn't feel like I did anything with the dog either. The grin showed up and ta-da. Maybe that was all it took? To embrace the darkness and let it know what I wanted? That seemed like a slippery slope.

I gripped the warm metal knob and turned it. Gears clicked and whirred inside until the door popped outward. "Out you go," I said to the monkey. It bolted away without another word. I watched it go, scurrying across the lawn, and took a deep, satisfied breath.

Kail appeared, walking between flashing neon signs, slow-clapping, until he stood in front of me. "I was beginning to wonder if you'd ever figure it out or if you were going to chase that thing around all night. Love what you've done with the place, by the way," he added, pointedly looking around me to the knob.

Don't kill him. Don't kill him. "Screw you," I seethed.

He patted my head, and the walls behind me cracked. "Time

to leave."

The foundation shook, and I braced myself in the doorframe. "What's happening?"

"Changing a nightmare isn't exactly a painless process," Kail said, eying the new knob. "It's probably a little pissed."

"What is? The building?"

"Building or not, it's still a nightmare. You had to feel that it was alive while you were messing around in there."

Dust burst from the ceiling, coating me, and I darted outside just as rubble fell into the doorway, sealing the exit.

"So dramatic." Kail straightened his jacket. "Let's go."

"Go where?" I asked, my mouth dry, heart racing. Was that supposed to happen? "Do you have another hidey-hole for us to crawl into?"

"Task number three awaits."

"What?" I shrieked. After hours inside with a deranged nightmare, he wanted me to do something else?

Kail smiled sarcastically and sauntered up to the chain link fence. The realization of what he did settled over me. That bastard set me up! If I got myself out, cool, but if I didn't… How long would he have left me in there? I stomped across the lawn after him.

Do.

Not.

Kill.

Him.

"What's task number three?" I asked skeptically.

"Don't worry. It's nothing you haven't faced before." He pried the fence away from a pole. "After you."

I stood beside Kail at the edge of a garden full of rotten vegetables, a single step away from cracked, parched ground. My heart fluttered wildly in my chest. At its center stood the rock the firefly had left me at when I first returned to save the Sandman, back before I was the Weaver. Not that he needed it, or that the human-me could've done much. But I remembered all too well what it felt like to be similar to that rock: utterly and completely alone. What it felt like to have my friends and family turn their backs on me. To have the Sandman walk away. Every step I took across the Barren killed me a little more inside.

"You have to face your fear to overcome it," Kail explained when I remained silent and still. He waved his hands in front of us. "Behold! The thing that ensnared you last time."

I didn't want to think about how many things frightened me

during my first solo trip to the Nightmare Realm, but this was by far the worst of them. "You're insane if you think I'm going out there," I said, my voice unsteady.

"Your fear is holding you back."

I crossed my arms. "I'm not doing it."

He huffed. "Have I steered you wrong yet?"

"You trapped me in a museum with an angry, poop-flinging mammal," I countered. "That's about as wrong as you can get."

"He flung poop at you?" he asked, too hopeful.

I glared at him. "Be glad he missed."

Kail's laugh was the first genuine one I'd heard. It was warmer than I expected, and even though it was at my expense, I was glad for it. It meant he wasn't cold through-and-through. The relief only lasted until he opened his mouth again.

"Go out there, survive, and meet me back here for a surprise," he said, clapping me roughly on the back.

"Everything you do is a surprise, Kail, and it's never a good one."

"You can't say I don't excel at my job." He watched me playfully. "You'll like this one, I swear."

"Bull."

He held up two fingers and put on a fake smile. "Scout's honor."

"It's three fingers," I said in a flat voice.

He put his ring finger up to join the other two. "Better?"

"I'm not doing it." I turned to walk away, but he was in front of me in the blink of an eye. "I'm *not*—"

He lifted me over his shoulder and stepped into the Barren. The shock of his actions didn't wear off until we were about two feet into the soul-sucking landscape. I shoved away from him and twisted until he finally dropped me on my feet. The effects of the landscape were immediate, sucking away the little joy I had left. The loneliness, the worthlessness… I launched myself at Kail with a roar. Unfortunately, my movements were sluggish here, weighed down by desolation—by my fear of it—and he sidestepped me easily. Soon, I would be a useless heap. Crushed by the solitude of this landscape. Just as I was when Kail and Rowan dragged me out of the Barren so they could use me to kill the Weaver.

"See you on the other side," Kail said with a wave.

Then he turned and walked away. The sight of his retreating back twisted my stomach.

"You can't leave me here!" I screamed, but he had another opinion on that, so I made to follow him. Only, my feet felt frozen to the ground. The hollowness of the Barren inched up my body, and I struggled to shove down the rising panic. Last time I was here, I gave up. If Rowan and Kail hadn't saved me, I would've languished forever. But things were different now. Kail would've preferred me dead last time. *Maybe not so different, then. Could* I die though? The Barren would make for a horrible replacement as Weaver which alone should give him pause.

Ha! Who was I kidding? Kail would let me die without a second thought. He hated me.

No. I shook my head. This wasn't right. Kail was helping me. This place just wanted me to think he wasn't.

Maybe he really *wasn't.* I needed to know what his ulterior motives were. My nails dug into my palms. *Keep it together.* I owned the Barren; the Barren didn't own me. Besides, I was only a few feet into… I spun, searching for something other than the desolate landscape. Nothing. Just the Barren in every direction.

Even the mountain I saw the last time was missing. But how? I was barely five steps into this place.

"Kail," I screamed. But he couldn't hear me—or he didn't care. I didn't even know where he was at this point. With a steadying breath, I swallowed my rage. The emptiness surfaced in its place. *Nope.* Anger was better. I let it bubble back to the surface. New plan: Escape. Beat Kail. The grin twitched, amused.

"Okay," I whispered to myself. "I am the Weaver. I am the Lady of Nightmares." I inhaled and exhaled slowly through my mouth. "Got that, Barren? You don't sca—"

A harsh metallic clang sounded right behind me. I spun on my heel, and my heart exploded. Before me stood a woman in a suit of silver armor molded tightly to her body. Intricate chain mail covered both arms, and a heavy leather hood reached up from beneath her collar to hide her hair. The most haunting feature was easily the flat metal mask covering her entire face. Other than the narrow slits that served as eye holes, the only marking was the Roman numeral three stretching from forehead to chin.

I struggled to move my feet, to keep myself from letting the Barren swallow me. *Escape.* I had to run. *Run.*

But before I could act, a fist full of metal plates slammed into my nose. Stars exploded behind my eyelids. Hot blood and tears flowed down my face before I even hit the ground. I gasped for breath only to choke. I forced my eyes open, the lids already swelling, to find the nightmare crouched over me. She reared back for another blow. My mind reeled at the thought of the pain those plates could inflict a second time, and my training took over.

My body moved without having to think. I scrambled back,

flipped to my stomach, climbed to my feet, and ran in one seamless move. The Barren made it feel as if I were carrying a small elephant on my back, but I couldn't just lay there, getting pummeled, let alone by a nightmare. A thing I was supposed to control. I scanned the horizon until I found the rock again. The clink of metal told me the nightmare was right on my heels. Then my head snapped back, my feet flying out in front of me, and a scream escaped my throat. The armored nightmare twisted my hair so hard I was sure I would be bald afterward.

She leaned in until the cool metal of her cheek brushed against mine. "You let Mare back in," she whispered in a light voice that somehow also vowed to end me on the spot. Then she slammed me face-first into the dry ground.

The world spun around me. Dizziness erased all coherent thought. There was another blast of pain as my head slammed into the ground again. The grin surfaced, its teeth bared in pure rage, and darkness burst outward, forcing my hands down to splay on the dirt. The knotted thread of the Barren echoed the feeling of despair through my bones.

Sulfur broke through the mind-numbing pain, and my stomach heaved. The pressure on the back of my head disappeared, and the grin gnashed its teeth. *Get up*, it seemed to say. I listened, trusting the darkness, and dragged my feet up from under me. My head swam. My vision was spotty, and my brain tried desperately to shut off, but I had to get to safety. To the Sandman.

No. Not the Sandman. I couldn't run back to his promised safety without at least trying to find it on my own. If it was the Sandman or die, I would turn to him. Otherwise, I needed to turn to myself.

I stumbled to the side and searched for my attacker before she could strike again. Instead, I found a wide circle of saturated dirt. The nightmare was waist deep in the center of it, clawing her way to the edge, but the more she moved, the more it tugged her down. She said something, but I didn't hear the words. Didn't care to hear them, either. All I knew was that, at the edge of the Barren, I could collapse. I left her there with mud inching up her breastplate.

The weight of the landscape rolled off me like rain on a window. I smiled at that. Maybe. My mouth was too numb to be sure. But I did know I conquered this place. At least, in a way. There were worse things out there than being alone. I was alone just now and look at what I accomplished. My magic worked perfectly under duress, though all I wanted was some pain medication, an ice pack, and sleep. Lots of sleep. Unless the magic could do that, I would pat my own back later.

***

It felt like a lifetime before I stepped back into the spoiled vegetable garden where Kail said he would wait. My eyes were practically swollen shut, and I saw everything through a curtain of eyelashes. There was every chance this wasn't the right place, though the air had the same tang of decay. I fell to my knees, not caring if Kail was nearby, and carefully lowered my aching body into a fetal position. Soggy cabbage was like a pillow beneath my head. *Soft.* I nuzzled into it, letting it cradle me. A quick catnap, then I would find help.

"Nora?" Kail called. It was far off, I thought, but perhaps not. Reality was fading in and out. Heavy footfalls echoed in my ears. "Nora!"

Kail's hands were on me, lifting me up. I groaned, wanting nothing more than to lie back down.

"What happened?" he barked when I ignored him. If I ignored him. Was he talking a second ago? He gave me a quick shake, and my brain rattled against my skull. "Hey," Kail coaxed again.

Fine. Answer him, *then* nap.

"I—" I coughed blood all over his mask. "Hate you."

"*What happened?*" he asked again, his voice raw.

"I conquered the Barren." I leaned into his grip, letting it hold me up since it was obvious he wasn't going to let me go. Maybe I could sleep like this—

"Nora?" Kail gently tapped my cheek. "Hey, stay awake."

"But I'm tired," I whined.

"You probably have a concussion, among other things. Don't fall asleep."

"I'm the Lady of Nightmares," I said, the words slurred. "Immortal. Strong."

"Yes, yes," he said as if he were talking to a child, and he lifted me into his arms. "Stay with me, Oh Powerful One."

My head nestled perfectly into the crook of his neck. Today he smelled like pumpkin spice, and I wondered, abstractly, if my family had celebrated Thanksgiving without me. "Your surprise better be worth it," I mumbled.

"Stay awake, and I'll tell you all about it."

My eyes slid shut, and I forced them open as much as I could. "Wouldn't that ruin the surprise part?"

"You slipping into a temporary coma would ruin it too." His hands tightened around me. "I found them. The nightmares that killed your friends."

My breath caught. "What?"

"Rowan promised to take care of the culprits if you killed the Weaver, didn't she?" He sounded defensive. Annoyed. "I figured if she wasn't going to keep her word, it fell to me to get it done."

I shifted in his arms and wheezed. "Why?"

"Think of it as my apology for not stopping Rowan."

Apology. Ha! As if he was capable of such a thing. I couldn't deny the appeal of his gift though. Natalie with her eyes in her hands and Emery with her arms sliced to ribbons. Coils of black swirled through the fog surrounding my mind, clearing it away. My friends would be avenged as brutally as they were killed. Blood would flow, black or red. Mindless or intelligent. Their lives were mine, and I would take them with the entire force of the Nightmare Realm behind me.

This time, when the darkness grinned, I grinned back.

***

The pounding in my head broke through the blissful silence. My eyes cracked, the lids heavy and swollen, but my vision was no longer obstructed. I sucked in a crackling breath. Everything hurt. Places that I didn't even know existed. But at least I was alive. And awake. I wasn't sure how long I'd been out—just that, at some point on the way here, I gave into exhaustion—wherever *here* was. I was grateful for the cushioned surface beneath me. There were lumps, sure, but it was a thousand times better than the ground.

"Nora?" It was a hesitant whisper, jarring, considering the source.

I blinked my eyes open and stared up at Kail's masked face as he leaned over me. "Ow," I moaned and batted at the tip of his beak.

He let out a breath that was half-laugh, half-relief. "It took you long enough. I was beginning to think I'd have to kill those nightmares myself."

Ah, yes. The nightmares that killed Natalie and Emery. Everything flooded back to me—the Barren, the armored woman, the magic rushing to save me. "How long have I been asleep?"

"A day and a half." Kail sat on a chair beside the bed and brushed the hair from his forehead. A wet cloth hung off the side of a basin with small bits of green leaves scattered on the tabletop. "How do you feel?"

Better than I should. I eased into a sitting position. "Where are we?"

"Here." Kail held out a wooden cup of water with more tiny leaves floating on top. "This will help with the pain."

I scowled. Rowan had tried to give me something to ease the pain of her touch, and I was glad I refused it. "I'm fine."

He glowered. "Don't be stubborn."

"Why am I always getting head injuries around you anyway?" I snapped.

"Maybe because you pick fights you can't win?" He shoved the cup into my hand and wrapped my fingers around it. "Now drink this. You'll heal quickly thanks to your magic, but this will take the edge off."

"Fine," I said, because I needed relief. Any relief. If Kail wanted to hurt me, he would've done it while I laid there unconscious. "But I need something to write on."

"If I leave, you'll dump it out," he accused.

I downed the entire thing in three gulps. It tasted like grass with a bitter kick, and when it was gone, I threw the cup at him and wiped my mouth on the back of my hand. "Paper. Now."

He batted the cup away before it hit him. It clattered against the concrete. "I doubt there's any here."

I scanned the small, dank room. No, not a room—a cell. Three walls were covered with names and tally marks, the fourth with thick black bars. Thankfully, the door was wide open. "Are we in a prison?" I asked.

"See? Not all my safe houses have trap doors."

I glowered at him.

"I needed somewhere to keep your presents," Kail said with a shrug. "It's as good a place as any."

"I'm sure there are a million other places to lock things up around here." I sighed. It didn't matter—he was right. It was probably one of the better options. "I need something to write on, Kail."

He reached under my pillow, searching.

"What are you—"

"When in Rome." He winked and produced a crude shank. Someone had wrapped half a roll of duct tape around the handle of a warped spoon, filed to a point. "I think there's some free wall space by your head."

I groaned and snatched the sharp object from him. It didn't have to be a fancy image, it just had to get my point across. The more I concentrated on the scraping of metal on concrete, the more my head throbbed, but the shape of the armored woman's face gradually took shape on the wall. Not my best work, but it would do. "What is that?"

Kail stared at it a moment before speaking. "It's Three."

"Three?"

"One of the Hours."

"The Hours? You mean the nightmares that destroyed the Blood Tower?" I asked. Kail nodded, and I swallowed hard, shifting to tuck the shank into my back pocket. "She attacked me in the Barren. Something about my letting Mara back in."

"Ah." Kail stretched his back. "Well, yes. That's bound to be an unpopular move."

"It was an accident. I didn't know she hitched a ride."

"Your intentions won't matter when she decimates the entire realm for the fun of it."

My stomach twisted. The Sandman warned me—unlike with the Weaver, I *had* listened. My mistake was letting Mara think there was a chance. Or maybe it didn't matter either way. She had made up her mind that she was coming, and there had been no changing it. Lying to her had seemed like my only way to return to the Nightmare Realm without the Sandman. I chewed my bottom lip to keep it from quivering. I was such an idiot.

"Don't worry, Lady," Kail said, interrupting my self-pity party. "I'm sure the Sandman will come up with a plan. If he's good at anything, it's that—unless you get in his way yet again." It was a slap in the face yet said without accusation.

"I don't want to rely on the Sandman to fix my mistake," I said quietly and flicked my gaze up to meet his.

His good eye changed slowly, switching between colors almost lazily. "We have to concentrate on Rowan. No one wins when they're fighting a war on two fronts."

"You're right." I slid off the lumpy cot and took a shaky breath. Moving seemed to push the ache from my muscles, so I bent my joints a few times. "How do I look?"

Kail stood with a smirk. "Two black eyes have never looked so good."

I made a *tsk*ing sound with my tongue. Black eyes were a vast improvement from what I was sure I looked when I stumbled out of the Barren. "Show me these nightmares."

"Now?" His eyes widened.

"Do we have anything better to do?"

"That's a loaded question, Lady. We obviously do," he answered cynically.

I rolled my eyes. "Your ex-girlfriend can wait another day. Let's go."

Kail shrugged and led the way down a hallway full of identical cells, down two flights of stairs, and around a corner. He paused, his hand on a door that said *solitary confinement.* "She's not, you know. For the record."

I bounced on the balls of my feet. The nightmares were close—I knew it. "What?"

His jaw twitched. "Rowan. She's not an ex. Or a girlfriend."

"Oh." That wasn't what I expected. I wondered why he cared what I thought on the matter. I hadn't even meant it when I called her that. "Okay."

"Anyway." He cleared his throat. "I should probably warn you that one of them is pretty strong."

"Don't care," I said and hurried past him into a dimly lit corridor.

Something lunged at the first door on the left, and I peeked curiously through the small window to find a giant wolf-man standing on his haunches. He was covered in coarse, wiry grey hair, his snout pressed in so he looked like a pug with giant fangs.

Long pointed claws extended from his hands. He stared out at me, part fear, part hate, part something else.

"He killed Emery?" I asked Kail without looking away from the growling creature.

"I don't know your friends' names," he said with a stiff shrug.

I scowled. It had to be. Something told me this thing wouldn't have bothered asking his victim to hold their own eyes. More likely, he would've eaten them. So. How to make him pay? Werewolves, wolf-men, whatever: they weren't up my alley. All I knew was that they were rumored to change on a full moon, and a person had to shoot them with a silver bullet to kill them. With the nightmare version, all bets were off.

"Does silver affect him?" I asked Kail.

"I wouldn't know."

"You wouldn't know?" I stared at him. "You caught the thing."

"I *lured* it, if you want to get technical. No silver required."

"Worth a shot, then," I mumbled and put my hand on the wall beside the door. The grin rose up, searching for the bundle of thread that was the prison. It came easily without my resistance, and with a quick flick of my magic, molten silver coated every surface in the room. It dripped from the ceiling, flowed down the walls, swirled across the floor. The wolf-man's howl was immediate. His paws sizzled as he jumped from one to the other. The molten liquid ate away at his fur, his skin, his bones. My heart ached at the gruesome sight, but the grin held my resolve firmly between its teeth. He deserved to die for killing Emery. He slammed against the door again, his wild eyes begging me through the small window to make it stop.

"You shouldn't have touched my friend," I said, almost as if my voice weren't my own.

The wolf-man's cries slowly faded as he thrashed, trying desperately not to touch any silver. But there was no escape. I stood there watching, waiting for the moment he drew his last breath.

And I reveled in it.

When his chest finally ceased rising, when he was little more than a skeleton, I turned to Kail and let out a short breath. "Next."

Kail eyed me warily and pointed to the next cell down. "Permission to rescue you if things go bad?"

I snorted. "Sure."

He slid the bolt open and pulled the door outward with a loud screech. Inside the small, musty room, I eyed a figure strapped to a gurney. A straight jacket and brown sack over its head hid its true form.

"What's this?" I asked calmly, stalking around the table. My power crackled in my veins.

"The most beautiful nightmare in the Night World," Kail said in a careful voice. "So beautiful, in fact, that you'll feel unworthy to look upon her and will—"

"Claw your own eyes out. Got it." I swallowed hard at the memory. "How did you catch this one then?"

He looked at me like it was obvious. "Do I strike you as insecure?"

"Far from it." I took a deep breath and steeled myself. "Let's see, then."

Kail stepped up to the gurney and ripped the sack off the nightmare's head. The room exploded with golden light. It was like staring into the sun, at the purest thing in existence. And when she smiled, I felt no bigger than an ant. A thing to be trampled. Indeed, someone—some*thing*—like me shouldn't look upon her perfection.

"Nora," Kail whispered.

His voice snapped the nightmare's hold on me, and anger blossomed in my chest. *Natalie.* She was pretty and smart. Funny. Loyal. And this… this *thing* made her believe she wasn't. I stared into the nightmare's wide blue eyes and saw no remorse.

"Beautiful." I glanced at Kail over my shoulder with a wicked gleam in my eyes. "We can fix that."

My magic swelled, ready, but killing her that way would be too easy. I took the shank from my back pocket and studied the crude workmanship. *Perfect.* Everything that she was—her golden skin, perfect profile, and glimmering hair—ruined by everything she wasn't. A fitting end.

With the first cut, the nightmare shrieked so hard the gurney shook. It cracked open the box of emotions I'd carried around for months and months. The anger, the hurt, the sorrow, I carved it all into the nightmare's flesh. I took my time doing it. Each new cut flared with golden light that dimmed quickly, leaving behind a blackened wound. I swept my hand over her face, her neck, her collarbones as easily as I would've used a pencil on paper. Her red blood ran thick down the shank. My grip slipped more than once on the taped handle. I felt the blood dripping off my elbows, and I didn't care.

When the nightmare was finally still and the golden glow nonexistent, I dropped the shank to the floor. "I feel better now," I told Kail in a stale voice.

"I'm sure you do," he said in a tone I couldn't quite decipher.

"Look at your arms."

I lifted my bloodied hands and sucked in a sharp breath. Beneath the crimson was my own pale skin. No more black. The Weaver's magic was really, truly mine. Fully absorbed. I flexed my fingers. What was I capable of now? A true smile broke across my face.

Kail smiled back, a strangely genuine expression, and pointed down the hallway. "The showers are that way, Lady Nightmare."

For the first time, there was no condescending tone in the title.

Chapter Eighteen

The Sandman

My spies were dying faster than I could make them. An unfortunate side effect of my magic, but at least seeking out new ones kept me from dwelling on Nora. And Mare—I was still having trouble wrapping my head around that problem. The Weaver had experience under his belt when we banished her, but Nora…

I shook my head and focused on the task at hand. Baku crept along the forest ground beside me. The incline to the top of the cliff appeared nearly nonexistent, but it was all an illusion. My thighs started burning halfway to the peak. Now that we were nearly there, I barely noticed it. There wasn't room to worry about personal comfort when we were approaching nightmares as perceptive as the Watchmen. They had one job, one base desire: defend what they were told to defend.

"Remember," I whispered to Baku. "We aren't here to cause a scene. You can't eat these."

Baku's lip curled in annoyance, but his eyes were resigned.

It was smart of Rowan to pull the Watchmen from their assigned landscape to overlook the Keep. The how was the most concerning thing about it though, unless the Weaver had stationed them there before without my noticing or removed their assignment altogether so they could roam where they pleased. My insides twisted at how much I truly neglected the Weaver during his binding. Too little, too late seemed to be my new motto. I needed to rectify that.

As Baku and I crested the top of the hill, solid forms of six giant stone men dotted the far side of the clearing. Some were the color of granite to blend with the rocky outcroppings, others a mixture of browns and greens to blend with the trees. If they shifted so much as a centimeter, their appearance changed to match the backdrop perfectly. The six of them worked as a team so I only needed to secure one to see what all of them saw. The trick was getting close enough. Luckily, their hearing was nowhere near as good as their eyesight.

Baku and I wove between trees, hiding behind thick trunks and boulders until we reached the edge of a wooded shelter. One of the Watchmen turned toward our hiding place in increments—his head, his torso, then his legs. His marble eyes looked out from beneath a sculpted warrior helmet. I cringed. Their hearing wasn't exceptional, but that didn't mean they couldn't hear at all.

I eased a handful of sand from my satchel and dropped it to the ground, directing its path toward the nightmare. It would take twice as much, maybe more, to inhabit something this size, but it could give us valuable information. No, not us. *Me.* It would give *me* information that I would have to get to Nora without her knowing how I came by it. The sand snaked through the sparse tufts of grass and eased into the cracks of rocks, staying as hidden as possible.

The Watchman began to turn back to the cliff but paused. With lightning-fast speed, he slammed the spear in his right hand against the shield in his left. The boom echoed down the hill. Baku bristled, and I pressed myself against the closest tree. One by one, the other five Watchmen twisted toward the forest. Then, in perfect unison, they aimed their spears straight ahead.

"Run," I told Baku.

A spear sliced through the tree right above my head. I ducked and rolled to the side as another soared straight toward my chest. The forest groaned around us as we fled down the mountain. Another spear hit the ground directly in front of me, and I flung myself sideways to avoid running into the swaying stone handle. The fourth ripped through my sleeve before tearing apart a tree to my left. It crashed down, taking me with it, and pinned my leg to the ground. My shin bone shattered under the weight. I swallowed the pained cry that rose in my throat and took a series of shallow breaths.

The Watchmen followed the path of their weapons and reduced the forest to splinters beneath their feet. Each of their steps was worth two dozen of my own. My magic tugged at me, asking to go home, but I couldn't leave Baku. The Watchmen wouldn't kill me; capture me, maybe, and give me to Rowan, but she could never keep me. Baku was another story.

I pried my leg out from beneath the rough bark with a

strained scream. *Run.* I only had to make it out of range of the spears—there would be no prying myself out from one of those. But my leg threatened to crumble beneath me. Baku still hadn't made it far enough to lose them, so I called on the rest of the sand in my satchel. It swept him up and carried him as far as it could before my concentration broke. I nearly vomited as I fell to the ground.

"Over here," I shouted to buy Baku more time.

Using the trees to prop myself up, I hobbled back up the cliff-side. The thunderous footfalls of the Watchmen slowed. I let out a wordless cry to draw their attention, then found it ringing true as I slipped on a mildew-covered rock. Rocks and roots battered my body as gravity pulled me down a slick, muddy trail. When a fallen trunk finally brought me to a halt, I laid there for a long moment, groaning. Bone protruded from my lower leg. I sat up carefully, cringing, and tugged the small bag of emergency sand from beneath my tunic. There was just enough to heal my leg, or at least lessen the pain until I got home.

A twig snapped behind me. Before I could even turn my head, someone latched onto my arm where the spear had ripped the fabric. Red silk flashed in my peripheral vision.

Rowan.

Her name was all I had time to think before the pain of her touch filled me. It cut and burned and suffocated. My magic clawed at the beach in a desperate bid for escape. With a final clear thought, I yanked it back. If I wanted to know what Rowan was doing, where better to be than the Keep? For the Night World, for Nora, the pain would be worth it.

I drew a deep breath and let the agony in.

When my vision cleared again, Rowan had my arms tied around a post at my back. The coarse rope grated against my skin, and the pain of my broken shin lit up my mind like a firecracker. But I stayed still. If I lost consciousness, my magic would drag me back to the beach. Rowan knew that too—it was an open secret in the Nightmare Realm—so she would be careful until she got what she wanted. Whatever that was. Now I simply needed to find something useful to make the upcoming pain worthwhile.

Pieces of straw littered the floor, and I took in the otherwise empty space with growing disappointment. I was going to have to escape from this room and sneak through the tower to learn anything meaningful.

"Hello, Sandman," Rowan said from behind me, her breath hot on my ear. She smelled of licorice and blood. "I know you can hear me. Let's have some fun."

I lifted my head, a gargantuan task, and met her red-flecked eyes as she circled to stand before me. "I think we have different definitions of fun."

"Of course we do." She raised a knife to my chin. "I know what will happen if you pass out, but there are ways around that."

The knife left my chin and nicked my neck. It didn't cut deep enough to hurt, but that wasn't her goal. She plucked the now-broken string holding my bag of sand away from my neck. Her fingers skimmed my skin in the process, sending sparks of pain straight down into my marrow. I ground my teeth to keep quiet, instead directing my anger into my gaze as it followed the pouch. It didn't matter if the sand was in her hands or mine—as long as it was in the same vicinity, I could call on it. But she didn't know that.

"There." Rowan's bright red lips lifted, and she tossed the pouch into the far corner of the room.

Then I saw it.

As Rowan turned to make the throw, everything clicked.

Harsh lines marred the base of her skeletal wings, black and crackled, as if she had been burnt in a fire. I drew in a small breath. Kail had shown me how to defeat her. All this time, the information was right in front of me, but I hadn't given it half a thought because of who it came from. Could he really want Nora to succeed? It was hard to realize everything could end without a single battle.

"Now…" Rowan ripped open the front of my shirt with the knife and cocked her head at the sight of my tattoo. "That's it? The source of your power? I thought it would be… bigger."

My jaw clenched. I had what I came for, so when the edges of my vision began to fade, I let myself succumb.

A quick burning shock lanced my chest before I could fade out. I gasped, the room coming back into sharp focus. Rowan stood in front of me, licking my blood from the tip of the blade. I looked down with sickening dread. She had sliced just above the moon tattooed there. An inch lower and it would've taken months to heal. This would only take two days, maybe three. But I couldn't let her see the relief on my face, so I hung my head as if I were defeated.

"Get comfortable, Sandman," she crooned, content. "We'll be spending a lot of time together."

The distinctive clip of approaching high-heeled shoes filled the stairwell behind Rowan, and she rolled her eyes. "What is it this time?"

A short woman covered in scales practically bounced into the room. Two tiny horns protruded from her green hair, and her dress was made from dripping seaweed. "There's trouble in the courtyard, your queenship," she chirped.

Queenship?

"It can wait," Rowan snapped.

"Unfortunately not," the woman said. "The Devourer has eaten through half your guard already."

Red flared up beneath Rowan's pale skin. "Your *friend* has come to save you?" she hissed, whirling on me.

"He's probably just hungry," I said with as much defiance as I could muster. *Baku, what are you doing?*

"Let's hope your Dream Keeper is a bit more loyal then." She threw the knife to the ground and stormed up the stairs, the scaled woman following close on her heels.

What did that mean? More loyal than who? I strained against the ropes. Whatever Rowan had heard about my tattoo, it didn't need to be intact for the sand to call me home. It only hindered my ability to wield it—a rather large problem at the moment, but it could've been worse. By the time Rowan returned, I would already be cocooned by sand.

Then I would find Nora.

And she would kill Rowan without ever setting eyes on her.

Chapter Nineteen

When Kail returned to the prison mid-afternoon with two horses in tow, I almost locked myself in the nearest cell. They were the same black creatures with clawed feet that carried me from the Barren the first time. Unsurprisingly, he wasn't riding the one that once tried to bite me. My new-found pride wouldn't allow me to be a chicken, so I swung into the saddle made of smooth bone and took the reins. My feet swung at the horse's sides, my legs too short to reach the stirrups attached to the seat by a ball and socket joint. I considered altering it for a second, but the memory of the crumbling museum was too fresh to try.

I glanced back at the brick prison hidden beneath climbing ivy. Concealed among the foliage were faces that screamed obscenities, but beyond that, inside, were the remains of two slain nightmares. Now that the adrenaline had worn off, I wanted to feel guilty.

But I didn't.

I was glad. Satiated.

"Lady?"

"Hm?" I forced myself to turn from the prison and my thoughts. Kail simply motioned me forward. "Bite me, and I'll turn you into dog food," I told the horse before nudging him with my heel. He didn't show the slightest hint of defiance this time, but I kept an eye on the back of his head anyway. From my peripheral vision, I watched Kail. "Where are we going? And don't give me a vague answer."

He smirked as if I stopped him just in time from doing exactly that. "The Blood Tower."

"What?" I asked in disbelief. "You *do* remember it was on fire the last time we were there, right? Is there even a tower left to go to?"

He shrugged. "I wouldn't know, but luckily, Halven and I have you."

"Halven?" I hadn't seen him since he left me with Kail that first day. While I now realized that earned him points in my book, I wouldn't say he *had me*. Nor Kail for that matter. There was still his ulterior motive hanging over our friendship. I cringed at the term. Was Kail my friend? Or a reluctant mentor? "What does he have to do with anything?"

"A lot." Kail hesitated. "He's my brother, you know."

I whipped my head sideways to look at him. His brother? They did have similar traits. The masks, the weirdly elaborate clothes. Halven was much more dramatic in appearance, but Kail made up for it with his sparkling personality. I snorted. "I didn't realize nightmares had siblings. Is it one of those solidarity things between all nightmares or is he your *brother*-brother?"

Kail was silent for a moment, and his hand absently moved to the center of his chest. He seemed to realize it and quickly grabbed the reigns. "He's my brother," he said stiffly.

Oh. That clears things up. I leveled a stare at him. "So you both came from one cord or you were next to each other or—"

"It's not important," he snapped. Then he took a shallow breath and, when he spoke again, sounded much calmer. "I'll teach you that later. First we have to get your loom."

Interesting. I filed his reaction away. "I suppose you know how to weave?" I asked as if he hadn't lost his temper for a hot second.

"No, but you will."

"I hate to break it to you, but I don't even know how to knit a scarf."

Kail sighed. "You didn't know how to bring giant dogs to life or create doorknobs out of nothing before either, but you did it. Listen to the magic, not your doubts."

Was that… I scowled at him. Was he offering moral support? Did we cross into another dimension without my realizing it?

"You'll thank me for everything one day," he said confidently after a moment.

And there he was.

If he was truly loyal—and that was a big if—letting him live would be enough reward.

The threads shifted gently along my arm, and I startled. I had first noticed it during my time in solitary confinement: almost a caress where before they kept a vice-like grip. I couldn't be positive, but it was almost as if they sensed my acceptance. That I now embraced the grin living inside me. That I wanted to be here. To harness their power. They could now relax without fear that I would rip them away as I might have before. No longer were they a parasite. Our relationship was too symbiotic for that. I watched the frayed end thump against the pulse point on my wrist, then suddenly something tickled the skin beneath my sleeve. The threads, now coiled loosely, slithered across my chest and circled my neck. My heart jumped into a frantic rhythm.

"Kail," I called, my voice wavering. Before he could answer, the other end of the thread settled peacefully in the hollow of my throat. When I looked over to him, he smiled wickedly. "What's it doing?"

"It just wanted more room." He eyed the newly visible end as it beat to my pulse like the one on my wrist. "The Weaver used to work them into his clothes to avoid the whole necklace look, but it suits you."

"Was that a compliment?" I joked to hide my unease.

He leveled his gaze at me. "We should use this time for another lesson."

I groaned.

"Pay attention to your surroundings," he continued. "Feel where we are and use it to guide you. The Nightmare Realm is large and has a tendency to confuse even the oldest of nightmares, but the Weaver could navigate it with his eyes closed."

"Does that include you?" I asked, searching my mind for anything that resembled a compass.

He paused. "It never used to, but things change."

"What kind of things?"

"If you're talking, you're not paying attention," he said with a clip to his voice, and he spurred his horse ahead of mine.

The faster I learned, the faster I could be done with his lessons. Then, once I had what was mine, I could see the Sandman again. My chest ached at the thought of him. Days passed since I'd seen him. What was he doing? Was he okay? I hated myself for sending him away, but he didn't want to let me learn. To let me face the dangers. He wanted to fix them for me. That didn't stop me from recalling the way his kisses felt or the way his fingers fit perfectly between mine.

Focus, I reminded myself. There was more than one reason I needed to do this alone. Distraction was one of them. The grin appeared, sarcastic yet ready to help. There was no swirling darkness leaking out this time, but a knowingness filled me. It was almost as if the grin had sprouted limbs as my hands directed the horse to the right.

"This way," I shouted to Kail.

***

The Blood Tower wasn't nearly as bad as I expected. Fire had scorched the outer walls, but they were still mostly intact, save for the bits of rubble cause by the impact of the fireballs. The front door lay bent on the ground outside, the hinges ripped from the frame. "This was broken from inside," I said, stepping carefully over the dug-up gravel. "Maybe that means the dog escaped."

"Maybe," Kail agreed. But he wasn't looking at the tower. His gaze swept over the area surrounding us, eyes narrow. "Halven should be here by now."

"If he's anything like you, he's probably waiting to make a dramatic entrance." I leaned through the doorway, blinking until my eyes adjusted to the dark interior. The stench of smoke permeated the air, and the walls inside were singed black. Dead tarantulas littered the floor like a carpet. No new ones had sprouted in their place. *Good riddance.*

"We shouldn't stay long," Kail said, suddenly at my side. "I'll do a quick sweep to make sure none of Rowan's minions are inside while you fix it. If Halven hasn't shown up by then, we get what we need and get out of here."

Before I could disagree, he disappeared inside. The spiders crunched under foot, and I placed my hand on the tower to see if I could feel how much damage was done. The blackened stone was still warm. I closed my eyes and searched for the ball of thread. And searched and searched. But it was nowhere to be found.

"All clear," Kail said between quick breaths. I opened my eyes and looked at him with wide eyes. "What?"

"There's no thread," I said softly.

"Look harder." He moved around me and searched the surrounding area for his brother again. "If the thread died, the tower would disappear."

Look harder, I mimicked behind his back, then turned my attention to the tower again. *A little help?* I asked the grin. It surfaced slowly, almost reluctantly. *Lazy,* it seemed to accuse, but I felt it reach into the ruins of the Blood Tower. The withered, throbbing pain echoed through me, and I gasped. The thread *was* there. Huddled. Bound tightly into a tiny ball. I stroked the aching threads soothingly as if it were a wounded bird. The ball shivered and loosened before reaching out to greet me.

The rest happened in a single breath. One inhale that seemed to burn my lungs to ash. The scent of sulfur exploded around me, and I tried to wrench my hand away from the suddenly scalding stone wall. I think a cry escaped from my throat, but it seemed as if I were only a passenger in my own body. Sounds dulled. Vision tunneled. The ground beneath me felt like shifting tiles.

And then it was over.

The stone was cold, the grin gone. I stumbled backward into Kail, tears streaming silently down my face.

"Well done," he said, impressed.

Exhaustion washed over me as I blinked up at the tower. Blood flowed between the stones again with such force that droplets sprayed outward. The old door still sat on the gravel while a large, elaborate black steel door stood in its place. Red metal studs formed a swirling design.

"My Lady," said a painfully hoarse voice.

I turned to find Halven bowing before me. "You're late," I said without an ounce of annoyance. I was too tired for that.

"Forgive me. I underestimated how much slower traveling could be with an army."

"A—what?" I looked between the brothers. "What's he talking about?"

"You told him you needed one," Kail said, irritated. "And Halven lives to serve. Where did you think he was this whole time?"

Scaring Dreamers. Lurking in dark corners. Off doing whatever it was nightmares did in their free time. "Why didn't you tell me?"

"You had to concentrate on your training," Kail said. "An

army is only as strong as its leader."

With a large enough army, I could crush the entire rebellion without using up all my current thread. My chest burst with hope. "Where is it?" I asked Halven.

Halven pointed around the tower where the Blood Army once congregated. I raced forward, all trace of exhaustion gone, and froze at what waited there. Hundreds, maybe thousands, of nightmares sprawled on the ground. They were still alive—their shifting limbs and labored breaths proving that much—but they couldn't crush a soda can, let alone Rowan.

"What happened to them?" I asked, deflated.

"Tired," Halven groaned. "We walked for days."

"They'll be ready to fight on schedule?" Kail asked.

Halven nodded.

"Good." Kail turned on his heel. "Let's go check your clock."

The brothers walked back around the tower together, but I stood there, staring. An army. *My* army. Guilt twisted my stomach. The Sandman said the Weaver relied too much on his nightmares. Look how *that* turned out. And here I was. Doing the same thing. Because, honestly, what had *I* done? Turned a thread into a giant dog? Altered a few buildings? Tortured nightmares? I wanted to be better than the Weaver, but I was following in his footsteps. When I became *this*, I told the Sandman we could create a united Night World, but now… Now I saw the power in what I had. Saw the potential in what I didn't. All these nightmares spread out before me, ready to fight for me, because they believed I would do what was best for them. Or maybe because they were mindlessly loyal. Either way, I understood the Weaver a little more now. His connection to the nightmares warred with his longing for the Sandman's friendship. He told me he wanted things to go back to the way they were before, and so did I. More than anything. The grin surfaced, a contemplative thing. I sucked in a deep breath and hurried after Kail.

"That shouldn't be a problem yet," Kail said, and I followed his voice to the room where he had given me the knife. "Where's Rowan?"

The large hand on the clock moved with a series of soft clicks.

"As expected," he murmured.

"What is?" I asked, and the brothers both startled.

"Rowan's still at the Keep." Kail pointed to a symbol on the clock that looked like an upside-down triangle on a stick.

I stepped closer to the mantel. A dozen gold symbols were emblazoned around the black clock face. "How do you know?" I asked curiously. Surely there was some rhyme or reason to it, but it all seemed like hieroglyphics to me. Were there only twelve nightmares he could find? Who were they?

"Halven asks the clock. Each of the symbols is a location."

I crossed my arms. "Even I know there are more places than that."

"These were the original landscapes. It narrows things down by telling Halven the nearest landscape, then he focuses his energy in that direction to pinpoint the person specifically. It's faster this way."

"You seem to know an awful lot about it," I said carefully.

Kail shrugged.

I squinted at him. "Back to what you were you saying when I walked in. What won't be a problem yet?"

The brothers exchanged a look—or Kail did, at least. Halven turned his masked face in his brother's direction. "Mara's hiding out in a cave at the moment."

"Ah, yes. Her." I chewed on my bottom lip. "Where's the Sandman?"

Halven stiffened.

"What?" I scoffed. "Do only nightmares show up on there?"

"Dreamers, sometimes," Halven rasped.

"I'm sure the Dream Lord is fine," Kail added. "He's giving you the space you asked for."

I winced. He was right, but I wanted to see him. Almost *needed* to.

"Take heart, Lady," Halven said kindly.

I forced a smile, then glared at Kail. "I like your brother so much better than you. Maybe *he* should train me while you manage the rabble outside."

"*Please.*" Kail snorted. "I'm the best nightmare you could get help from."

"I don't know about that." I glanced at Halven. "He talks a lot less than you *and* is nice when he does."

Kail bristled. "Sorry, Lady. You're stuck with me until my eye is fixed."

"Is that all it takes to get rid of you?" I reached toward his face, and he jerked backward.

"How about you practice changing a few moving targets first?" he said, his pupil blown wide. "My eye is a lot more complicated than a doorknob."

"Arrogant bas—"

"Shall we call it a day?" he asked loudly. "I'm exhausted, and you look like you're about to fall over."

Now that the shock of the army's arrival was beginning to fade, the drained feeling crept back in. But I had done it. Fixed the tower. Returned charred remains to their former glory. I smiled to myself, and the grin matched it, equally satisfied. Wanting to be alone, I nudged it.

But it didn't budge.

In fact, it grew.

Panic clawed at my chest. The door I locked the grin behind had disappeared, and the darkness grew heavy in my veins. *We need each other*, it seemed to say with startling clarity. I took a shaky breath. It wasn't wrong.

Besides, we both knew I was only *trying* not to like it.

"What's next?" I asked.

"Now, Lady, we get some rest." Kail flopped down on the couch and put his hands behind his head. "Tomorrow, you take control of your realm."

Chapter Twenty

The Sandman

Hours could have passed. *Days.* It was hard to tell. All I knew was the white-hot pain in my chest. The sand worked fast once it dragged me home, burying me within seconds, but the wound was still there. Skin grew like new over the cut, but beneath, the trapped sand wrestled with interior repairs. Rowan hadn't cut me that deep, but the amount of blood flaking on my skin made it seem otherwise.

I reached up to shake the sand from my hair and winced. How was I going to be of any help like this? I eased back onto the beach and took long, deep breaths. It felt as if a fever was in my bones, making everything ache. But there were other ways to help Nora while I healed. Smaller ways, like getting her a message, would be enough for the moment. She needed to do this alone, after all.

And she had Kail.

Jealousy sparked along my nerve endings, but I shook it away. Nora loved me. This wasn't about us, and Kail was far from being a threat in that respect. Sure, he got to see her every day, all day—a thing I'd never been able to do myself, but one day, maybe I could. I wouldn't lose hope that we would eventually reunite the realms. Forever was a long time.

But what worried me most was why Kail told me how to kill Rowan instead of telling Nora. It seemed like he wanted Rowan dead, so why go through the effort of putting on a show? There must be a reason. Kail never did anything without one—it was just rare that anyone knew what that reason was.

A little longer, and I would get dressed, track Nora down, and tell her everything. This information was too important to trust to a messenger, even one as trustworthy as Baku. And, perhaps, part of it was my desire to see her. Just to make sure she wasn't doing something ridiculously stupid again. I winced at the flash of heat the thought brought along with it and shoved the anger back into its box. Everything in its time.

"Sandman," a voice called down its cord. A voice I knew well enough from five years inside Nora's dreams. "Help me sleep."

I immediately stood on shaky legs and yanked the cord hard, hurtling myself into the Day World with a pained scream in my throat. My legs buckled as the soft blanket of sand became a braided area rug that did little to soften the blow when my knees hit. I fell forward into a puffy bedspread, buried my face into the soft material, and panted for a moment before composing myself enough to stand.

Katie stared slack-jawed at me from the other side of the

bedroom. "It worked," she said in an incredulous voice. "It—it worked."

"Yes." I caught a glimpse of another form under her sheets and stumbled back a step. "Who—"

"Kellan's a sound sleeper," Katie said in a rush. "Plus, he's high as a kite tonight, so if he sees you, don't worry about it."

Don't worry about it. There were an awful lot of things I wasn't supposed to worry about lately, and, in my opinion, they were all very much of concern. Katie rolled her eyes and rushed up to the bed, shaking Kellan violently.

"Don't do th—" I began to protest.

"See? He's out." She let out a disbelieving huff as she turned back to me. "I can't believe it worked."

"It's nice to see you coming around to the truth," I said carefully. The Dream Realm was already pulling at my center. "I'm sort of in the middle of something, so if this is some kind of test—"

"Oh my God. *Oh my God.* Is that blood?"

I stepped around the bed and gripped her upper arms carefully. The strong scent of alcohol permeated from her. "Katie, listen to me." My magic rippled. In another ten seconds, I would be hurtling back to the beach whether I wanted to or not. "We have to finish this conversation somewhere else."

"Wha—"

As quickly as I could, I pinched a bit of sand that was trapped between my shirt and tunic and threw it in her face. The next second, she slammed to the floor. It wasn't my best moment, but it was the only option I had left, because this time, when the beach called me home, there would be no denying it.

If it was any consolation to Nora's sister, my landing back

on the beach wasn't much better. The sand cradled me, softening the blow, but the impact made every warm, throbbing piece of me flash red-hot. My vision was still blanketed in white when a pair of hesitant hands brushed the hair from my face.

"Hey," Katie half-shouted. Or maybe it just felt like she did. "Are you okay?"

"Sorry about your headache," I mumbled.

The hands disappeared. "My what?"

"You'll understand when you wake up." The sand moved to cover me, but now wasn't the best time for another burial. If Katie was going to accept the truth, for Nora's sake, I couldn't risk scaring her off. "Just give me a second."

"Okay," she whispered so softly I barely heard.

I steeled myself by taking deep breaths and focusing on my center. Whatever strength I could pull from the sand within the next few heartbeats, I did, though it wasn't much. My vision cleared, and I forced myself to sit up, but that was all I would be doing. Katie knelt beside me, her face paler than pale as she stared into my pavilion. I knew what she was looking at.

"Nora gave them to me," I said. When she turned back to me with a wild, confused expression, I added, "The drawings."

"This is it, isn't it?" Katie practically flopped backward, propping herself up on her hands. "This is where she came every night. She tried to tell us…"

"Breathe, Katie," I said gently, and she gulped down air. "The place Nora and I met is just under the brightest star, near the water, but yes. This is the Dream Realm. I wouldn't have brought you here if I had another choice."

Her eyes darted back to my chest. "What happened? Is Nora okay?"

"She's fine. I will be too, but you caught me at a bad time."

"Is she here?" Some of her shock gave way to concern. "I know she won't believe it, but our mother is having a horrible time dealing with everything. We all are. So I mean—I thought, if she wasn't with you, you would know where she went."

And there it was. The question I knew was coming. I ran both hands down my face. How was I supposed to tell her what happened? Did Nora even *want* her to know? If she did, she would've found a way to let Katie know, but maybe now... There was no easy path to take.

"She's not here," I said simply.

"Then where is she? I think she wants us to believe she ran off to New York, considering all the work she put into faking an internship, but maybe it was to throw us off." Katie inched closer with each desperate word. "If she's fine, but she's not here, then where is she? *Please.*"

There was no denying how deeply Katie felt Nora's disappearance. It was all over her face, in every syllable of her plea, and she had called me. *Me.* Who she didn't believe existed. And Nora loved her. Nora loved her so deeply that she risked everything to track Katie down in the Nightmare Realm. No matter what happened between them, Nora wouldn't want her sister to be in this much pain. Katie deserved the truth.

I sighed. "Would you like the full version or the quick one?"

"The quick one," she answered immediately.

I nodded. "After we saved you, Nora killed the Weaver, which transferred his magic to her. She rules the Nightmare Realm now."

Katie blanched. "Actually, I think this merits the full version."

It absolutely did. I waved toward the pavilion. "Make yourself at home. This is going to take a while."

Katie was much less patient than Nora had been as I laid everything on the table. The explanation took so many detours that half of it didn't sound logical even to me, but sometime near dawn, I told her of the last time I saw Nora. I left out the part about her haggard appearance.

"So you just let her go off with this other guy? This—this *nightmare*," Katie screeched. "But you *think* he's helping her?"

I swallowed a groan. We'd been over this. "I'm not, nor have I ever been, someone who would force a person to do something." The Weaver, maybe, but that was different. Nora's story wasn't the same as his. "Your sister is smart and capable, Katie. A lot more than anyone likes to give her credit for."

Katie glowered. "She's also ridiculously impulsive. Care to take a stab at where that can get her? Oh, that's right. *Literally* stabbed. By some evil, manipulative tree-woman."

I closed my eyes and willed away the image Katie's words inspired. When it was safe to speak again, I met Katie's gaze and held it. "I promised Nora I would step back so she could figure things out, but don't confuse that with not caring. Every star will fall from the sky before I let anything happen to her. It doesn't matter if the entire Night World collapses. The balance could leave us with nothing but a single stone to stand on and I would step off so that she could survive."

Katie paused to study me. "You really do love her, don't you?"

"She is my soul. Without her, I am nothing."

"Why?" she asked curiously.

I frowned. "Why?"

"Why do you love her?"

Was there supposed to be a *why*? Did love have to make sense? I'd never loved anyone the way I loved Nora. At the time, when my feelings toward her began to grow, I wondered if it was because she was the only person I had significant contact with. It was me, the beach, and a silent Baku without her. It took nearly three months before I accepted that my feelings were real and not because I was lonely. I loved Nora because there was a connection between us that had nothing to do with magic. Her smile lit her eyes, which lit something in me. She had five different laughs, was a talented artist, and had a fortitude that never failed to fill me with pride. Things were easy between us. We were two halves of a single piece, fitting together in each jagged place.

"You're blushing." Katie smirked then, half-glad, half-troubled. "Whatever your reasons, you've got it bad, Sandy. Make sure you don't confuse her right to be an idiot with my right to be alive. I love Nora with my entire heart, but letting her hold the fate of all mankind?"

"She's not holding it alone," I said quietly.

"No." Katie sighed and eased back on the pillows. "I suppose not. But still…"

She wasn't wrong about her sister. My Nora was kind and smart and compassionate, but she was also impatient to a fault. First with killing the Weaver, then returning to the Night World with Mare in tow. If she didn't learn to slow down and think things through, there was no telling what the consequences would be. Suddenly, seeing her again felt increasingly urgent.

"Mind if I stay?" Katie asked. "I'm not ready to wake up and face the real world yet."

I shook my head, though she was no longer looking at me. "Stay as long as you'd like."

"Thanks." And then, after a long pause, "Can I come again? I promise not to get in the way, but it feels like I'm closer to Nora here. Like I'm seeing her in a different way, and I want to understand." She huffed. "I'm probably not making sense."

"You are," I assured her. This was the place where Nora could always be Nora. Even though she wasn't here, it sometimes felt like she *could* be. "Open the drawer on the end there. Take one of the pouches and fill it with sand to use whenever you'd like."

"I'm sorry I called you a freak," she blurted.

My eyes widened, and a laugh burst from my chest. The pain sent me backwards into the sand.

"Sorry about that too," she said nervously.

I smiled and tried not to wheeze too loudly. "I'll live."

"You better." The drawer thumped open then shut again. "Someone needs to look out for my little sister."

I sobered, hoping against hope that both of us were wrong about that. *Please, please let us be wrong.* My exhaustion won then, dragging me into a state of fitful slumber with Nora's name playing on repeat.

Chapter Twenty-One

Nora.

I shifted under the covers.

Nora.

Pulled them up over my head.

Nora.

My eyes flew open. That voice. I recognized it. The Sandman's voice was more familiar to me than my own. I gathered the blankets tighter around me. But how? It felt so very far away now that I was awake, and I couldn't be sure I had really heard it at all. He sounded wrong. Too frantic. Wild. My gut twisted.

"Kail?" I whispered. "Are you out there?"

Silence.

I looked inward to the Sandman, shifting through my own feelings to see if I could catch some glimpse of his. Anything to feel a little less alone. But, unsurprisingly, his walls were barred tight. I lingered anyway. Would he feel me if I reached out? If I knocked on that barrier between us, would he answer after I told him to leave me alone? I shook my head. Of course he would. But doubt still nipped at me as I lifted a finger and tapped three times.

For the briefest of moments, his mental doors cracked, and a burst of pain shot up my leg. I flew out of bed and buckled to the ground with a yelp. "Sandman?" I hobbled around the room, throwing on the first clothes I found. His doors slammed shut again. I beat against them with my mind, begging to be let in, but they didn't budge.

"Kail!" I raced out of Rowan's old room and paused. My thoughts sparked all over the place, making it impossible to focus on my own magic. Desperate, I shouted his name again.

He sauntered down the hall, seemingly out of nowhere, shirtless. His brown skin was covered in a senseless pattern of black lines. "Yes?"

"We have to go." I quickly retrieved my bookbag from inside the door and tossed it over one shoulder. "Now."

Kail squinted at me. "Go where? We don't march until dawn."

"Something's wrong with the Sandman."

"Ah." He scratched the back of his neck. "About that."

Hot fury flooded me. "You knew?"

"There may have been a rumor circulating through the troops last night."

I gripped his beak. The smooth white of his mask darkened

beneath my hand. Cracks spider-webbed up the curve toward his face, the spaces between peeling away like old paint. "What rumor?"

"Nora." His good eye flashed violently. "Stop."

I tightened my grip. "Tell me!"

"He's with Rowan," he said with tangible fear as he gripped my wrist. "Please. I'll explain everything."

"Explain fast," I demanded without relinquishing my hold.

"He was trying to infect the Watchmen." He winced. "Rowan found him and took him to the Keep."

I shoved him into the wall. Half his beak crumbled, leaving a burnt, jagged crater in place of its curve. I wiped the residue on my jeans and adjusted my bag over both shoulders. "Get whatever you need," I instructed. "We're going." He remained against the wall and dragged air in through his mouth. I raised my brows. "*Now.*"

"He let himself be caught," Kail said in a tone I'd never heard him use before. Defeated. Like he knew this was a battle he would never win. "He could've let the sand call him home at any time, but he didn't. For whatever reason, he wanted to be there."

"Were part of my instructions unclear?" I raised my hand to grip his beak again.

"Fine," he snapped before striding back the way he came. "Give me two minutes."

The threads pulsed against my arm and neck. *Soon,* I promised them. They could come out and do their job soon. All of them. If Rowan thought I would let her take the Sandman, she was mistaken. She had my Keep. My loom. But she would never have my heart. I proved that much when I took the knife from her. When I plunged it into the Weaver's chest to protect everyone—the Sandman included. I was wrong then, but I wouldn't be wrong now. The Nightmare Realm was mine and she was done pretending otherwise.

"This is a horrible idea," Kail muttered as he brushed by me on his way to the staircase.

I stormed after him. "Did you really think I'd leave him there?"

"I *think* the Sandman is perfectly capable of taking care of himself, just as he's done since the dawn of time. Rowan is a fool to think she's caught him." He shouldered out the front door. "But what I think obviously doesn't matter, does it? I'm just a stupid nightmare. What would I possibly know about anything? Especially compared to the newest member of our world."

"Watch yourself," I warned in a voice not quite my own.

"He *wants* to be there," Kail said again, insistent.

I scoffed. "Why would he? He's not a masochist, and he certainly wouldn't want to become bait to lure me in."

"And here I thought you knew him better than anyone," Kail snapped.

"I do."

"No." Kail kept walking, his shoulders stiff, in what I assumed was the direction of the Keep. "You know a different Sandman than the rest of us. He's always been *good*, as subjective as that is, but when he's around you, he's almost human. When he's alone, he blazes a path of destruction through this place."

"What's that supposed to mean?"

"It means, the last time you were in the Blood Tower, he didn't just look for you. He murdered every nightmare he came across." His expression turned stony. "Didn't know that, did you?"

I wasn't going to dignify that with an answer. Wasn't going to feed into Kail's agenda. The last time I was in the Blood Tower, I would've rejoiced to hear he killed them. The only thing that had changed since then was me.

"Really, *Lady*," Kail continued. "Aren't you even a little concerned that the Sandman was traipsing around your realm, messing with your nightmares?"

"They weren't *my* nightmares then."

He leaned a bit closer. "They're yours now."

I opened my mouth to reply, but nothing came out. Nothing could when Kail made such a valid point. I hadn't known the Sandman was a killer then, but that didn't matter. It was in the past. Maybe they attacked him first. There were a lot of things only the Sandman could clarify. And I would let him. One day, when this was all over. What *was* important was that he wasn't killing any of the nightmares now. Infecting them—taking their minds—was another matter. Until he proved otherwise, I trusted the Sandman in my realm. With my life.

"Well, as you've so keenly shown that you're able to exert your will," he said sarcastically, motioning to his mask, "why don't you bid the entire army to follow us? Might as well get everything over with at once, right? Priorities and all."

I shoved past him, my shoulder knocking his arm. "Stop talking before I burn off the rest of your face."

"At least try to remember what those threads are for. They're all you have until you learn how to weave, and Halven did a lot of work to make sure you kept them." He caught up to me and grabbed my arm. "Actually, you know what? If I'm going to march you toward Rowan—who, might I add, probably wants to kill me *slightly* more than you at this point—I want my eye fixed first.”

“You were going to lead me to her in a few hours anyway.” I ripped myself free of him and skirted around a puddle surrounded by a ring of three-eyed frogs. A hundred more puddles dotted the next quarter-mile, filling my head with croaks from their inhabitants. “What’s the difference?”

Kail leapt over a pile of what looked like beige bird eggs covered in jelly. “Look around you. Where’s the army? Where’s Halven?”

I rolled my eyes. “He’s *your* brother. Where did you see him last?”

“Asleep!” he shouted. “Because it’s the middle of the night!”

“It’s technically always night here, Kail,” I quipped, weary. It was the darkest part of it, but I wouldn’t concede the point.

He let out a frustrated groan. “Please, just think about this.”

“Hm.” I held a finger up to the edge of my mouth. “Okay, thought about it. Not leaving the Sandman to be tortured by your maniacal friend.”

“So torture is only okay if you’re the one doing it?” He waved to his face. “Look at me.”

I refused. If I did, I might waver. Or, more likely, I would slam my fist straight into the gaping hole, snapping the entire beak clean off. “You’re the one that said I needed to be feared. Besides, you can still see out of your eye, can’t you?”

His jaw twitched. “It’s. My. Eye.”

I glared at him, unamused. “And your mask is your mask. You’ll live.”

“I regret every minute of helping you,” he snarled.

I stiffened at that. If Kail wasn’t helping me, he would likely be helping Rowan instead. He never struck me as the type to sit on the sidelines to wait and see what happened. Then again, he was the embodiment of the unknown. There was so much I didn't know about him. So much I didn't understand. And chances were, I never would. Especially since, after this was all over, I was booting him back to the Blood Tower where he wouldn't be able to harass me anymore. That day was still too far in the future to plan, so for right now, as much as I loathed it, I needed him.

"Fine. Your eye or your mask? I'll try to fix one now and the other after we get back from the Keep."

"If you die in there, Rowan won't fix either one," he said, eyes glittering with rage. "You may not know this, but I'm rather vain."

I rolled my eyes. "Shocking development, but let's be real. If I fix both now, what incentive would you have to not turn on me?"

"Would you like a list?" He held up a finger. "Let's start with *Rowan wants to kill me.* I chose a side—*your* side. There's no going back for me now."

"Pick one," I said, cutting off his tirade.

He exhaled slowly and spoke through his teeth. "The mask."

I swiveled to face him and set my palm over his charred beak. The grin twitched lazily, lending me its power, and the curve rose up beneath my hand until his mask was as good as new.

"There. Happy? Now let's go."

Chapter Twenty-Two

The Sandman

When Nora tapped against my mind, phantom pain answered. I scrambled to regain consciousness and shove it down before it was too late, but I wasn't quick enough. By the time I pulled myself together to send her another message—that I was fine—her mind was whirling too fast to listen. It was a massive tornado of worry and anger, crushing any calm thought I sent at it, which only left me with one option. I had to find Nora before she did something stupid, like tackling Rowan head on. I climbed from beneath the sand to find Katie gone and eased the strap of my satchel over my head. I winced as the new skin over my cut stretched from the movement. It felt as if there were shards of glass inside my chest, but I could function well enough for this.

Baku lounged near the water's edge, and relief washed over me. He climbed to his feet as I neared. "You made it," I said. He shot me a look as though the mere thought that he wouldn't was offensive. I chuckled. "It's good to see you."

He nodded once and eyed my ripped shirt. I should've taken a minute to change so Nora would believe that nothing was wrong. *Too late now.* It was everything I could do to keep moving forward; there was no way I was going to backtrack.

I cleared my throat. "Any idea where she is?"

Baku trudged by my side into the Nightmare Realm, skirting around the place burned by the acid rain. He cast a glance in my direction that let me know his exact thought: *idiot.*

"You didn't have to come," I said playfully to lighten the mood.

He exhaled in what I interpreted as a sarcastic laugh.

"We won't be long." I hoped. Her magic registered within this side of the realm, which was a small miracle, but it was moving in the direction of the Keep, which was decidedly not. "I need to talk to her for a second. That's all."

The only thing that might keep me true to my word was that I needed the sand for another day. After that, I would be able to resume normal activity. The pain might linger for a few days, but it was of no true consequence. In that much time, Nora would've already destroyed Rowan's tree and taken the realm. By the time we had to join forces against Mare, I would be as good as new.

On and on we walked, following the trail left by Nora's magic. Baku leaned into me at one point to offer his support, but I could walk on my own. By the time the Keep was in view, I was beginning to regret not taking him up on the offer. The Watchmen looked down at us accusingly. Was there no other

215

path she could've chosen? Their stone eyes bored into me, angry at having missed their mark and annoyed at not being able to leave their post to finish the job.

Baku snorted. I followed his gaze to find Nora near the base of the cliff with Kail behind her. My heart leapt, my legs pumping before I even realized I was running or that Baku had taken off in the opposite direction.

"Nora," I called.

She stopped mid-step and stumbled forward, while Kail simply turned to face me.

"Finally," Kail called back. "I was beginning to think we'd actually have to go in there to save you."

"In where?" I stepped up beside Nora. She still hadn't faced me, her eyes fixed on the ground, but just being next to her made it easier to breathe. With her blond hair flowing loosely over her shoulders and the pink knit sweater she wore, it almost seemed as if she didn't belong here. *Almost.* Because the threads circling her neck told the truth. "Are you okay?"

There was a pregnant pause.

"Define 'okay'," Kail drawled. "Does walking away from your army to launch a suicide—sorry, *rescue*—mission, count as okay?"

"Can you give us a second?" I asked Kail, and he backed away. Indeed, wishes *were* sometimes only wishes. Of course Nora would mount a foolish attempt to save me. I knew she would the moment she felt my pain. "Nora, look at me."

"No," she said, determined.

I placed a hand gently on her shoulder, and she shivered beneath the touch. "Why not?"

She was silent for a heartbeat. "Because, Sandman. I'm

supposed to be figuring myself out and claiming the realm, but do you know what I'm doing instead?" Her voice grew tighter, more irritated, by the second. "Instead of marching my army to the Keep this morning as planned, I rushed here to save you. But Kail was right: you obviously let yourself be caught, or you wouldn't be in front of me. So now, I'm having trouble deciding if I'm angrier at you for going with her or myself for not believing it."

She was going to make her final stand today? Without sending word to me first? It was one thing if she didn't want my help, another to take on her enemy without giving me a heads up. A *goodbye* in case things went poorly. If she failed, if I hadn't had another moment with her—how was I supposed to live with myself? Did she understand my feelings for her? Truly and completely? Even now that things were different? Did I understand hers? We deserved a five-minute conversation before she marched off to her potential death.

"Were you going to tell me?" I breathed. "So I could see you again before—"

She spun around, and I drew in a sharp breath. Faint reddish-purple bruises fanned out beneath her gold eyes. "So you could tell me not to attack? So you could blame Kail for something out of his control?" She held her hands up. "Or how about so you could see that my hands are back to normal? Care to ask how I accomplished *that* one?"

"Nora, I—"

"I'll tell you." Tears rimmed her eyes, but I wasn't sure if they were caused by sorrow or rage. "The secret to absorbing the Weaver's power was torture. I carved up the nightmares that killed my friends, and I didn't even think twice about it."

"Nor—"

"And that's not all I've done. Kail's mask? I burnt half of it to ash with my bare hands because he tried to talk some sense into me, and I only put it back together because I needed his help. Not because I regretted it."

I wrapped my arms around her and held tight. If she wouldn't let me talk, this was the next best thing. Despite the terrible things she just told me, I loved her. No matter what she did or would do, she was the brightest star in my sky. "Shh," I said quietly. "None of that matters. You're doing what you need to. It will calm down one day, and you'll be able to control your actions." *Urges*, the Weaver had always called them. After banishing Mare, after drawing a clear line between Day and Night, his mind became a more volatile place, just as mine became less so. If the Weaver could control himself, if he could learn to be more pragmatic with his violence, Nora could too.

"Of course it matters." Her hands gripped my shirt, and she buried her face in my chest.

I winced against the pain but held tight. "Not to me. When I said always, I meant it."

"I'm sorry," she said quietly. "I—I can't be—"

Kail cleared his throat.

I glared at him over Nora's head. "There's a reason I came," I said into her ear. "I realized something important."

She stared up at me, gold eyes gleaming, and continued to hold me close. "What?"

"Kail showed me a tree that he said used to be Rowan." I toyed absently with the ends of Nora's hair, wrapping them around my fingers, though all I wanted to do was kiss her. "When I was with her in the Keep, I noticed her wings were burned."

"So?"

"So, I set the stump on fire that day. It burnt out within seconds, but it was long enough to do some damage. I think if you destroy the nightmare she *was*, it will kill them both," I explained.

She glanced at Kail, who had crept closer. "You knew about this?"

He sighed loudly. "Obviously."

"Then what was all *this* about?" she shouted, pushing away from me to advance on him.

"Training," Kail ticked off a finger. "Gaining loyalty."

She slammed her palms against his shoulders, and he stumbled back. "I could've trained in the Keep."

"Which is why I told *him*, thinking he would understand. But when he didn't, I took it as a sign. You've got an army now, and, when you take the Keep back, it will be with a show of force. No one will doubt you then."

"An army *Halven* built," she argued.

"Nora," I said gently, scanning the area in case the Watchmen alerted anyone. The trees remained still. "He's not wrong about the show of force, and it's my fault for not realizing what would happen if—"

"Stop. I don't want to play the blame game right now," she said. My chest crackled, the sound like plastic crumpling, and Nora glanced at the torn fabric of my shirt. "What was that?"

"Nothing important." I rubbed the skin just below the tattoo where it wasn't sore. The movement shifted the ever-moving magic beneath, and there was a small pop. "I have to get back to the beach, but there's one more thing I wanted to tell you."

Her eyes widened with worry. "Tell me what happened."

I shook my head. "Your sister called to me tonight."

"Katie?" She jerked back in surprise. "Why?"

"She was looking for you." It was all I felt right saying, especially now. Her mother was a sore subject, and she didn't need to be distracted if she was about to take down Rowan. "I told her everything. She took it well, considering."

Nora chewed her bottom lip, looking askance. "Thanks. I'll… I mean, can you make sure she doesn't come here? Use your sand on her until this is all over?"

So she doesn't become a weapon to use against me again, is what Nora didn't say, but she didn't have to. "Of course," I promised. "She already has some."

"Okay, thank you." Nora closed her eyes and took a deep, centering breath. "I'll check in with you soon. After I take care of a few things," she said, glancing at the Keep in the distance. It was smart not to say her plan out loud with so many ears nearby—it was enough of a risk that I had.

"Stay safe."

She nodded and turned to Kail. "We're going back to the tower to have a little chat."

I took her wrist before I could stop myself. Nora looked over her shoulder at me, and her expression softened. "I love you," I said, wistfully.

She turned, stretched up on her toes, and kissed me. "Wait for me?" she breathed against my lips but didn't stay for my answer.

Letting her walk away was like watching the sun go down for the final time. When she was out of sight, Baku nudged my leg with a tusk. "I'm okay," I said, my voice hoarse. But I wasn't.

Chapter Twenty-Three

Nora

Maybe I deserved this pain. This exhaustion.

The hurt was no less than what I put my family through. Katie had called out to the Sandman, for crying out loud. How desperate was she? There had to be something I could do to ease their fears. I couldn't go back, and Katie couldn't come here. The last thing I needed was something snatching her up again or her seeing me like this.

And then there was Kail's betrayal.

I definitely, absolutely deserved that, but I didn't expect to feel so stung by it. Kail was good at what he did. At making me believe he was on my side even though I knew he was up to no good. It was hard to tell which bothered me more—that he lied or that I bought it.

"Are you going to ignore me the *entire* walk back to the Blood Tower?" Kail asked in the cool voice he used the first time I met him.

"Ideally."

"You're not going to snap my mask off or stab my other eye?"

"Don't tempt me," I warned.

"You're angry with me," he said, suddenly chipper. "I'm willing to let bygones be bygones if you think hurting me again will help you get over it."

I stared at him harder. Was he serious? Was this another ploy to win me over to his side so he could use me like a puppet? Or was that honestly what he expected of me? Was it what Rowan had done? I balled my hands into fists. "I won't apologize for what happened earlier, if that's what you're fishing for."

He snorted. "I don't expect you to. That's the ruthlessness that will save you."

"Then what?" I whirled on him, arms raised to my sides. "What do you want me to get over, Kail? That we've been running all over the Nightmare Realm like fugitives for weeks now, *hiding*, when this all could've ended the moment I got here? That you lied and lied and lied? Every day, you spun your web around me, but do you know the worst part? I was starting to believe you were on my side."

"We weren't simply hiding, and you know that," he said quietly.

"Oh, right. I was *training*. Learning how to use my magic so I could claim my realm when *I should already have it*." I stepped closer and poked his chest. "You were going to let me risk my life—all those nightmares' lives—for what?"

He hesitated. "The show of strength would've earned you the surviving dissenters' loyalty."

"What makes you think I'd allow survivors?" I ground my teeth together until they ached. "How about some straight answers?"

The corner of his lip twitched. "When have I ever given you a straight answer?"

"Exactly my point." I ran a hand down my face, forcing myself to calm down. Kail filled in the blanks when it suited him and talked in circles when it didn't. It was time that changed. "You're going to tell me the truth. Now."

He lowered his chin, cocking his head to the side. "About?"

"Why did you show the Sandman the way to defeat Rowan? Why didn't you take me right to the tree?"

"I wanted you to trust me first," he said warily.

"Trust you?" I burst out laughing. I couldn't help it. "You wanted to earn my trust by lying to me?"

He bristled. "I *did* help Rowan last time you were here. Would you have believed me if I took you there right away? The Sandman didn't even bother to think on what I said until now. Besides, Halven and I wouldn't have let Rowan kill you."

The laugh died in my throat. "There's nothing you could ever do that would make me trust you."

Except he had made me trust him already. Barely. Day after day, he worked a little magic on me. Not real magic like mine, but his own twisted charm. Each new thing he taught me was another fold of a paper airplane. But now I tossed that plane into the wind and watched as it dove nose-first into the ground.

"Then it really shouldn't bother you that I omitted things," he said with a stiff shrug.

"What's your motive?" I demanded. "You said you had one."

He thought for a moment—really thought. "I think I'd rather wait and tell you when you're in a better mood."

Then he turned on his heel and strode away. I gaped at his back for a long moment before my mouth caught up to my brain. "Hey, you don't get to walk away from me," I shouted, storming after him. "You were the one who started this whole conversation. I was perfectly fine with the silence, but *no*. You just *had* to pick at it, didn't you? Well, now it's time to fess up before I decide to throw you to Rowan as a parting gift."

When he didn't turn around, I snagged his elbow and attempted to pull him to a stop. "Keep walking," he said in a deathly low voice and easily extracted himself from my grip.

Oh, no. He wasn't going to feign danger to avoid the truth. "After you answer my question."

"Remember how Three attacked you in the Barren, and I didn't ask questions?"

"What about it?" My fingers unconsciously went to my healed nose.

"You did kill her, right?" His eyes slid to mine, one flickering too quickly. "That's how you got away?"

"Not exactly," I said slowly as my nerves began to tingle. "Why?"

"Don't look back but—"

I threw a glance over my shoulder.

"Or ignore me. What else is new?" Kail droned.

"I don't see anything," I whispered.

He sighed. "Three of the Hours are following us, so the sooner we get back to the Blood Tower and the army, the better."

"What do they think killing me will accomplish?" I hissed. "It's not going to make Mara disappear."

He *ts*ked. "Mara? What does she have to do with this? The Hours are working with Rowan."

"No," I said slowly. "If they were working with Rowan, Three wouldn't have tried to kill me. She would've taken me back to the Keep for Rowan to do it. She was mad that I brought Mara back."

Kail's body grew more rigid, and he eased sideways to stand closer to me. His eyes were the only part of him moving as he scanned the riverbed on our left all the way to the landscape of dense yellow fog on our far right. "That makes sense," he said finally. "Unfortunately, that means we can't reason with them. First you killed their creator, then you sent an Ancient back to destroy their world, which in turn will destroy *all* the worlds. They're probably seeking vengeance."

"I didn't *send* her back," I shot back defensively.

"There you go again." Kail slid an arm around my shoulders to encourage me to walk faster. "Splitting hairs."

I fought the urge to turn around and search for the Hours. My heart slammed into my chest with enough force I swore it would break through bone. Rowan wanted me dead. Twelve nightmarish knight-like people were hunting me. I couldn't push the Sandman further away if I tried. My family thought I ran away, and the only person standing in my corner was someone I could no longer believe in.

Someone I never should've believed in to begin with.

"This is your fault. I could be in the Day World living my real life right now," I told him.

"You wound me with your accusations," he said sarcastically.

"I clearly let you know my feelings on the matter before Rowan sent you off with Elkmar. Don't blame me for your choices."

Elkmar. The shadowy nightmare with ribbed horns and webbed hands that was meant to deliver me to the Weaver after Rowan gave me the knife. He still filled me with unease. The clicking of his voice, the way he stayed so close no matter how I changed my gait… A shiver ran over me. Where was he these days? "Why would you go along with it if you—"

"Really? *Now* is the best time for this conversation?"

I attempted to step out from beneath his arm, but his fingers dug into my shoulder. "You can talk and walk at the same time."

He grunted in frustration. "We all have our weaknesses, okay? Just… leave it alone. Please."

I opened my mouth to let him know just how much I *wasn't* going to let it go—but had he just said *please*? An arrow whizzed by my head. I tucked my face into Kail's side with a small shriek.

"Be fearless," he said into my hair. "Duck."

"Wha—"

Kail slammed us both to the ground as a hail of arrows soared through the sky, landing around us in a perfect circle.

"Run!" I ordered, climbing to my hands and knees.

"No." He pressed me harder into the ground so I couldn't move. "If the Hours wanted you dead, you would be. Six doesn't miss."

"Or they want to make me die a slow and painful death." My voice rose so high it cracked.

"We don't care about the method," said a deep male voice. "Only the outcome."

Kail's arm shifted, allowing me to scramble to my feet. Three stood before me, her arms folded tight across her chest. Beside her was a second woman in similar armor, a long black braid trailing over her shoulder, the Roman numeral six on her mask. She nocked another arrow but kept it pointed at the ground. The third nightmare, the one that had spoken, wore a black fur cloak around his shoulders that nearly hid all the shining metal beneath. An X was carved over his face mask.

"Hello, Ten," Kail said, dusting himself off.

Ten didn't acknowledge the greeting, his eyes remaining on me. Though I couldn't see them, I felt them, like nettles. It was ages before the burning ceased, and Ten spoke. "Three has something she would like to say." When the woman beside him didn't speak, he gripped her arm and pulled her forward a step. "We discussed this as a group," he whispered to her.

"I'm sorry for trying to kill you," she said as unapologetically as possible. Ten cleared his throat, and she added, "Lady."

My eyes widened in surprise. She was seriously apologizing? Because someone made her? Like a scolded child reluctant to admit to poor behavior? I glanced at Kail who looked equally perplexed. "Um." I elbowed Kail hard in the ribs.

"Ow! What was that for?" he mumbled.

"Say something," I hissed from the corner of my mouth.

He opened and shut his mouth a few times. "Like what?"

"I don't know. Think of someth—"

"Lady," Ten interrupted. "The Hours have decided to honor you as the rightful ruler of the Nightmare Realm as long as you have a plan to deal with Mare. If you don't, we will remove you."

I blinked in surprise and eyed Six's bow. The grin sneered. *How dare they?* They were giving me an ultimatum? As if it were up to them. The only one here that should be making decisions was me, and right now I had half a mind to turn them into a living Dali painting. You're welcome, Dreamers. Hope you enjoy your melting clock-people. I filled my lungs until they were near bursting and opened my mouth wordlessly.

"And," the Hour continued, "as a show of good faith, you'll heal Four."

Oh, good. *More* demands. "If I don't?"

"She's a little busy at the moment," Kail interjected. He flashed a quick look in my direction as if begging me not to freak out.

"This can't wait. Neither can Mare," Six said in a light, airy voice. "You need to kill her now before she regains too much strength."

I huffed. "Yeah, well, like Kail said, I'm busy."

"If Four dies, you die," Three spit.

Kail leaned into my side. "Healing the Hour might be faster than arguing about it."

"What happened?" I asked reluctantly.

"Mare attacked him. We've brought him with us, there." Ten pointed behind them.

While I couldn't see anything in the direction he indicated, I did notice the blood coating his metal gauntlet. Not just a few drops either. My shoulder ached at the phantom memory of Mara's claws, but I had worn no armor. Assuming Four dressed like the other Hours, he was covered in it, so how was he that bloody? It might be worth healing him simply to see what Mara was capable of against a real opponent. Again, I wished the Weaver's memory of Mara lasted a bit longer.

"I'll look at him," I agreed.

Kail gave no outward sign that he approved or otherwise, which was both helpful and stressful. I didn't want him second-guessing me in front of the Hours, but a bit of validation would've gone a long way. It would have to be enough that he stayed beside me when the Hours lead me toward their injured comrade.

Nestled beside the river, directly beside a chain that disappeared below the water's surface, Mara's victim laid lifeless. Blood seeped into the short, bleached grass at the water's edge, then into the stream itself. Small parasitic worms coasted on the surface, soaking up the murky red liquid.

It took me a long moment before I allowed my gaze to seek out Four's wounds. The silver breastplate was dented an inch deep, and chunks of his arm were missing, along with the protective chainmail. Claw marks on his neck left him nearly decapitated. Both legs were turned at unnatural angles, and there wasn't much of his body *not* covered in crimson. I hardly believed he wasn't dead already.

"Not the safest place to leave him," I commented. "Who knows what lives at the other end of these chains, and with all that blood? It's like you were asking for trouble."

"Clearly, we were in the right," Three said defensively. "Now heal him."

Was she giving me orders again? Where did she get off? I—

Kail touched my elbow. "All or nothing, Lady."

Kill all of them or none of them. One was more satisfying, the other more expedient, and I wasn't exactly out on a leisure stroll. There were other things to do, so I crouched at Four's side. With a sigh, I placed a hand on his chest, wincing against the feel of his blood beneath my palm. The thread squirmed weakly, though still very determined to survive. The grin helped—urged my power into the thread, pumping it full of strength.

Just before the final pieces were tucked neatly back into the knotted ball, I broke contact. The dent remained in Four's breastplate, though less pronounced, the scratches on his neck still red and angry, and his arms were now covered in scabs. Four moaned weakly.

"Good as new," I lied.

"Finish it," Three commanded.

I stood, feeling even smaller than I was in Three's shadow. "He'll live. Now, if you'll excuse us."

Six's bow flew out in front of me before I could make it more than two steps. "If Mare can do that to one of us, imagine what else she's capable of."

A chill ran up my spine. "I'll deal with Mara. As soon as I finish my other business."

"You have an army now," Three snapped. "Let them take Rowan out while you deal with the real threat."

I barked a laugh, which was probably not the wisest idea, and Kail glared at me. "I'm going to kill Rowan with my own two hands, thank you. Who do you think you are? You can't tell me how to rule."

"Lady or not, you're no nightmare," Three snarled, lunging at me.

Ten yanked her back by the collar before I could react and dragged her away. "We will have words with her again, Lady," Six promised. "But be warned. Next time we see you, you will need to have a plan ready, or we will appoint a ruler who does."

"Your friends are leaving." I motioned behind her where Ten and Three continued to move away, practically dragging Four between them. "Might want to go with them."

Six made a small sound of annoyance in the back of her throat, though I wasn't sure who it was directed at, and hurried after the others.

"See?" I hissed the moment they were out of earshot. "This has nothing to do with Rowan and everything to do with that evil hag."

Kail cuffed the back of my head. "Do you have any idea what they're going to do now?"

"Talk to Three again, obviously." I rubbed the back of my head and started walking toward the Tower. "I bought myself some time to come up with a plan, at any rate."

"Right. Time. From the Hours," he said in a dull voice. "And when that time runs out, they'll expect you to take down an ancient being. If you don't? *Poof*, you're dead."

I stepped over the chain, and at the other end, a large metal cage broke the surface of the water. Small ripples, like those made from a light spring rain, danced around it. The grin widened as something inside gurgled.

I grimaced, ignoring the tormented sound. "Mara was always going to have to die, but like you said, one thing at a time."

"And you choose now to start listening to me? Mara will kill you before you can even raise a sword."

"What did you want me to tell them, Kail? That I was busy? Because that was *so* helpful," I snapped.

"This is serious." His eyes narrowed to slits. "You do know what's in the Ever Safe, don't you? And what will happen if you don't take care of Mara?"

"I don't even know what the Ever Safe *is*," I admitted. My head throbbed. Rowan, Mara, Hours, the liar next to me. There was only so much more doom and gloom a girl could take. "But go ahead. We have a long way to go so you might as well enlighten me."

He let out a small huff. "Story time really isn't my thing."

"*Make* it your thing."

He waved his hands out in front of him, and his voice took on a monotone edge. "A long, long time ago, before the world as you knew it—"

I silenced him with a look. "Cliff notes version."

"Boring," he said with a dramatic sigh. "Basically, this place used to be full of what we call the Ancients. Blah, blah, blah, the Weaver and Sandman came into existence when your world needed to balance things out, or some such nonsense. That whole bit's kind of iffy for me. Anyway, things went down. They locked the Ancients in the Ever Safe where they've been dormant ever since."

Seemed like a non-issue then. "What does that have to do with Mara?"

"She escaped. Clearly." He made eye contact with me and held it. "Everything you've been hearing about her destroying our worlds? It's because she wants to open the safe and let her friends out to play."

My stomach dropped. I assumed she wanted to come back because the Day World sucked so much for us, but if Kail was right… My mouth ran dry. *Screwed.* I was so screwed. "Can she do that?"

"If she didn't know how, would the night lords have messed with the balance to exile her?" Kail's gaze dulled, his thoughts taking him far away.

"Perfect," I mumbled around a lump in my throat. "Just perfect."

Since I was going to die—either by Rowan before I found her stump or by Mara after—I needed to do a better job of saying goodbye. My family needed closure. There was only one way to do that given my current situation, so it would have to do. I poked at the grin in hopes that it would have a better idea, but it snapped its lips shut.

Fine. That settled that then. Option number two it was.

Afterward, I would make things right with the Sandman. Who knew—he could already have a plan. Maybe it was time I tried to remember the girl who thought we could unite the realms. The grin thinned, but it didn't have to like everything I did.

***

When Kail and I finally dragged ourselves back inside the Blood Tower, my feet felt raw. Almost as raw as my nerves. But nothing else attacked us along the way. A few mindless nightmares stopped to watch us with something like reverence, and a tall flower with a face waved her leaves in greeting. The only thing keeping me from falling asleep right there on the hallway floor was the fact that tonight could be my last chance. I paused beside Halven, where he waited just inside the door, and waited for Kail to shuffle to the staircase.

"We leave at dawn," I announced to both brothers. Then I whispered so only Halven would hear, "Meet me outside in two hours."

Chapter Twenty-Four

The Sandman

Katie flopped down on the edge of the pavilion with a plastic bag. "Good evening, Mr. Sandman," she said in a poorly-executed English accent.

"Hello again." I didn't bother climbing out from my half-buried state. It felt too good with the sand covering my bare torso to get up before it was necessary.

"I come bearing gifts." Katie dug into the plastic bag and produced a spiral notebook. "My mother was tearing Nora's room apart earlier, so I liberated this."

Her notebook. "How did you know where to find it?" I asked carefully.

Katie pointed to the drawings on the wall. "No one gets that good without practice, so I may have done a little digging of my own. Don't tell Nora though."

"Your secret is safe with me." I eyed the notebook hungrily. Nora hadn't let me go through her drawings in a long time, and it would be a lie to say I wasn't curious. I knew I shouldn't look, that it was private, but the temptation was palpable. "Why did you bring it here?"

"Are you kidding me?" She reached back in the bag and pulled out a large box of colored pencils, setting both items on the pillow beside her leg, before stuffing the empty bag into the pocket of her plaid pajama pants. "My room isn't safe from expert snooping, and I clearly can't go back to college in the middle of this crisis. If my mother saw this, she would absolutely lose it. It was either try bringing the pictures here—victory!—or use them to start a bonfire."

I nodded, glad she opted for the first choice. "I'm sorry. About your mother." I looked away then, toward the stars. "If it wasn't for me, she and Nora would've been closer, and you wouldn't have to deal with her invading your space so often."

Katie snorted. "Maybe. Or maybe she's always been like this."

"You don't have to say that to spare my feelings. I know what I've done," I said quietly.

Her laugh filled the beach. "Please. Like I care about that. You've definitely screwed a lot of stuff up, but credit needs to go where credit is due. My mother's issues are her own. Plentiful as they are."

"Okay," I said, strangely amused. "Then, in your opinion, what do I need to apologize to you for? You deserve that much from me."

Silence fell as Katie picked at her bottom lip, her gaze

faraway. "Nothing," she said after an eternity. "If I had believed Nora, she wouldn't have hidden so much, and if I knew, then maybe I would've had a pouch of sand to keep me from the Weaver when I needed it."

I sat up then, sand cascading down my chest. She couldn't find me completely blameless. If the situation were boiled down to bare facts, I stole her sister away. She had the dream because of me, the Weaver went after her to get it, and now—

"So *that's* the tattoo, huh?" Katie said with a playful smirk. "I'm dying to know why Nora saw you shirtless way back then."

"Back *when?*" I asked and hurried into the pavilion for a shirt. The black fabric clung to my body, putting just enough pressure over my breastbone to make it uncomfortable.

"The day we saw you at the mall, Nora said you had tattoos." Katie wagged her eyebrows. "Interesting development."

"She was talking about the ones on my arms," I clarified. "Not my chest."

Katie burrowed into the pillows. "Sure. Whatever you say."

I leaned my back against the wall, legs crossed. "What about Kellan?" I asked, feeling slightly defensive.

"He's gone. I broke up with him." Her words were unbothered and lacked emotion. "Jen came home for Thanksgiving and wanted to meet up, so... you know." She waved a hand through the air. When I stayed silent, she added, "We talked. I begged forgiveness and plead with her for another shot."

"I knew what you meant." Because I felt like doing the same thing with Nora—but at the same time, it was her that needed to apologize. She asked me to wait, so I would. I would wait forever, but there were still conversations that needed to be had.

"I hope you two work it out. Nora told me you guys were great together."

"So." Katie forced a cough, her voice rising, and motioned to the notebook. "Have you looked at them before?"

I stared hungrily at the cover and shook my head. "She didn't talk about drawing much. I had to ask for the ones on my wall."

"Maybe you should." She gave me a pitying look before snuggling deeper into the pillows and closing her eyes.

Katie was giving me privacy to take her advice, but I wasn't entirely sure I should. These were Nora's. If she wanted me to see her drawings, she would've shared them herself. Then again, she wouldn't have left the notebook behind if she didn't want anyone to eventually find it. Nora admitted more than once that her mother went through her belongings and would again after she was gone. Maybe she wanted her mother to see what was inside.

Against my better judgment, I slid the glossy black book into my lap and cracked it open. The first page was a spectacular rendering of the beach. So was the second, as well as the third. Pages and pages of a starlit sky, then one of Katie with her pink hair, followed by a portrait of Natalie, then Emery. Me with my hood up and another with my hood down. And finally, drawn with a regular pencil, so light that the page almost looked blank, was a knowing grin. Who would it have been if she finished?

I went to shut the book when Katie quietly said, "There's one more."

I jumped at the sound of her voice breaking my reverie and carefully turned the page, the crisp crinkle of it loud in the silence. My heart dropped. I wished I hadn't seen this until I was alone. Maybe not at all. Mostly, I wished Katie hadn't seen it. My finger traced the pencil marks in the corner. It was another one of me, this time with my head on Nora's pillow as I slept. She captured every shimmering mark on my bare arms and followed the path across my collarbones, where the tattoos disappeared beneath the sheet. It wasn't hard to figure out when she'd drawn this. I had only been shirtless in her bed once. Heat flooded my face, and the ache in my chest had nothing to do with my healing body. With shaking fingers, I closed the notebook and placed it back on the pillows.

"I'm never going to see my sister again, am I?" Katie looked up at the sky, the bright stars reflected in her watery eyes, and her chin trembled.

"You will," I promised. "Someday, when she's ready."

The silence that followed was a heavy, painful thing, but something about it felt easier with Katie there. A shared sadness stretched between us. I hadn't realized how much I needed another soul to share the burden, if only for a few minutes.

"You two look comfortable," drawled a familiar voice. "Moving on so soon, Sandman?"

I flew to my feet and faced Kail. "How did you get in here?"

"Like Mara's the only one who knows how to hitch a ride?" He flicked a piece of hair from his forehead. "Baku's back."

There were only a dozen things wrong with what he just said. "Where is he?"

"He'll be along when he wakes up," he said casually, eyeing Katie with interest.

My jaw hung open, speechless.

Kail huffed. "Oh, don't give me that look. He wanted to eat me; it was purely self-defense."

I scanned behind him for Nora, but she was nowhere in

sight. "What are you doing here, Kail?"

"I'll give you two guesses." He looked around me to Katie. "Should we talk in front of the human?"

"Is it about Nora?" Katie eased to her feet and took in Kail from head to toe. A worried gleam shone in her eyes as if she thought he would snatch her away at any moment. It wasn't impossible.

"Ah." Understanding lit Kail's face. "You must be the famous sister. Is she around?"

"Is who around?" I asked.

"Nora, obviously. Who do you think?" he snapped, suddenly impatient.

My pulse roared, my magic grating against my insides. *Stay calm. Think. Process.* "What do you mean, 'Is she around'? She's supposed to be with *you.*"

He made a low, thoughtful noise in his throat. "Well, this is less than ideal."

"Nora's supposed to be with him?" Katie asked. "*This* is the guy?"

"She could do worse," Kail quipped. "A clown, perhaps."

The blood drained from Katie's face at the mention of clowns. If Katie was afraid of them before the Weaver trapped her inside a cave with one, she had to be absolutely terrified of them now.

"Enough," I demanded. Kail pulled a piece of yellowed paper from inside his jacket and held it out. I accepted it only to find Nora's handwriting filled the center: *I'll be back soon. Wait here.* "What does that mean?"

Kail scowled at me. "I'm pretty sure it means she'll be back soon and for me to wait there."

"Give me that." Katie ripped the letter from my hand. She scanned the words a dozen times, as if something new would appear before clutching it to her chest. "Where did she go?"

"Well, I rather thought she'd be here," Kail said cynically.

My insides flipped. "You're telling me you don't have any idea where Nora is?"

"I'd ask Halven to find her, but he seems to be aiding and abetting her little jaunt."

"Let me get this straight." I sucked in air, trying desperately to keep myself from murdering Kail on the spot. No burst of emotions broke through Nora's walls signaling she was in trouble, so that had to count for something. "Nora took off with your brother? And you have no clue where?"

"As I said, I *had* an idea." He motioned around us at the never-ending sand. "It didn't pan out."

"You were supposed to be taking care of her," I shouted. White-hot rage blasted through my head. I trusted Kail against my better judgment because Nora seemed to, but he couldn't even keep track of her, let alone stop her from storming the Keep when she thought I was held captive. For someone as old as he was, he was completely incompetent. He had *one job*—keep Nora safe.

"Don't try to pin this all on me," Kail shouted back. "If you hadn't dragged my name into this earlier—"

"Don't you dare," I said through my teeth. "She had a right to know about the tree. You might be okay with lying to her, but I'm not."

"Oh, *that's* rich." Kail laughed, stepping close enough that we nearly touched. "You lied to her for years."

A knife to the gut. "And look how things turned out."

"Wow. You two are being ridiculous." Katie stepped between us and held her hands out to keep us apart. "I don't give a rat's behind whose fault it is, but one of you better come up with a way to find her, *pronto.*"

I inhaled, and a shudder ran through my body. *Don't kill him.* Nora needed him. *Him. Not me.* The thought barreled through me like a freight train, but now wasn't the time. "Katie's right," I admitted reluctantly.

"She's definitely with Halven," Kail said slowly. Then, to Katie, he added, "Before you get your panties in a twist, he's trustworthy."

"Oh, I highly doubt that," Katie scoffed.

"What about the army?" I asked.

Kail's lips parted in disbelief. "If the army was missing too, would I have assumed she snuck away to visit her lover?"

"You two are talking like Nora's your prisoner," Katie sharply interjected.

"Of course she isn't," I said, her outburst stealing my anger. "But she's still learning to use her power."

"And you remember our realm, don't you Bubble Gum Princess?" Kail smirked. "Nice dye job, by the way."

Katie blanched. "You seriously trust this guy with my sister's life?"

"Don't worry. If I was going to hurt her, I would've done it a long time ago. She's rather infuriating, though I'm sure you know that." Kail smiled, then paled. "Oh, look. Someone's awake."

Baku stormed toward the three of us, swaying slightly on his feet. A cloud of glimmering sand followed him down the nearest dune.

"That's my cue to leave. I'll wait at the Blood Tower in case she comes back," Kail called as he raced in the opposite direction.

For a moment, I entertained the thought of keeping him locked inside the barrier. Let him sweat a bit. But now wasn't the time to be petty. I sighed and, with a quick flick of my wrist, opened the barrier into the Nightmare Realm just long enough for him to escape. Baku chuffed at my side, his brindle fur sparkling with sand.

"Sorry, but you'll have to wait a little longer to eat that one." I looked Baku over. "Are you okay?"

He nodded once and eyed Katie.

"Katie, this is Baku. Baku, meet Nora's sister."

"My head's about to explode," Katie said in a strained voice, and she wobbled where she stood.

"You should probably sit down." I took her elbow and eased her down onto the pillows. "I need to talk to him for a minute."

Katie wordlessly tucked her head between her knees.

I knelt beside Baku, my chest aching worse than before, and lifted a handful of sand. Tapping into his dreams, I let the grains fall from between my fingers, and what took shape chilled me to the core. The Blood Army marched behind Rowan, her face a thing of fury. Then, from behind the red mist, another large group of nightmares broke away, veering right while Rowan kept left.

"She knows," I breathed. "About the tree. She knows we know." I stared at the dream, hoping for a clue about where the second group was headed. "Where did they go?"

Baku shifted his feet nervously and gave a small shrug.

My stomach twisted. One battalion to protect the stump,

another to hunt Nora down. That's what made sense. I would've done the same thing in Rowan's position. "We have to find Nora. *Now*." And warn Kail. If he was going back to the Blood Tower alone, he might run into them before he got there.

"Katie." I put my hands on her shoulders. "Stay here as long as you want—Baku will stay with you. When you're ready to leave, all you have to do is wake up."

She looked up at me with wide eyes. "Tell me she's going to be okay."

"It's Nora." I did my best to smile reassuringly, but my entire being screamed in terror. "She'll always be okay."

Katie glanced over at Nora's drawings again and winced. "You better hurry."

Chapter Twenty-Five

Nora

Halven stopped at the edge of a black and white floor caked with dried muck. With no walls around the tiled area, a breeze sent dry leaves rustling across the surface. I gagged at the pungent scent of rotting meat that it brought along with it and swatted at the swarm of tiny flies that greeted us. Couldn't Detective Bell have been afraid of kittens or something? A rhythmic thwacking drew my attention to the table in the center of the floor. A squat, wrinkled nightmare with green skin and no nose stood on a tall stool. His long, pointed ears shook with each thud of his meat cleaver. Blood splattered around him as he hacked at what looked like ribs. Entrails, piles of skin, and fur covered nearly every inch of the table, and unidentifiable liquid dripped from the edges.

"That's disgusting," I said from behind my hand.

Halven shrugged and pointed to the far end of the table. I squinted, and a human figure took shape near the table leg. A large man with dark skin was gagged and bound to the blood-slick wood.

"Detective Bell." I let out a relieved breath. "Thanks, Halven."

"I'm at your service, Lady," he rasped.

The Weaver had used Detective Bell against me before, so I didn't see a reason not to use him for a bit of good now. He said he was sorry, and I believed he meant it. Maybe he felt guilty enough that I shouldn't feel bad for hijacking his body. Either way, this was my only feasible option. I needed Bell in particular. My parents knew him, trusted him, and I doubted they were aware that he was no longer a detective. In fact, I was banking on it.

Darkness swelled in my chest. It was probably dangerous to try this without any of Kail's instructions, but the grin hadn't let me down yet. I had to trust my power. Trust myself. Besides, Kail's *instructions* were basically to toss a problem at me and wait to see if I sank or swam.

"Lady?" Halven asked, concerned.

I brought my head up, shoulders squared. "Wait here. We'll go back to the Blood Tower when I'm finished."

I called upon every ounce of confidence I had and strode out to the table. *Please don't be one of Rowan's.* But Halven was with me. I trusted him at least this much.

The nightmare looked up from his work to reveal pupil-less white eyes covered in pulsating blue veins. "Lady Nightmare," he said in a high, shocked voice. "I didn't do it!"

"Do what?" I asked suspiciously.

"Anything." He blinked rapidly. "I swear it."

Halven stepped up behind me, and I let out a breath. "Watch him," I told Halven in a low voice, then nodded at Bell. "I need to borrow your Dreamer."

"But I'm hungry," the nightmare whined like a small child.

"I'll give him back when I'm finished. It won't take long."

"Yes, Lady." He pouted. "Thank you, Lady."

I knelt in front of Bell and picked at the knotted rope around his wrists. He shrieked and thrashed at the touch. "Enough," I shouted. "Relax. It's Nora."

"Nora?" His pupils blew wide as he focused on my face. "Run! Run before he catches you."

My hands stilled, the knot still intact, and I sat back on my haunches. There wasn't time to chase Bell all over the Nightmare Realm. This would have to happen here. With a deep breath— one I instantly regretted making this close to the spoiled meat— I reached inward toward the grin. It was waiting for me, lips curled in contemplation, and a wisp of black guided my hand until my pointer finger pressed against Bell's forehead. His mind exploded through me. Every fear, every want, all spread out before me like a buffet on Halloween. Only, instead of chocolate severed fingers and ghost-shaped Peeps, they were the real thing. I gasped at the shock of it all, but the darkness urged me onward. Deeper and deeper. Until I came to a small orb of glowing light.

Take it, the grin seemed to say.

I wrapped my fingers around the gentle warmth, and the ground fell out from beneath me. My body felt as if it was expanding. Changing. Rational thought came and went. Up and down. Side-to-side. Dizziness dug its claws in deep. Then it stopped in an instant, a head-on collision at eighty miles an hour. My neck whipped back. My ears rang so loudly I felt it echoing in my skull. I sat up gingerly and massaged my head. Only it wasn't *my* head. Not unless someone had shaved it in the last sixty seconds, and if that was the case, there were going to be *big* problems.

But it only took a moment to understand I wasn't in the Nightmare Realm. Instead, I was in a room lit only by a small television atop a dresser. A striped comforter covered the lower half of my body. No, not mine. Bell's. I did it. I was in. I flexed his hands, testing out the motions, and the mattress shifted beside me.

"What's wrong, baby?" A dark-skinned woman, her hair covered with a colorful scarf, leaned up on one elbow, frantically blinking the sleep away.

"Nothing," Bell—I—said. The darkness guided me from beneath the covers. Coaxing—but not forcing—his actions so they seemed natural. "Just a bad dream."

"I told you not to watch that movie before bed," she half-mumbled, rolling back onto her side.

I padded across the room and grabbed a pair of pants from the back of a chair. I stood back and let the grin do the work as it led him through the steps of making himself presentable.

"What are you doing?" the woman asked.

"I'm going to take a drive," I said, Bell's voice robotic. "Clear my head."

The woman didn't say anything else after that, and within five minutes, I was driving to my house in a silver sedan.

I stole glances in the rearview mirror every so often. His facial expression remained blank the entire trip, and the grin kept trying to poke at his thoughts. *No.* I snapped the unspoken order at it. This already felt uncomfortable—I didn't need to know Bell's deepest, darkest secrets. I wondered if he was aware of what I was doing or if it felt like a dream. Maybe neither. Maybe he would have flashes of this later and wonder, like he seemed to with what happened before.

I parked his car in my driveway, walked to my door, and knocked. Panic burst in my chest, and I scrambled to back away. To exit Bell's head. Suddenly, I didn't want to do this. To see them. But the grin held tight as Paul answered the door. His mouth parted, and he stared for what seemed like an eternity before slipping outside. "Detective." He closed the door with a soft thud. "Tell me you're not here for the reason I think you are."

"What reason would that be?" I pressed. The darkness seemed to shush me.

Paul paled. "A homicide detective shows up in the middle of the night while my daughter is missing—"

"No, no," I said. "Nora's fine."

Paul blew out a breath. "Come in. My wife will want to talk to you."

Ha! My mother had threatened him with a lawyer the last time he had me at the station. But the grin ignored me, and I followed Paul into the living room. Everything was in perfect order which somehow made seeing my house again worse. My favorite blanket was folded over the back of the couch and the dancing stuffed turkey remained at the center of the coffee table even though it was well into December now. The automatic air freshener periodically spritzed a pumpkin spice scent into the air. Usually by now, the tree would be up in the corner and our stockings would be tacked up above the television. Seeing the house Thanksgiving-ready, like it was when I left, was a gut-punch.

"Val?" Paul paused at the top of the stairs. "Can you come down here a minute?" I heard my mother mumble a reply, then Paul turned back to me. "Would you like a cup of coffee?"

I shook my head just as my mother appeared at the top of the stairs in holey sweats and a stained sweater. Her hair was matted with grease, and I swore it had thinned since I left. Her dead gaze found mine, and she started down the staircase like a zombie. The closer she got, the more the shock wore off, and I realized that she was wearing *my* sweater. One I wore to bed a lot during the winter, printed with the words 'I don't do mornings'. Except when I left, it was in much better shape. Had she been living in it? I sneered at the thought. Clutched in her hand was a small stuffed bear my dad gave me when I was little that I hadn't seen in years. If only she had held me as close.

"You remember Detective Bell, don't you?" Paul said gently.

"Hello," I said. "I have some good news and some bad news, if you'd like to come sit down."

"Good news?" My mother perked up and rushed into the living room. "You found Nora?"

I nodded. "She called the precinct from a restricted number when she found out you reported her missing. She's safe in Nevada with a friend."

"A friend? What friend?" She twisted to look at Paul with wild eyes. "She doesn't know anyone in Nevada."

"Is it her boyfriend, Ben?" Paul asked. "Have you found him yet?"

Ah, crap. I hadn't thought about the fact that the Sandman wouldn't be Day Walking anymore. Of course they would think he was either with me or guilty of something. Probably the latter, in my mother's case, since she liked to believe the worst of everyone. "They're together," the grin made me say.

"She wouldn't do this to me," my mom insisted, nearing hysterics. "There's no reason for them to run off together. We never stopped them from being together. Why would she—"

"Mom." Katie rushed down the stairs, glaring at Bell as if she knew, or at least suspected, it wasn't really him. "It's true. Nora called me too."

Paul shifted to address Katie. "She called you? When?"

"Tonight. I was going to tell you." The lies rolled easily off Katie's tongue. "She wanted you to know that she loves you and she's sorry."

My mother leapt to her feet and began pacing. "Send someone to bring her back. She's a minor."

"I'm afraid it's not as simple as that," I said.

"Maybe we should go to Nevada and talk to her face-to-face," Paul suggested.

"You're right." My mother squeezed the tiny bear so hard I expected its head to pop off. "I'll pack right now. We'll catch the next flight out and talk some sense into her."

"Mom," Katie implored. "We can't just show up and hope we stumble into her. She wouldn't tell me where she was staying, let alone what city she's in. It's a big state."

"Your sister lied about an internship and then took off in the middle of the night with her boyfriend. I'm going to track her down and drag her back by her ears if it's the last thing I do," my mother insisted and headed for the stairs. "I don't care if I have to comb every square inch of Nevada to do it."

"Katie's right, Val," Paul said. "Please think about this. We should go, but only once we have a plan in place." Paul followed her up the stairs, his voice fading away.

Katie stepped closer to me and narrowed her eyes. "Nora didn't call, did she?"

"Of course she did," the grin insisted, though I didn't know why it bothered.

"Liar." Katie waved a hand through the air to cut off any forthcoming denial. "I don't know what's going on here, but I do know where she is. If you talk to her again, tell her that Rowan knows, and she's marching."

My breath caught. *How?* How did Rowan know? How far was she from the Keep? I pressed forward to beg for details, but the darkness was faster. "Who is Rowan?"

"I hope Nora gets there first," Katie said with a knowing scowl.

The grin flew into action, sending Bell's body racing back to his car. The tires squealed as I sped away from my house. I took corners so fast the vehicle nearly tipped, and at the first red light, I slammed the car into park. The darkness pulled back, and I struggled to hold on. I couldn't leave him in his car in the middle of the street—a million things could happen after I let go. But the grin bared its teeth, insistent.

In the next moment, I was back in the Nightmare Realm beside an unconscious Bell. I sucked in a breath, my heart pounding a mile a minute. There was no time—he was on his own now. I stood and wheeled on Halven. "We have to hurry."

"Goodbye, Lady." The green creature resumed his chopping, but I blocked it out.

Rowan knows. There was only one thing Katie could've meant.

"She knows we're going for the tree." I looked at up at Halven and knew that behind his mask, his face reflected my own fear. "We have to get there first."

"Kail—"

Kail. He could handle himself, but I needed that army. Just in case. I held my hand out. "It's too far to walk. Do the thing you did to me at the Doll Maker's."

Halven didn't hesitate as he clasped my hand and sped us back to the Blood Tower.

Chapter Twenty-Six

Nora

The Blood Army's moans filled the courtyard of the tower and carried into the neighboring tundra where Halven and I stopped. Rocks rolled away from the sound, bumping into each other, into us, with tiny, surprised *oofs*. Small pixie-like nightmares dressed in furs fled from patches of dried grass, filling the air like a swarm of dragonflies, tiny sacks in their arms. Halven and I stood there in mutual terror.

"This isn't right," I breathed. It didn't make sense. Why would Rowan be *here*? If she thought I was heading for her tree, what purpose would she have coming to the Blood Tower? "Where is the army? Why aren't they doing something?"

Halven shook his head.

"'No' what?" I whisper-yelled.

He pointed to the top of the tower where a plume of red mist billowed upward. "You don't have one anymore," he croaked.

"No. No, no, no. They can't *all* be dead." There were so many—and the Blood Army was the main force I expected to face. My army should've been prepared to fight them. My mouth ran dry, and I stepped forward. Halven put his arm out to stop me. "We have to do *something*," I insisted.

But what could we do? My army was dead. And Kail—no. There was no way he was dead too. The army may not have been ready, but he always was. He was the king of hidey-holes and escape routes. A virtual Houdini. The Blood Tower probably had more hidden passages than Paris had Catacomb tunnels.

A scream rose above the low moaning, and the familiarity of it cut me in two. *Oh. Oh, no.* Kail was alive... but he hadn't escaped. After the quaking pain of his cry, I wasn't sure if I should be glad he was still breathing.

Halven was the one to step forward this time, but I dug my fingers into his forearm. "I know another way inside." His chest rose and fell with heavy, labored breaths, but that was the only part of him to move. "Come on, before it's too late."

That got his attention, and he locked my hand in a death grip. "Where?" The question was harsher than usual.

"There's a hidden door beneath all those teeth on the—"

We were running then, faster than ever before. The wind stung my eyes, and each inhale felt like I was suffocating, but the discomfort was nothing compared to the gut-wrenching fear. It was like thinking the Sandman was dead all over again. Like turning on that lamp in Emery's living room and knowing what I would find when I looked up. I shouldn't care if Kail lived or died. What I *should* be doing was racing to the trees while I knew Rowan was occupied. But maybe she wasn't. Maybe someone else led the Blood Army here. I shook my head. It didn't matter who was hurting Kail—it only mattered that I stop them.

A blanket of teeth crunched beneath our feet. If one didn't look too closely, they could be mistaken for pebbles ranging from the whitest of whites to yellow to black. "The door is—"

I took a shuddering breath and tried to regulate my breathing. To calm down. Focus. It was buried somewhere near the center, but I hadn't been paying much attention when Kail and I escaped the fiery attack. Halven and I didn't have time to dig through this entire place, so I jabbed at the grin. It popped open with impatience. I let go completely, and the darkness urged me forward. "Here," I shouted, and fell to my knees a few paces away.

Halven joined me, and we scooped handfuls of teeth out of the way. Some of them still had bloody roots attached, others slimy with what I assumed was saliva. The small piece of rope finally appeared. Halven wrenched the hatch upward and a shower of teeth flew into the air. More funneled into the dark opening with a chorus of tiny pings. I jumped inside, teeth pelting my head, catching in my hair, with Halven right behind me.

The door slammed shut, casting us in darkness, but my feet moved as confidently as if the tunnel was brightly lit. The walls stretched out in front of me as solid shadows, and Halven's outline was perfectly clear against the grey haze. Another scream echoed somewhere overhead. I shivered, my fury needing an outlet, and ran.

"I can't reach," I huffed when we reached the overhead

door.

Halven reached up and paused to let out a long, shaky breath. Then he eased the trap door open a crack. After what felt like an eternity of him looking into the room above, he lifted it open the rest of the way and climbed out. A moment later, he reached down for my hand, swinging me up with graceful ease. I shook teeth from my hair. Focus. I had to focus. There was no telling how many things were lurking inside the tower right now.

A loud thud bounced down the hallway. "Where is she?" Rowan shrieked.

Her voice slithered over me, blinding me with rage, and I barreled from the room. I didn't think. Didn't pause for a moment. The blackest part of me ruled my movements, and I let it take me straight to Rowan's old room. What I found inside had my own lips mimicking the grin's internal sneer. Rowan's burnt wings blocked the doorway, but between the charred branches, I saw Kail, bloodied and broken on the floor.

"Just kill me," he wheezed, blood gushing from his mouth.

"You'd like that, wouldn't you?" Rowan growled.

She bent and grabbed Kail's chin. Her touch ripped a cry from his throat and brought every scream I'd ever heard crashing through me. Starting with Katie's. Ending with my own. No more—there would be no more screaming because of me.

"I'm right here," I said in a deadly voice.

Rowan whipped around, her red-flecked eyes wide. "Dream Keeper. I was looking for you," she said confidently.

"Oh." I released a mirthless laugh. "I think you mean *Lady Nightmare*, though I'm not sure how you could make that mistake. This is your fault, after all."

Her expression tightened. "You left the Nightmare Realm

before I could congratulate you."

"*Kill* me. I left before you could kill me. We're past pretending otherwise."

My gaze slid to Kail, his head hanging in defeat, and anger roared in my ears. *End her now*, the grin demanded. Energy crackled over my skin, and I lunged. Mindless. Unseeing. My body was a wild, reckless blur of magic. I was in the backseat, watching myself move with an ease that couldn't be taught. My shoulder slammed into Rowan's chest, and she tumbled backward into the giant bed.

But instead of yielding, she gave me a predatory smile. "The Weaver's magic has done wonders for you." *Imagine what it could do for me.* She didn't say it, but the thought hung in the air between us.

Until I smashed through it, fists flying.

They each met her face with a sickening crunch, and the sureness faded from her eyes. My next blow met her palm. Her fingers dug into the back of my hand, and the blazing pain had me crawling back into the driver's seat. A scream built rapidly in my chest, and it wouldn't be long before it escaped. Whatever force oversaw my body slammed down on the gas pedal. My body moved without my mind, twisting and turning in ways neither the Sandman nor Kail had ever trained me. I tried to stop it. To move another way. *Any* way that would show I still had control.

But nothing worked.

Rowan was off me. My hands were around her throat, and the pain registered behind a brick wall. She slammed me into one of the Keep's walls. Her wings rose higher. Shifted. The tips pointed at me. And then Rowan screeched.

With her grip loosened, I scrambled away, gasping for air, and my limbs slowly returned to me. *What was that?* My heart became heavier with each beat. Kail stood in the center of the room with half of Rowan's right wing in his hands, and Halven slipped in front of his brother in a protective stance. My mind scrambled to find a solution, but my thoughts were twisted with the agony of Rowan's touch. I was just now able to feel the terror at having my body stolen away.

Rowan shot to her feet. I punched her again. She sailed sideways, her head cracking against the wall, and slumped to the floor, knocked out.

"Tie her up somewhere before she regains consciousness," I croaked to Halven. He was covered from head to toe, making him the only one of us who could safely touch her. I needed a minute to still my shaking body and relearn how to move properly. "Then find me something to kill her with."

Halven nodded and swept across the room, where he gripped Rowan by the crown of raven beaks adhered to the top of her head, dragging her from the room. Her intact wing snagged on the door frame. With one swift kick from Halven, the offending piece of burnt branch crumbled into ash, and the two of them disappeared down the hall. And, just like that, I was alone with Kail. Without a single idea of what to say or how to act.

"You're picking up on the whole grand entrance thing," Kail said after a long, heavy moment. "I had ideas on how to teach you that particular skill, but I suppose this will have to do."

I cut him a sharp look. "You're welcome."

"For?" he asked in a pained voice.

"Saving your life."

He laughed and slid down the wall to sit beside me. *When had I sat down?* "I'm pretty sure *I* saved *your* life," he said lightly.

"What?" I blurted, and he tossed the broken branch at our feet. "That doesn't count. Halven and I didn't have to sneak in here, you know. We could've let Rowan kill you and gone for the stump instead."

"*You* didn't have to save me, true." He sighed and dabbed carefully at his bruising jaw.

I opened my mouth to say I should've let him die but swallowed the words. Kail's cheek was already swelling, and there was a huge dent in the mask above his right temple. Each shallow breath ended with a crackle. Bones in one of his hands jutted out at unnatural angles, and scratches marked the side of his neck—yet still he hadn't told Rowan where I was. My note hadn't been very specific, of course, but he could've told her that I would be back. To hide and ambush me when I walked through the door. There had to be a million ways to double-cross me just waiting inside his head.

I cleared my throat and shifted to kneel in front of him. "This doesn't change anything," I said carefully. "If you told me about the tree sooner, none of this would've happened."

He gave me a sad smile. "I didn't protect you to change anything."

"Then why? You could've easily played your cards to save yourself."

"I told you." He coughed and clutched at his ribs. "I have my reasons."

I rolled my eyes. "When I got here, you said these ulterior motives of yours depended on my humanity, which I assume means you'll want a favor one day. You might as well fess up while I'm feeling generous."

He closed his eyes and licked the corner of his cracked lip. "Perceptive."

When he didn't elaborate, I bit down on my tongue. *Later.* When Rowan wasn't tied up in the other room—when she was dead. "I need gloves. And a turtleneck, maybe. Does your brother have spare masks lying around?"

Kail cracked his eyes open, unamused. "Do you have spare faces lying around?"

I opened my mouth, only to shut it again. *Touché.* "Are you going to help me kill her or not? I need to be able to touch her without worrying about her shredding my insides again."

"I'm afraid I'll have to sit this one out." He winced. "But you're welcome to raid my closet for gloves. Or, you know, take the easy route and use the gun in your bag."

"You went through my stuff?" I shouted. Lies. Snooping. More lies. It shouldn't surprise me, but he'd made such a big deal out of my trusting him. And he'd actually succeeded to a degree. I stared at him as his muscles twitched beneath his skin, and my anger left in a whoosh. He bore the pain well—well enough that I knew it wasn't his first rodeo. After decades—maybe longer— at Rowan's side, how could it be? He deserved to watch her die. I licked my lips. If I could heal Four, I could heal him too. I pressed my hand against his chest before I could change my mind.

Kail jerked. "What are you doing?"

"Shut up," I snapped, then called on the grin.

It unfurled, and the magic flowed from my fingertips, finding Kail's knotted thread without a drop of effort. The thread throbbed against the magic, and the grin did the work, as always.

It tucked gold fibers back in place, smoothed down snagged bits, and molded it all back into a neat ball. Except for the frayed end—that still dangled helplessly. I nudged the magic at it, but Kail pushed my hand away.

"Not that," he said hoarsely.

I looked him in the eyes and startled. His blue eye flashed colors in unison with the other. "Your eye is better," I whispered.

"About time," he muttered, though he couldn't seem to help the boyish glint that surfaced in his irises. He stood. "Come on, Lady."

He was halfway through the door before I climbed to my feet. "Kail?"

"What?" he asked without turning around.

"You said I could've left you here to die…" I chewed my bottom lip for a moment. It wasn't what he said, but how he said it. "Why couldn't Halven have done the same?"

"Ah." He cracked his knuckles. "Careful, Lady. You might stumble upon all my secrets."

"Something tells me *you* don't even know them all," I joked.

"You might be right," he said with a laugh as he stepped into the hallway. "Let's go. You've got a murder to commit."

Murder. The word twisted my gut. I knew it was what I was going to do—what I had already done. On top of torture. But it didn't feel right to be so numb to it. I winced. Now was not a good time to regain my conscience. Rowan had to be dealt with while I had the chance, so I stood tall and followed Kail.

Outside, the Blood Army's moaning took on a deeper note, and I glanced out the nearest window. Each robed figure drifted toward the same point, circling their unseen prey. *No.* Deal with Rowan first, the Blood Army second. Whatever nightmare they were attacking was—

"Sandman?" His name left my tongue before I could stop it.

Kail leaned back on his heel to follow my gaze. "Ah. Don't worry. He can handle himself."

"Don't worry?" It felt as if I were the one out there, surrounded by the enemy. "He can't possibly take that many on by himself."

Kail snorted. "Looks like he's doing fine to me."

A silver tornado made of sand blew a path through the onslaught. Still, my heart raced. I remembered exactly how that mist felt. The Sandman needed help. The grin puckered in obvious denial at the idea of assistance.

"I may have told him you were missing," Kail admitted, nonplussed.

"I wasn't missing." I sucked in a breath. "Wait—you what? How? When?"

He shrugged. "I got your note and assumed you'd be there."

I gripped the windowsill. "So you what? Went to drag me back?"

"Oh, I don't think the Sandman would've let me drag you anywhere. You, on the other hand…" He winked and pressed a stone in the wall to open a hidden door.

"Not another step," Rowan ordered from inside.

I froze, a million curses on my tongue. Halven's back was pressed against Rowan's front, a long, jagged piece of her broken wing pressed against his throat. Before I could move, before I could speak, Kail let out a low wail at the sight of his brother in danger. "Don't," he pleaded. The word was brittle and desperate, and it nearly ruined me hearing it from him.

"I could do it," Rowan said. "Take you both out, then the

girl. But the Sandman is another story."

"Rowan." Kail sounded small. Lost. "Please."

"Send the Dream Keeper in, and I'll let him go."

Kail shook with fear, or maybe anger, but he didn't move. I shoved him aside. Despite the ruffles around Halven's neck, Rowan's weapon placement was perfect.

"Let him go," I demanded.

Rowan dug the tip in a little deeper, but Halven didn't move a muscle. "You're not in any place to be making demands."

"Nora," Kail begged. "Let her go."

"*What?*" I spun on him. "Are you kidding me? This is the moment we've been training for."

He shook his head. "Let her walk out of here. Promise the Sandman won't touch her on the way out, and maybe she'll let us all live to fight another day."

"I'd much rather see you all dead," Rowan snapped.

All of us.

Kail and Halven wouldn't matter much to the Dream Lord fighting an army singlehandedly, but I would. And no matter what he believed about the balance, the Sandman would never let anyone get away with killing me.

"You could kill us all," I agreed slowly. "But then you would die too. What you didn't see inside the Keep the day I killed the Weaver was that I died too." Not true, of course, though it felt like I had. The words flowed so easily, it didn't feel like a lie. "The magic killed me and then brought me back as this. So I suppose the question you need to ask yourself is whether or not you would have time to be reborn before the Sandman finds you."

She hesitated. The grin inside me gnashed against my self-constraint. *End her, end her, end her*, it chanted. Let Halven die. Let anyone die, as long as she did too. Now. While she was in the Blood Tower. Trapped. Alone. Vulnerable.

"You'll never survive this realm," Rowan spat, holding Halven against her chest. They moved toward us in unison without her hand leaving the weapon. "Every day you breathe is another day borrowed."

I shrugged, feigning confidence. "Take it up with my bank."

"Move," she insisted. "I'll release him when I'm outside."

Don't you dare, the grin warned me, but the desperate look on Kail's face as he obeyed was enough for me. This wasn't letting Rowan escape—this was saving Kail's brother. This was earning the loyalty he had given me. *No.* More than that. This was a way to keep my humanity in a place built for the inhumane.

We followed Rowan all the way to the front door as she used Halven as a human shield. "I know you think you've figured out how to win," she said, slipping the door open with her heel. "But you'll never succeed."

"We'll see," I vowed.

Rowan shoved Halven toward us a split second before the door slammed between us. I bolted around the brothers and threw it open again, but she was already halfway across the tundra, surrounded by what was left of the Blood Army. The ones the Sandman managed to kill lay scattered around the tower, their bodies slowly evaporating into red mist. There was no getting past it—we were trapped until the bodies finished decomposing unless we wanted to be boiled alive.

"Rowan," I screamed so loud my throat burned.

Mistake, the grin chastised. *Big, big mistake.*

It wasn't wrong.

Chapter Twenty-Seven

Nora

The steady thud of a meat cleaver greeted me, followed immediately by the stench of what could only be a dozen corpses. They were skinned and chopped into large sections, rotting away on a tall table. I held my breath as I approached a small green nightmare standing on a stool beside the table. "Where is she?" I demanded, the sense of déjà vu not lost on me.

The creature didn't bother to look up from his work. "Who, Dream Lord?"

"You know who."

"She left." He paused to slide a pile of rancid meat across the table and resumed chopping. "Needed to borrow my Dreamer, then took off in a bit of a hurry."

"Your Dreamer?" I asked, confused. The nightmare nodded to the other end of the table, and I picked my way closer, avoiding the thick liquid dripping to the floor. My eyes widened. "Detective Bell?" The Dreamer muttered incoherently as his eyes darted around behind his lids.

"She broke him," the nightmare complained. "He's not scared anymore, but he won't wake up either."

I pressed my fingers against his throat to find a pulse. It was barely there, unsteady and fading. "What happened?"

"Don't ask me." He waved his knife at Bell and kept talking. "The Lady took him sleepwalking and stayed in his head the whole time. Fried his brain, I suppose, but he'll still make for some tasty meat. Chop him up and—"

I tuned the nightmare out and stared at Bell. Sleepwalking was foreign to me. The *how* of it. The Weaver never stayed. He went in, did whatever brainwashing he had to do, and got out. Anything could've happened inside Bell's head while Nora was in there. "I'm sorry," I whispered. Hopefully, he would wake up with no lasting effects. I reached for my satchel. After everything he'd been through, starting with the Weaver's first murder, he deserved the peace of the Dream Realm.

 Blood bubbled from Bell's mouth. His head fell back, and his eyes rolled so far back all I could see were their whites.

"No fair," the nightmare cried.

I gripped my sand, but in the next moment, Bell vanished. "*No!*"

"She didn't say she was going to kill him," the nightmare whined to itself.

I leveled a stare at the creature, my heart thumping wildly. "Which way did Nora go?"

"Not sure. Halven took her," he said, pouting.

I reached out with my magic until I found Nora's. That way. *The Blood Tower.* She was on her way back to the very place Rowan would expect to find her. A low, frustrated scream lodged in my throat. Until this was over, Nora had to stop taking off without thinking, and we needed to know where she was. All of us—me, Kail, Baku, Halven. As unlikely as it was, we were working together toward the same goal of putting Nora in her rightful place. While I understood her desire to figure herself out, she needed to believe in us. Not even I was delusional enough to think I didn't need help from time to time. I didn't *like* needing someone like Kail to watch Nora's back, but what I liked made no difference.

With a shallow breath, I forced myself to stand and move in the direction of Nora's power. I ran a hand through my hair, holding it off my forehead. My jaw ached as I clenched it shut. I was angry with Nora, but I should be even angrier. It wasn't possible though. She was in a bad place right now and doing what she thought was best, even if she was actually selecting the worst option. I kept telling myself during my entire journey through the Nightmare Realm.

When I reached the Blood Tower, I froze, my heart dropping. Whatever I expected to see at the Blood Tower, it wasn't this. Rowan was supposed to be marching the Blood Army to defend her tree stump. That's what made sense. The second set of nightmares should've come here, not Rowan herself. Nora could already be halfway across the Nightmare Realm for all Rowan knew. So why?

But Nora wasn't halfway anywhere—she was inside. Her anger raked along my mental wall like thorns. Fighting the entire

Blood Army wasn't at the top of my to-do list, but there was no getting around them. I stayed away from Nora all this time and still it came down to this. There would be ways to fix her image later if she survived. I steeled myself for what had to be done, and *only* what had to be done. If I held back now, Rowan might not realize I'd regained my strength until it was too late. She had already underestimated me once when she took me to the Keep.

The weary, heartsick boy in me had no place here so I looked across the tundra through the eyes of the Lord of Dreams. I registered everything with lightning precision. Tower entrances, Blood Army weaknesses, numbers, the density of the red mist. Alone it meant nothing. Together, it gave me an exact plan of attack. I took my gloves from my belt and shoved my hands inside to protect my skin.

"Forgive me, Nora," I said without an ounce of apology and snapped my hood up.

As I ran toward the tower, I felt nothing. Not the anger and vengeance I felt when I scoured the Nightmare Realm for Nora the first time. Not worry for her wellbeing because she already had help—and her own strength. I didn't even feel the burn of the army's mist where it snuck into the crevices of my clothing. I felt nothing except perhaps resignation. This wasn't Nora and me anymore. This was Dream and Nightmare. Day and Night. And it was my duty to protect all of it.

The Blood Army drifted toward me as a unit, circling me. I poured half of my satchel to the ground by my feet and waited. Waited for them to come closer. To press together into a tighter pack. Then I swept my arm out. A tornado ripped through their ranks, snuffing them out. The other robed figures wailed and pressed forward to fill in the gaps.

"I don't have time for this," I mumbled and lifted my hand again.

Only, my arm froze midair. Rowan's red silk gown caught my eye from the doorway. She hugged Halven to her chest, a jagged stick in her hand. I noticed right away a large portion of her wings were missing. The Army swiveled away from me, moving toward her instead. I regained myself and threw my hand out to make another twister. More figures fell, but not enough. The door slammed shut. Rowan was alone. And running. The Blood Army circled her, their mist seeming to propel her faster and faster. I took two steps when Nora's voice cut through me.

Her scream was for Rowan, but it obliterated my sense of nothingness. It felt as if my heart started beating anew, and my stomach dropped. *I'm in trouble.* How could I be what the universe needed if, even in these circumstances, Nora filled my every breath? Unfortunately, there was no cure for love. Not that I would take it if there were.

"Sandman," Nora called, waving me forward.

I jerked, and the first true blast of pain went straight through me. Red mist rose through the entire courtyard, higher and higher, as the bodies evaporated. I rushed from the carnage and over the threshold before any of the blistering cloud could make it inside. The door barely shut behind me before Nora's arms wrapped around my middle.

"Hi," she breathed.

"Hi." I melted into her, my anxiety falling away. "Are you okay?"

"Fine." She stepped back and cleared her throat. "We're all fine."

"What are you doing here?" Kail's two flashing eyes scanned

me critically.

I pushed my hood off and glared at him. When had she fixed him? Last I knew, she was fuming over his earlier omission and refusing to make his requested repairs. "Finding Nora," I said simply.

"You were supposed to check between here and the trees," he said grumpily.

"Obviously she wasn't there," I snapped.

"Enough. Let's all take a minute. Or five," Nora said. She eyed the red mist pressing against the windowpane. "We're clearly not going anywhere right now."

"The tunnel—" Kail started.

"Five minutes," she barked. "Then we'll meet in the room with the clock to make a plan."

I watched her walk away, shoulders squared, and instantly knew how she was going to spend that time. It made sense that she would want to hide her weakness from Kail and Halven, but was I included now? Would she still allow me to see her vulnerability? I wasn't brave enough to find out. But, in those minutes, Nora was going to crumble under pressure only to pull herself together, stronger than before.

"She's stalling," Kail said with a sigh.

Halven shook his head. "Our lady is right. Without a plan, we're going into a fight blinded by hatred."

"We need options." I massaged my temples. "You have five minutes to fill me in about this tunnel."

Kail studied me for a long moment, then led the way into the tower.

Chapter Twenty-Eight

Nora

We were not trapped in this forsaken tower of death. I refused to allow it. But no matter what part of the Blood Tower I touched, it was the only knot I could feel. Nothing beyond the walls, nothing within them. Some part of me knew it wouldn't be possible to change anything without touching it, but I couldn't help trying. The grin turned smug, and I punched the nearest surface, which happened to be a decorative metal sculpture that spiraled up from the floor. My knuckles throbbed, the skin peeling away, and the grin seemed to chuckle.

"Fine," I whispered at it. "Do you have a solution?"

Silence.

Of course.

Because the grin wasn't an actual, physical thing—it was just part of the magic. It didn't have a mind of its own even if it felt like it sometimes. *Okay.* Think. Rowan came here believing she had the upper hand. I was sure she didn't expect things to go as they did, so what would her backup plan be? Retreat to the tree? Plan another ambush?

"Hey." Kail poked the back of my head. "When you say five minutes, do you usually mean twenty?"

I whipped around. "Oh, I'm sorry. Did you have somewhere else to be?"

"It would be good to know for future reference," he said.

"Bold of you to assume we'll have a future." What did I know about any of this? I was a seventeen-year-old high school drop out from the Day World. My biggest problems should be picking out the perfect prom dress, studying for the SAT, and applying to colleges I didn't want to attend, but no. Instead, I had to become an expert at strategy so I could plot the death of my mortal enemy. I shouldn't even *have* a mortal enemy.

Kail rolled his eyes. "Everyone's waiting to hash out our next move."

There was no more stalling. No more hiding. I stared down the grin, letting my resentment harden my nerves, and joined the others. Halven stood in front of his clock and the Sandman sat on one end of the sofa, pinching the bridge of his nose. He smiled when I walked through the door, and I couldn't help but return it. *God.* He was the most beautiful man in existence. It was all I could do not to bury myself in him right there in front of the brothers.

"It takes about six hours for the bodies to disappear and the mist to dissipate," Kail said. "Are you sure you don't want to take the tunnel?"

"Can Halven whisk us all across the Nightmare Realm at once?" I asked. Halven shook his head without looking away from the symbols.

"It would take longer to go through the tunnel and backtrack in the direction of the trees than it would to wait," the Sandman said, his tone dry. He had probably told them the same thing a dozen times while they waited for me.

"It would take the same amount of time," Kail corrected.

Anger flared inside me, and I said, "In that case, there's really no benefit to leaving just now."

"Let's not get sidetracked," the Sandman said and placed his hands on his knees. "It doesn't matter how we get there—it matters what we do after."

I took a seat beside him, careful to avoid physical contact. We needed to focus on the plan, and if I touched him, I would give into the urge to fold myself into him. To soak up the warmth, the love, of him instead of feeling like a rock plunked into dark, icy water.

"We should all lay our cards on the table first," I said. "There seems to be a lot of things the four of us are sharing with one or two others instead of with the group." Not that we were really a group—more like pairs. Me and the Sandman, Kail and Halven, me and Kail. But we hadn't been a cohesive gathering until now. "I'll start," I added when they were silent. I turned to the Sandman. "Those bruises you saw? I was attacked by one of the Hours, who are also responsible for burning down the tower."

"The Hours?" The Sandman sat up straight. "Rowan has the Hours behind her?"

Kail snorted. "That would make our lives too easy."

"They're upset about Mara," I said, cutting a look at Kail.

"Some more than others," Kail added. "Three wants her dead. Six and Ten want a plan to take care of the problem, or they'll kill her. The others could be anywhere in between."

"If they kill you, they'll be the new Weaver," the Sandman stated.

"Not sure they thought the process through," I admitted. "Anyway. Your turn."

The Sandman cocked his head and locked eyes with me. "I don't have any secrets. You know I've been making spies and that I let Rowan capture me. There's nothing else to tell."

My first instinct was to scream *liar*, but while the Sandman hid things sometimes, he didn't lie. Especially not to my face. My heart throbbed painfully with guilt for even thinking it. "Okay." I looked to Kail. "Go ahead. And remember we only have six hours."

He crossed his arms and leaned against the wall beside his brother. "Sure. Believe everyone but me."

Yup. I shrugged. "I'll always believe the Sandman, and I haven't asked Halven yet."

"Kail and I will tell you the same thing," Halven supplied in his usual raspy voice. "Forgive me, but it's easier for him to explain."

"Not yet," Kail hissed.

Halven looked away from the clock for the first time. "Then when?" he asked his brother.

"No," I interrupted with finality. "Now is perfect."

Kail shook his head. "You won't agree yet. We still have to prove ourselves."

"Put us back together," Halven blurted so quickly it sounded as if his throat were made of gravel. He coughed and rubbed at his breastbone. "Please, Lady. It hurts to be apart."

Pieces clicked together. The frayed end of Kail's thread, the cryptic answers when it came to Halven. They weren't brothers. They were the same nightmare cut in two. Kail's ulterior motive was to be whole again. Even the grin's lips parted in surprise. I sucked in a breath at the agonized look on Kail's face and Halven's rigid stance. The Weaver wouldn't put them back together because he didn't care how they felt about being apart. That's why he needed my humanity. My heart cracked a little for them both.

"That's why Halven couldn't leave you to die?" I asked in a low voice. "Because if you die, he dies?"

Kail clenched his jaw and nodded once. "Pain aside, I don't particularly like having my biggest weakness wandering the Nightmare Realm alone."

"It's safer to wander than to work with Rowan," Halven said softly.

"I didn't have a choice," Kail snapped, his face instantly red. The break in his voice nearly did me in as he said, "Go ahead, Lady. Get it over with. Tell us you won't help so we can let go of the hope."

The backs of my eyes prickled with tears. *That* was what he wanted. Why he was helping me. I wasn't sure why I felt it so deeply, but it was a weight lifted to know his reasons weren't underhanded. "Of course I will." My voice wavered, and I felt my face flush.

They said nothing, but Kail's eyes fixed on the floor. Had they really thought I wouldn't do it? After all they'd done for me? But an image of Kail's crumbled beak flashed before me, and my ears rang with the fight we had when I found out he knew how to kill Rowan. Why *wouldn't* he expect me to refuse? He betrayed me with the knife many months ago, and he probably only knew the unforgiving nature of the Weaver and Rowan. He was right to want to build loyalty and trust first.

"After," Kail finally said. "When you've got your loom back and have practiced on something else first. It's a lot harder to put things back together than it is to rip them apart."

"Okay," I agreed.

The Sandman reached over and took my hand, squeezing gently. His expression said everything he couldn't say in front of the others, and my heart swelled. *I love you, I love you, I love you.* But also, a painful twist deep beneath that. *You don't deserve him*, it said. And it was right. So, so right. I squeezed his hand back anyway.

"So, where's Rowan?" I asked Halven.

"The trees," he said, pointing. "The Blood Army too."

The Sandman tensed. "I saw what Baku saw—there should be more than the Blood Army with her."

"A few." Halven confirmed.

"Does it say where they went?" The Sandman's violet, starlit eyes scanned the clock almost frantically.

Halven rubbed at his throat. "Who, specifically?"

A crease formed between the Sandman's brows. What had he seen exactly? Another army? "Where's Baku?" I asked, trying not to think about it. One disaster at a time. "Is he going to help?"

"He does what he wants when he wants," the Sandman said in a distant voice.

"Oh, he'll come," Kail said with certainty. "At the end. To eat the corpses."

"We leave when the mist lifts," Halven rasped, steering the

conversation back on track. The four of us exchanged looks and nodded in agreement.

"And when we get there?" I asked.

"We fight," Kail said as if it were obvious.

"This is my first real battle," I said. "I'm going to want to fight with something a little more concrete."

"Trust yourself," the Sandman whispered. "Use what you've learned. Rowan may have nightmares on her side, but they aren't there. Even if they are, they'll switch sides if you give them reason to. Make a show of force."

"And the second you get the chance—" Kail dragged a finger across his throat. "It doesn't matter if it's Rowan or the tree, as long as you take one of them out."

Take one of them out. Right. That was the plan, and yet the action itself always seemed so far away. So *doable*, yet so unreachable. Standing at the starting gate turned out to be a whole other beast. Suddenly, I wasn't sure this was a race I could win. I was *not* ready for this. Not even a little bit. I was nothing more than a puppy who just learned to eat solid food stepping into a fighting pit with the top dog—but what other choice did I have? It didn't matter if I was ready; this was happening, and I was going to win.

I took a fortifying breath. "What about you guys?"

"We'll watch your back." Kail glanced at the clock. "Don't worry. I know all Rowan's tricks. You just worry about killing her and leave the rest to us."

Even now that I had all this magic, her touch was too much. Telling me not to worry was about as helpful as telling water not to be wet. The Sandman ran his thumb over my scraped knuckles, and I jumped.

"Sorry," he whispered. "I didn't mean to hurt you."

"You didn't. I just realized something." I smiled and turned to Kail. "Rowan's clothes?"

"What about them?" he asked, curious.

"Show me where they are."

He shrugged and pushed off the wall.

I moved to follow him into the hall when the Sandman grabbed for my hand again, stopping me in my tracks. "Can I see you later? Alone?"

"Please," I answered, my heart fluttering at the thought, and I gave him a quick kiss.

Maybe we really could win this. Together. All of us.

Chapter Twenty-Nine

The Sandman

This was the first time since I told Nora that I loved her that I was *this* nervous to see her. All our time apart washed away the moment she returned my smile in the sitting room, and holding her hand felt like it did the first time, sparks and all. I had to believe things wouldn't go badly when we left to face Rowan, but if they did—if they did, I wanted her to know how I still felt. I leaned my head on the doorframe of Nora's room and watched her chew her bottom lip as she stared at the clothing scattered over the floor. When she didn't notice me after thirty seconds, I tapped my knuckles on the wood.

Nora jumped at the sound, then smiled as her gaze fell on me. "Hi."

"Hi." I motioned to the heap of fabric. "Need help?"

Nora snorted and pointed to a pile of red silk in the corner. "Raiding Rowan's closet was a flop. All she had were three identical red gowns. I'm trying to decide what will offer the most coverage so she can't touch me, but I guess it doesn't matter what I wear. Nothing here would cover my neck."

"Layers," I suggested.

Nora plucked up a camisole, a t-shirt, and a purple sweater and tossed them onto the bed. "I should've packed some of my scarves," she lamented.

I stepped into the room, closing the door behind me, and took my gloves from my belt. "Here." They were too big for her, but it was better than nothing.

"I can't take those." She climbed to her feet. "You'll need them if you fight the Blood Army."

"You need them more than I do." I took her hand and set them in her palm, holding tight. "How are you?"

"I'm o—"

I silenced her by tracing a line across her forehead. "I mean in here."

Nora's breath caught. "It's like there's another person in there with me sometimes," she admitted with a grimace. "But it's getting better. I just need to get through this, you know?"

"I know." I pulled her against me, and she nuzzled into my chest. "We will."

We clung to each other for what felt like an eternity, silently soaking each other in. It was almost like before. *Almost.* A hint of sulfur clung to the air about her, where before she smelled like autumn giving way to winter—a fresh, crisp scent that was distinctly Nora. It was still there, under everything. All of her was. The Weaver's magic hadn't destroyed her completely, which meant there was hope. Maybe it wouldn't—maybe she really could be both. Her reaction to Kail's secret, that she didn't hesitate to grant their request, proved it.

"Are you sure I should go?" I asked.

She held me a bit tighter. "I'm sure."

"You've come so far without me…"

"I've learned a lot being here." She set her chin on my chest and looked up at me with as much longing in her expression as I felt. "But my head feels messy, so I'm going to listen to something else instead."

"Kail?" I joked.

"Ha-ha." She tapped her fingers over my chest. "My heart."

My own heart swelled painfully. I tried not to think about all the hurt she caused me. This could be our last time together for a while, and I wanted to enjoy it. There was plenty of time for anger later, because Nora would survive this battle if I had to kill Rowan myself—but I wouldn't dredge it all up now. She had to focus on what came next.

"Sandman," she whispered. "Where did you go?"

"What?"

"Just now. You looked like you were a million miles away."

I shook my head.

"We used to talk about everything," she said wistfully. "Now look at us."

"Now isn't the time," I said.

"Now is the only time. If I don't make it back tomorrow, I'll die with a lot of things left unsaid, and I don't want that." It wasn't said with fear, but resolve.

"You're not going to die, Nora," I promised.

"You don't know that." She stepped back suddenly and

covered her face. When her hands dropped, her gold eyes shimmered with tears. "I've done so many horrible things to you, Sandman. Why are you still here?"

I clutched the fabric over my heart. Another blow, though I knew she didn't mean it to be. My love for her was strong enough that I wouldn't walk away instead of trying to work things out. "I promised you that I would be yours no matter what, and I meant it."

"I don't—" She growled wordlessly. "I don't want you to be here because of some promise you made before I lied to you." I stepped forward, but she stepped back, keeping the same amount of distance between us. It sparked a match inside me. "Am I angry? Yes," I said, the words bitter. "But we can talk through it after you've taken your realm. I'm not here because of some sense of obligation. The promise will always be true, no matter how many lies you tell, because I've lied too. For five years, I kept secrets that would eventually destroy your life. *More than your life.* Because of me, there are a lot of devastated people in the Day World right now, and while I can't be sorry for saving the rest of the world, I *am* sorry for the cost. I understand lying when you feel it's the only option for the greater good. You did what you thought you had to do, and I don't blame you for it. I only wish you had *talked* to me instead. That, after everything, you trusted me." My voice cracked. "Have I not always done what you wanted? I admit I was being selfish about you coming back here because I didn't want to lose you, but if you insisted… You had to know I would've brought you here, Nora."

"I'm sorry," she said. Her voice warbled, and she pinched her lips together to stop them from quivering.

"It's not over, you know," I said with an edge. "Learning

who you are. You've barely scratched the surface, so when this is done, I'll give you the space you need."

Tears flooded down her cheeks. "Without you, I'm this other thing, but I don't want to be. I want to keep being Nora."

"You are." And she was. I wanted to believe she would stay that way forever, but some part of me knew she would eventually adapt to her surroundings. Maybe not to the extent the Weaver had, but enough. Besides, she was young. It was natural she would grow and change.

She shook her head and fell to her knees. "I'm sorry. This wasn't supposed to be about me. When you asked to see me, I wanted to apologize about everything, but especially—" She paused and wiped her face off. "Especially that last night in the Day World."

"You needed to distract me," I said and swallowed a lump in my throat.

"No." She winced. "No, that wasn't why. You said you were selfish for keeping me in the Day World because you didn't want to lose me. I didn't want to lose you either. And, before you say it, I know logically that I wouldn't have, but I stopped thinking logically a long time ago. I knew what it meant to you, but I didn't let it stop me. So just hate me, okay? I need you to hate me."

My heart broke for us both. Its contents were a swirling mass of anger and sorrow and regret. Everyone had their breaking point, and, while this would be it for some, I wasn't close to mine. Not when I understood first-hand how hard learning to be a new version of yourself was. Before the Weaver and I banished Mare, altering the Night World and ourselves, I was less kind. Just as the Weaver wasn't always wholly malicious.

Hot tears stung my check, and I joined Nora on the clothes-covered floor. "I love you." When she opened her mouth to issue a rebuttal, I stopped her with a kiss. "I love you, Nora. Always."

Her hands trembled as she cupped my face. "I'm sorry," she whispered softly.

"Shh," I said against her mouth and kissed her again. "We've forgiven each other. Whatever comes next, we'll figure it out."

Nora kissed me then, her lips scalding. It was a desperate thing seeking comfort. I matched it and poured every second of longing into her. Her touch erased everything, leaving nothing but us. This time, it was me who tugged off my shirt. Me who guided hers over her head. The black threads winding over her skin drew my attention, and she paused.

"I can't take them off," she said, drawing away.

My eyes met hers, and I pressed her hand against my exposed tattoo. "I can't take mine off either."

Her breath caught, a small smile appearing across her lips, and she climbed onto my lap. Our kisses softened and slowed, grew explorative. Until we couldn't take it anymore.

"Are you sure you want to do this again?" Nora asked.

My body shook in anticipation. "Absolutely sure. Are you?"

"Oh, I'm sure," she said with a hint of laughter.

And that was all either of us needed to hear.

That night, on the cusp of a new future, we brought the Dream and Nightmare Realms together. Only time would tell if we could keep it that way.

Chapter Thirty

Nora

Blue and white crystal pillars stabbed the sky in all directions. The columns stretched for miles, forming a dense maze of tunnels and holes for us to climb through. After an hour, I was covered in sweat and more than ready to level the entire landscape, but that would ruin the whole sneak-until-we-can't-sneak-anymore plan. And, on the other side of this ridiculous obstacle course, we would rendezvous—Kail's word, not mine—with the Sandman after he replenished his sand supply.

I leapt at the side of an extra wide piece of fallen crystal, searching and failing to find something to grab onto. Halven made climbing over it look so easy. Of course, Halven was practically a giant compared to me. But then, most people were.

Suddenly, Kail grabbed my ankle. I squeaked and kicked out.

"Kail!" I hissed. But he just grabbed my other leg and slid me up the side of the chipped pillar.

"Sorry," he said, sounding anything but. I straddled the crystal and glared down at him. "What? Would you rather keep practicing for your breakout roll as a rabbit?" He gripped my thigh, just above my knee, and pretended to yank me back down.

"No," I said quickly, squeezing my legs to stay put.

Kail chuckled and hauled himself up beside me with an embarrassing amount of grace. "A little trust, Lady."

"There *is* no trusting you," I mumbled. I was beginning to sound like a broken record.

He gave me a withering look. "I thought we were past all that."

I wanted to be, but there was no reason he would stay loyal after he got what he wanted. True trust didn't come with an expiration date. "You scratch my back, I scratch yours. Don't read too much into it."

"I won't kill you," he insisted, suddenly serious.

"Do you say that to all the girls?" I batted my eyelashes at him sarcastically. "Rowan trusted you enough to show her weakness, and look where that got her."

"For what it's worth, she didn't trust me either," he said, aloof. "Listen, I don't like being vulnerable. Halven and I waltzing around separately puts us both at risk."

It did. And it gave me something to hold over them. Halven was much better company. I could keep him at my side and use Kail to do my dirty work. It would serve Kail right for deceiving me for so long. I wrinkled my nose, annoyed with myself for even thinking it. "Who isn't trusting who now? I said I would put you back together."

The muscles in his jaw twitched. "All I'm saying is, if you do this for us, we will always be grateful enough not to stab you in the back."

"The Weaver was stabbed in the front," I deadpanned.

Kail rolled his eyes. "And make myself the most wanted man in the Night World? Pass. If the Sandman didn't kill me, everyone else would try. At least take comfort in my instinct for self-preservation."

Now *that* I could trust.

He slid down the other side of the pillar, landing neatly on his feet. I followed suit, though much less smoothly, and we walked the rest of the way in a strangely comfortable silence. My ears picked up on every little sound, just as Halven's and Kail's seemed to, but the three of us were together. For now. Maybe I should give them long-term benefit of the doubt. Or maybe that was what they wanted. Once they were put back together, who would they be? Kail or Halven? Neither? Which personality would stay, and which would go?

"Hey," the Sandman whispered, suddenly at my side.

My heart jumped, and I reached out for him. He took my hand. "Baku can't find any trace of Rowan's second group of nightmares, but the Blood Army is waiting on the other side of this landscape."

The tell-tale sign of red mist reflected through the crystal, distorted. We had to be close. "How did they know we were coming this way?" My voice shook. If the Blood Army was waiting for us, there was no getting out of this end of the landscape unseen, and it would be all too easy to send nightmares after us from behind. We would be fish in a barrel.

"We need to distract them," Halven said. "I'll go."

"Like hell you will," Kail shot. "We are not dying today."

"Someone needs to."

"No, they don't," the Sandman said. "They're not overly intelligent, right?"

Kail shook his head. "They follow orders. Nothing more."

The Sandman dipped his hand into his satchel and tossed sand straight up into the air. As it fell, the particles swirled into a shape. *My* shape. It wasn't a completely believable clone—the image was slightly grainy and partially transparent—but it was definitely me, down to every last freckle.

"Good enough for them?" the Sandman asked.

Kail nodded, impressed. "Should be."

Tiny wrinkles formed around the Sandman's eyes as he concentrated on the figure. She—it—disappeared to the left, and the Sandman motioned for us to follow him in the opposite direction. A few more hurdles, and the end of the crystal obstacle course peeked through the openings. Mist licked at the very edges, but there was only silence, which set me on edge worse than if the robed figures of the Blood Army had moaned. We approached slowly, all of us wary. My heart beat wildly in contrast, and I barely drew breath for fear something would hear. The Sandman looked down at me with a small smile. *It'll be okay,* his smile said. *You can do this.* I hoped he was right.

Suddenly, the Blood Army wailed violently.

My head swam. *They saw us.* This was it. We wouldn't even make it to Rowan. I closed my eyes and waited for the blistering pain.

"Nora," the Sandman whispered. "It's working."

My eyes snapped open to find the Blood Army drifting away from us. The mist receded, leaving a straight line of sight to a row of trees. Only, they weren't really trees at all. Dozens of stumps of various heights lined a dirt path, and the tall, scraggly trees lay to the side like a hundred corpses. "It's supposed to look like that, right?" I asked with rising dread.

They didn't have to answer. The Sandman and Kail both wore matching looks of shock while Halven shook his head in disbelief.

"We'll buy you time," the Sandman said. "As much as we can."

I swallowed hard. "But—"

He kissed me, quick and passionate. "Go, before they realize they're chasing the wrong Nora."

The grin rose to the challenge, forcing my feet to move. I didn't want to go. Didn't want to fight. To fail. Forget looking like a strong, powerful leader. I needed help. What were they thinking, sending me after Rowan on my own? The darkness in me didn't care how afraid I was, and it kept me on a direct path all the way to the edge of the tree trunks.

A loud growl echoed from the other end of the path. I stumbled on a pile of crushed red berries, but the grin widened. It only took a moment to know why. A dog—the first nightmare I created—leapt off one of the tall crystal pillars and raced after the Blood Army. I didn't know how he found me. Didn't care. Relief that he made it out of the tower swept over me, only to vanish the moment I heard a familiar voice.

"I was beginning to think my informant was wrong," Rowan crowed.

My brain fired a million thoughts all at once, but I understood zero of them. *Hot.* It was so hot here. The ground dropped out from under me, but the darkness broke the fall.

Black talons dug into my muscles, fused with my bones. The grin twitched eagerly as my hand reached unconsciously for a thread.

A flick of the wrist.

A puff of sulfur.

Beside me stood a creature nearly as tall as I was. Its elongated body was made of layers of thick, overlapping triangular plates the color of new copper. Its nose came to a sharp point, capped in tiny burrs. I didn't have to say a word for it to identify the enemy. Red berries popped under its hooved feet as it barreled toward Rowan.

The darkness didn't bother watching what happened next. Instead, it slammed my hands against the nearest trunk, and the grin pursed in concentration. The knotted thread that emerged was bigger than the one in the museum, bigger than the one in the Blood Tower. It shifted around itself like a ball of snakes, feeding the entire tree-lined path. How was I ever going to find the right piece in time? I would need to destroy the entire landscape.

The nightmare that went after Rowan let out a death squeal that rang in my ears and flamed my anger. I almost didn't look, but I had to. Rowan's jagged, broken wings bent over her shoulders, spearing the nightmare through the eyes. *More time.* The need for it pounded through me almost as fast as my pulse.

Two more threads exploded before I realized I pulled them from my arm. An orange dragon the size of my palm zipped overhead. The other—a purple alien-like creature with oozing pustules and wheels for feet—cackled. It was hard throwing them at Rowan when I knew their inevitable fate. Harder still not to lunge in and take care of her myself. Sadly, the Weaver's powers didn't grant me the same ability the Sandman's did. The nightmares *were* my power, my strength, and they were doing their job. I had to do mine.

I pressed my palms against the nearest stump again, feeling desperately for a frayed end. A weakened middle. Anything that would tell me where to press. How to destroy it. An orange blur thwacked the side of my face. I gasped as the small dragon flopped over, dead, at my feet.

"You're just like your predecessor," Rowan called, sounding almost bored. "But what you've failed to realize is that I'm the Weaver's strongest creation. I couldn't kill him, but there are no nightmares that can kill me."

More time, more time, more time. I pressed my palm harder against the rough bark. *Where are you?*

Rowan's wings flared behind her. The black blood of her victims oozed down the jutting branches and dripped onto the red silk of her dress. She eyed the thread on my arm with hungry eyes. "Give me the threads, Dream Keeper. You never wanted them anyway."

As if the threads were what mattered. Without the magic in my veins, in my head, my body, the threads might as well be given to the Doll Maker to sew on buttons. "I'm not a Dream Keeper anymore," I said with all the bravado I could muster. "I'm the Lady of Nightmares, and you will stand down."

Her laugh was genuine and harsh. "So much confidence." She stalked toward me. "Though I suppose it's hard not to feel like you've won when your lapdogs are circling."

Lapdogs. The darkness sent out a silent thrum that left me feeling as if I were in the passenger seat again. "It's only fair we do this one-on-one," I forced myself to say. "No armies. No tricks. Just you and me."

The grin snarled at me, the threads convulsing against my skin. *Relax*, I snapped at it.

"Come on," I goaded, abandoning my search for the frayed thread. "Let's get this over with."

Rowan plowed into me before I saw her move and knocked me off my feet. My back hit the ground, the air whooshing from my lungs, as she reached for my exposed throat.

Immediately, I wrapped one of my legs around hers and flipped us so I was on top of her. And that was the last thing I remembered. The Sandman's training, everything I'd learned since, all of it swirled in technicolor as the darkness regained control. I blinked rapidly, trying to get my eyes to focus, but it was as if I was looking through a frosted window. Things faded. Blurred. I floated away to that place where I'd been every night after I'd fallen asleep in the Day World.

The next moment, everything was crystal clear. I was on my back, and the large dog I created was dragging Rowan down the path by her broken wing like she was nothing more than a stick to play fetch with. I staggered to my feet at the same moment Rowan grabbed one of the dog's back legs. His howl of pain would forever scar my mind. I screamed my rage and leaned forward to tackle her. That was as far as I got before the grin peeled upward, and the blackness shoved me down to my knees. Things swirled again. Nothingness. Everything. Hypersensitivity followed by numbness.

The grin grew and grew, and my face bunched against it. The dog continued howling as he dragged Rowan to me. Mentally, I beat against the spreading grin, tears welling in desperation, but it ignored me completely. With one hand still pressed against the ground, pinning the frayed thread down, my other palm slammed against Rowan's chest. My vision blurred, allowing only snapshots to register. Rowan's panic-filled gaze. The frayed thread pounding violently at both ends. Creaking wood. Screams—so many screams. My throat burned as if I was the one crying out, but my teeth were bared in agonized concentration.

The world washed over me like a tidal wave. The sharp ache of the alteration. The shredding pain of Rowan's touch on the exposed skin right above the Sandman's glove. Flashes of gold as the thread knitted back together. Each reattached fiber sent jolts of electricity through every cell of my body. The darkness swept over me again, numbing me to the pain.

And then something cold and wet brushed against my cheek.

My eyes flew open with a startled gasp only to find the massive dog nudging me with his nose. *No.* Rowan hadn't won, or I wouldn't be here. But where was she? I flew off the ground and spun around. My heart stopped. Instead of a field of broken trunks, there was a path neatly lined with bare trees. A fresh layer of red berries coated the ground. More noticeable was the tree now towering over me. Branches were missing and broken, its trunk covered with charred bark.

"Oh," was all I could say. Hundreds of ravens croaked in response, their wings beating like drums overhead.

Rowan. The tree. Rowan *was* the tree. I wanted her dead, but this—this was almost better. In death, she could become a martyr. In life, she could become a warning. But to be so peacefully rejoined with her former self seemed almost like a reward. I scanned the other trees—all of them connected—and knelt in the center of the path.

There was no crippling pain this time, no black moment. It

was as easy as adding the doorknob to the museum door or turning a cell into liquid silver. The grin looked greedily on as the darkness helped me ease pieces of their thread away and mold it into something different. They were slight changes, all carefully calculated. A sense of hearing for Rowan, a voice for the others, causing just enough pain for them each to cry out in a chorus of different pitches. Paired with the rhythm of raven wings, even I was delightfully horrified.

"Let this be a warning to anyone who thinks they can do better than Rowan," I said to the dog. He hunched on the dirt, licking his leg. "Thank you," I softly told him.

He let out a small whine and glared at Rowan's trunk. Eyes narrowed, he stood and lifted his leg.

I gaped, the shock quickly fading, and I laughed. A real laugh. It was a weightless thing, a helium balloon pulling me up, up, up. Every moment leading to this had sucked something away from me. Stolen seconds, minutes, hours of my life exchanged for fear and doubt. But now—now I was buoyed by relief. It was over.

It's never over, the grin jeered.

But it was. *This* was. That deserved a moment of quiet victory.

Chapter Thirty-One

The Sandman

Nora was halfway to the broken tree line when Halven slammed face-first into the ground beside me.

Sand burst from my satchel in a protective bubble as I looked around wildly for the cause. Kail lurched toward his brother. I ground my teeth and sent sand out in all directions, searching. It found our enemy in record time—an invisible humanoid nightmare. The fine coating of sand revealed his form, a masculine body with hammers instead of hands. The sand wrapped around him like a second skin. "Duck!" I shouted.

Kail crouched just as one of the hammers swung at the back of his head. I squeezed my fists, and the sand squeezed too. The nightmare buckled under the pressure. He lay on the ground as stiff as a board. With another wave of sand scouring the area, I straddled the nightmare and slammed my knees into his upper arms.

"Kill it," Kail urged. He carefully flipped Halven over, examining him for wounds. "What are you waiting for?"

"Answers." My sand returned empty-handed, and I met Kail's angry stare. "Rowan knows too much about our movements, and I want to know how."

Kail flicked a look over my shoulder. "Not the best time for an inquisition."

I followed his gaze to find the Blood Army backtracking. They funneled straight for the fallen trees, and a curse flew off my tongue. "Watch this thing," I snapped.

"Where are you going?" he asked, laying Halven's head carefully on the ground.

"Watching Nora's back like you promised we would."

I lifted myself off the nightmare with a building sense of purpose and drew in a breath, letting it out slowly. With it, my qualms faded. I became the Lord of Dreams—a powerful being responsible for defending both worlds. For protecting them. Such was my penance for what the Weaver and I did when we banished Mare long ago, but this was about so much more. This was about Nora.

I stepped out from the shelter of crystal pillars, and the Blood Army paused. *Decisions*, I thought. Me or Nora. But orders were orders. Half of the robed figures shifted toward me, while the rest continued along their original path. It didn't matter— they would all be dead in a moment. Sand poured from my satchel to circle my hands. A silver glowing orb of pure dream magic hardened around both my hands, and sparks of navy blue popped with anticipation. I drew myself up and shot into the center of the red mist. The other sand I carried flew out in an attempt at snuffing the painful cloud, but there was too much of it.

That didn't matter either.

My lips curled in vengeful triumph, and I crossed my wrists in front of my chest. When I threw them back down to my sides, silver and blue light exploded through the Blood Army. I winced against the brightness as their moaning died off. My chest panged with the sudden explosion of power. I rubbed at my tattoo, reveling in the fact that I wasn't depleted like I would've been months ago. When the white light finally faded, I stared down at the entire Blood Army. Dead. A quick snap of my fingers and the last bit of sand I had domed the bodies, trapping their mist.

"That would've been helpful back at the tower," Kail screamed from the other side of the pillars.

I cast a wistful glance at the tree line before rejoining Kail and our prisoner. Nora was okay. If not, I would feel her die. And then I would beg Kail to kill me too, because Kail as the new Sandman was better than living with such a destructive loss. *She's fine.*

"I'm serious," Kail said the moment I was beside him again. "We waited hours to leave when you could've done *that*."

"We needed time to make a plan," I said. *I needed time to mend things with Nora.* A selfish thing, I knew, but a few hours wouldn't have made a difference. "Besides, I wasn't supposed to be helping, remember? Nora made that quite clear."

Kail huffed. "What do you call leveling the entire Blood Army?"

I cut him a hard look and knelt beside the still-glimmering

nightmare.

"Whatever," Kail mumbled.

Halven chuckled, and I jerked at the sound. "You're awake."
He held his arms up as if to say *obviously*. I shook my head to clear
the ringing in my ears. "Has he said anything?"

"We were waiting for you," Kail said, shrugging. "You're the
one with questions."

I rolled my shoulders. Of course Kail would still be difficult.
"Who told Rowan where we were?" I asked with an exasperated
sigh.

Silence.

"Do either of you have a preferred method of torture?" I
asked Kail and Halven.

"Break a finger?" Kail suggested, half-hearted. "Rip out a
toenail, maybe?"

I stretched my fingers in an attempt to control myself. It was
no wonder Nora broke his mask—too long around him and I
would probably break his *neck*. "Are you going to help with this?"

Kail crossed his arms. "Why do you assume I enjoy torturing
things?"

"I *assume* you want to know who Rowan has spying on you,"
I snapped.

Kail opened his mouth to reply when the nightmare
whispered, "Mara. It was Mara."

"Wow," Kail scoffed. "Just threatening bodily harm got him
to spill his guts."

"Hush," Halven said, leaning forward.

"How did Mare know?" I asked.

Silence. Then: "I don't know."

That was his answer for every following question I asked.

Where was Mare? He didn't know. Was Rowan alone in the trees? He didn't know. I pushed away from him with a strangled scream. There had to be more. Why would he know Mare told Rowan our location and not know anything else? I ran my hands through my hair and looked out at the tree line. The now *unbroken* tree line. I froze.

"Interesting," Kail contemplated. That wasn't the word I would have chosen. "Maybe she put them back up to find the one remaining stump."

A large, shaggy nightmare broke through the trees. I searched for Nora's feelings but only got a quick flash of exhaustion. The dog-like creature ambled away in the opposite direction, but nothing else moved. "I'm going down there," I said, the not knowing finally breaking me.

"Don't." Kail stepped up beside me. "Nora made him."

Nora made that thing? I shook the thought away. She was learning her magic, which included making nightmares. Kail nudged me with his elbow and motioned a few yards down, where another figure walked straight for us. I recognized that purple sweater. My heart ricocheted in my chest. There was no holding me back this time. I ran toward Nora as fast as my legs could carry me. The closer I got, the louder a hundred different screams became—unlike those of the Blood Army, but no less fearsome. I scanned the area behind her, waiting for something else to emerge from the trees. Nothing came.

Nora stopped where she was and waited for me. A tired smile tugged at the corners of her mouth. Her arms circled me when I reached her, holding tight. "It's done," she breathed.

"Yes." I ran a hand over the back of her head, toying with the ends of her hair. "What's that noise?"

"The trees."

"The trees?" I asked.

"I changed them." She sighed and eased out of my embrace. "This is the Nightmare Realm, and there's only one way to survive."

"One way?"

Something hardened in her eyes. "Rule by fear."

Concern flickered through me at the ease in which she said it. A bit tired sounding, yes, but the words flowed from her mouth as if they meant nothing. "It was Mare," I said, changing the subject.

She winced. "Mara? What was her?"

"She told Rowan where we would be."

"But how did she know?" Nora said loudly, eyes wide. "How do *you* know?"

I motioned behind us. "We caught an assassin."

"Did he say anything else?" she asked, quickly regaining her calm demeanor.

"Unfortunately not."

Nora hung her head and placed the top of it against my chest. "I suppose that means there's no time to catch our breaths, huh? What are we going to do about Mara?"

"We?" I asked.

She squirmed uncomfortably. "You worked together with the Weaver to stop her the first time, didn't you?"

Yes. And that was the thing that finally destroyed our relationship. "We did. I like hearing you call us 'us' though."

"We can do this, can't we?" She squeezed my hand. "Bring the realms together. Or, as together as they used to be."

"We can do anything." I took her cheeks in my hands and

lifted her head so I could see her face. "Including breathe, Nora. We can't run after Mare without thinking things through." She wasn't a nightmare—she was an Ancient. An Ancient that knew how to escape the Ever Safe where the rest of the old beings slumbered.

"Tell me what to do, and I'll do it," she whispered.

I was quiet for a moment as different scenarios played through my mind. We needed to know where Mare was and what she was after. If we could take her to the Day World again, she would be trapped. The alterations the Weaver and I did were still there—still strong. If Nora didn't have the dream in her, Mare wouldn't have made it back the first time.

"Give me the dream," I said haltingly.

"What?" she asked, confused.

"It's the reason Mare could come back with you. Both Nightmare and Dream magic together—"

"Yes," she said quickly. Understanding smoothed her features. "Take it."

I pressed the pads of my middle fingers against her temples, my palms shielding her eyes, and felt a pang of regret. This dream was what brought us together and eventually was what tore Nora apart. I was sorry I ever asked her to hold it—but at the same time, if I hadn't, we never would've fallen in love. No matter what Nora became, I trusted her with this information. It hadn't occurred to me to take the dream before, because—even if Nora could access it—she would never let the nightmares into the Day World. Not with her family there. This wasn't about trust, though. I closed my eyes and called my magic home.

It raced frantically to meet my call, and when I opened my eyes, a flickering orb floated in the air between us. I hurried to cup it in my hands without looking down at the sand-made images swirling inside. Without another Dreamer, it would be reabsorbed into me. But a Dreamer with a true heart and a true mind could fuel the magic themselves.

"I won't spy or step foot in your realm, so you can build a name for yourself, but give me use of Halven," I said quickly.

"Halven?" she blurted. "I promised I would put him and Kail back together, and I just proved I could do that."

I took a long breath. "No one knows that but the four of us. Everyone will think Halven is off doing what Halven does while Kail stays to help you. I need eyes here if I'm going to figure out what Mare is doing and how to stop her."

"Use Baku," she said defensively.

"Baku doesn't speak," I explained. "And everyone knows we have a relationship."

She chewed her bottom lip. "Fine. But only until you know what's going on."

"Of course." I kissed the top of her head. "Kail and Halven are where you left them."

Nora's gaze snapped up. "Aren't you coming?"

"No." I held the orb closer. "I have to do something with this."

She eyed the glowing sphere hidden in my hands and nodded. "But I'll see you soon?"

"Soon," I said, though I wasn't sure how long things would take. I smiled anyway. "You can do this, Lady Nightmare. Go on. They're waiting."

Nora toyed with the threads near her wrist until the worried gleam faded from her eyes. Her shoulders slowly squared. "I can do this," she repeated softly to herself and walked away from me.

I didn't watch her long. She was safe, she was strong, and she had allies.

Instead, I let the beach pull me home, my magic already skimming over the cords in search of one in particular. One that Nora would never dream of hurting, in case dealing with Mare affected Nora the same way it had the Weaver.

"What is *that?*" Katie cried, shocked.

I spun to face her, surprised by her presence enough to forget my search for her cord. "Katie. I was just coming to see you." This felt wrong. A betrayal, almost, but I also knew it was the best option for both worlds, so I held her gaze. "I have something important to ask you."

Chapter Thirty-Two

Nora

The walk to the Keep was fueled by adrenaline. Excitement. Anticipation. After I met back up with Kail and Halven, after they killed the assassin, everything became a blur. My eyes focused on what was in front of me—a clear pathway to the Keep. Nightmares bowed when I passed, Kail close at my heels. *Word spreads fast*, I thought but didn't look away from my destination despite the urge to take in each of their faces. The Lady of Nightmares would rule by fear, and no one feared a thing they knew. I watched Kail from my peripheral vision and understood him a bit better. We were all more than the face we presented to the world. I was Nora to my family. To the Sandman. Maybe to Kail and Halven. To everyone else, I would be something untouchable.

"Welcome home," Kail said with a small smile.

Another step up an incline, and I saw it. The Keep. Half walls rose throughout the entire lawn where before there was nothing. No, not nothing. The Sandman said the Keep was much bigger before his battle with the Weaver. I studied the lines that formed room after room and smiled. An imposing palace for an imposing position.

"Have them continue rebuilding," I told Kail. "I want it completed within the month."

Kail's eyes widened. "You could finish it yourself in a fraction of the time."

I could, yes. If I wanted a palace made of spies. The walls here could be like those of the Blood Tower—alive with nightmares—but I didn't want to be watched. First my mother, then the Sandman in my dreams, and here, it was Kail. Defensive measures would be taken to protect myself, but the walls themselves would be painstakingly built using whatever materials my nightmares could find. I wove my way through the construction. It seemed like a waste of resources with Mara still out there somewhere, but I would rule this place and these creatures in my own way. And I would do it without a permanent audience.

"Have them continue," I repeated and paused at the door to the Keep. The darkness grinned wide along with me. "Stay here."

"Lady." Kail bowed and took two steps back.

Inside, the stillness of the Keep washed over me, and I took my first easy breath. *Mine.* Finally. Lights flickered to life as I shut the door, revealing four other doorways and a set of spiraling stone stairs that wrapped around the entire interior. I stared at the hatch above, knowing exactly what was there, but before I ascended them, I peeked into each annexed room. The closest had a bed covered with a soft, gold-spun blanket, a chest similar to the one Kail had in the museum, and a bookshelf full of trinkets. The next room was arranged as some sort of a macabre living room—the moving heads of nightmares mounted to the walls would be the first thing to go—and the third housed only stairs leading to the basement.

The final room was instantly my favorite. A large oak table ran the length of each wall with floor-to-ceiling cabinets on either side of the doorframe. Papers covered nearly every inch of the table, and worn bits of charcoal crunched beneath my feet. The walls played host to hundreds of charcoal sketches of nightmares. Their eyes seemed to follow my every step, though I knew it was only an illusion. I plucked the nearest drawing off the wall, and a sense of peace settled over me. The Weaver's technique was good—more than good. Every imagined light reflected off a sketched bubble with a tiny person trapped inside. While I wasn't sure if the inhabitant was part of the nightmare or a rendering of what the bubble would do to Dreamers, I felt every ounce of the Weaver's creativity. It shook hands with the artist in me, eager to pick up a pencil. A brush. Anything that would get the sudden rush of creative thoughts onto paper. I smiled, biting my bottom lip.

There was work to do.

Nightmares to weave.

Mara to hunt.

Mara to kill.

These drawings would help until she was taken care of. The Weaver spent eons at this, so they were undoubtedly valuable outlines. Perfect for learning the loom. I set the bubble drawing on the table and slipped from the room, reluctant to go. But there was something else I had to see. Touch. Feel.

The hatch to the domed upper level creaked open. I slipped inside and tried not to remember the feeling of the knife as it slid into the Weaver's chest. The lingering scent of sulfur helped clear my head, but the rust-colored stain coating the floor like paint nearly sent me spiraling. *Blood.* This was the place where the old Nora died and I was born.

The loom creaked, seemingly aching for my touch just as much as I ached to touch it. The threads vibrated against my skin when at last I reached out and made contact with the machine. *More*, they seemed to say.

"Yes. So many more," I whispered, though I wasn't sure what they wanted more of. More of me? More nightmares? It didn't matter—I would give them both. I would give them everything.

The bench was still knocked over from where the Weaver once stood to face me, so I picked it up and sat behind the loom. A flash of power stole my breath as I ran my hands along the aged wood. It felt better than anything I'd done with my magic so far. Like I was finally alive again after months on my deathbed. A sigh rattled my body with a breath that wasn't mine, ripping the ecstasy away. I felt it with every drop of blood in my veins. Freezing. Burning. Tearing through me.

Then a voice slowly emerged inside me, gentle, playful even, but carrying a thunderstorm on its back. I recognized it at once.

"Lady, Lady, quite contrary," it crooned, "how does your darkness grow? With bloody claws and snapping jaws and pretty nightmares all in a row."

My blood drained to my feet in one painful whoosh, and I

gripped the loom so I wouldn't fall from the stool. The darkness thrummed. Swelled. Invaded and conquered every bit of my body. It couldn't be…

"Weaver?" I croaked.

"Hello, Keeper," the grin replied.

Acknowledgements

To all the readers following Nora and the Sandman's journey through the Dark Dreamer trilogy, I thank you from the bottom of my heart! You make this job worth every drop of sweat and blood.

The best CPs in the world: Lauren, Kalyn, Loretta, and Candace.

As always, my Saltmates!

Lindsay & Judy.

Priscilla, Katie, Elle, Melissa, Stacy.

My family: Dan, Ian, Ryan, Nonny, Kathy, Mom, Dad, Heather, and my Georgia family.

My heart is full because of you all!

Also by Amber R. Duell

Young Adult

The Dark Dreamer Trilogy:
Dream Keeper
Dark Consort
Night Warden

When Stars Are Bright

New Adult
Fragile Chaos
The Prince's Wing

Faeries of Oz series (co-written with Candace Robinson):
Lion (ebook prequel short story)
Tin
Crow
Ozma
Tik-Tok

Vampires in Wonderland (co-written with Candace Robinson):
Rav (ebook prequel short story)
Maddie
Chess
Knave

Once Upon A Wicked Villain (co-written with Candace Robinson):
Spindle of Sin
Tower of Shadows

About the Author

Amber R. Duell was born and raised in a small town in Central New York. She does her best writing in the middle of the night, surviving the daylight hours with massive amounts of caffeine. Her favorite stories are dark with a touch of romance and a villain you either love to hate or hate to love.

When not reading or writing, she enjoys snowboarding, embroidering, snuggling with her cat, and staying up way too late to research genealogy. She loves to travel and has visited more countries than states. Kissing the Blarney Stone and hand-feeding monkeys in the mountains of France will be hard to beat, but that doesn't stop her from trying to find the next real-life adventure.